BOTTOM DOG PRESS

HURON, OHIO

WANTED: GOOD FAMILY

JOSEPH G. ANTHONY

APPALACHIAN WRITING SERIES

BOTTOM DOG PRESS, INC.
P.O. Box 425, Huron, Ohio 44839
http://smithdocs.net

CREDITS:
General Editor: Larry Smith
Editor, Layout & Cover Design: Susanna Sharp-Schwacke
Cover Art: Library of Congress, Prints & Photographs
Division, FSA/OWI Collection LC-USF34-046298-D
Author Photo: Lexington *Herald-Leader*

DEDICATION:
To the African-Americans of Kentucky for their long,
brave, and inspiring struggle. To Susana Sharp-Schwacke,
Larry Smith, and staff at Bottom Dog Press for their expert
editing; to Jaqui Linder for first reading and careful thought.

WANTED: good family with plenty of help to raise 7 acres of tobacco and as much corn in Scott County. Good land, team, tools, fertilizer furnished. Fair four-room house, garden, chicken range. House has electricity. Plenty of work outside of crop will be furnished. Beds ready to burn. In good community on hard road near school, church, and stores. Do not call or write. Come and look at it before Thursday afternoon. Take Highway 27 to Sherman, KY. Turn left at Sherman on blacktop road.

J.G. Lawson, Huckleberry, Kentucky, Rt. 2.

CHAPTER 1
Rudy Johnson—March 1948, Lexington, Kentucky

I hear some people got plans for their life—actually sit down and sketch out what they think will happen. What they know will happen. How they do that? I don't know from one day to another what I'm gonna do. I'm looking for one thing and find something else. I'm going one direction and I ends up the other end of the county. I'm 36 years old, got four children and the best woman in the whole town of Lexington—in the whole state of Kentucky—and my right foot still ain't certain where my left foot's headed. Mamma tells me not to worry so much; she says that's just what colored people's lives are like—least ways poor colored people's lives. You got to scramble just to stay in place. And when you think you got a place all settled, along comes somebody—usually a white somebody, Mamma says—and you got to move on.

"You talking about Estill County again," I say to Mamma. Mamma's always talking about Estill County even when she isn't.

"No, I ain't," Mamma says. "I'm talking about Lexington, Kentucky, the place all the county-colored think is Mecca."

"You one of them," I say back. Mamma loves Lexington. Getting her to leave Lexington, even for an afternoon, is getting a turtle to leave its shell.

She just nods. "Yes, I am. I didn't say all the dumb colored, I said all the county-colored and I'm one of them. But just because Lexington ain't Estill County, that don't mean it Mecca."

Maybe I don't know what I'm looking for, but I know I ain't looking for some tenant farm in Scott County. Only nobody seems to be hiring—at least not hiring colored ex-G.I.s. And the ad didn't say white. Popped out at me in its own box right next to "The Colored Notes" in the *Lexington Statesman*. I'm not saying it was in *The Colored Notes*, but it close to it. "Wanted, good family with plenty of help to raise 7 acres of tobacco and as much corn." Well, we a good family. And between Nannie and the two older boys, we got plenty of help.

"You got to be kidding." Nannie give me the bad eye. "Just because it don't say white, butterhead, don't mean colored are welcome. If it's not in 'The Colored Notes,' it don't mean colored. Might as well be on the front page."

She crosses her arms like she does when I've got on her last nerve, as she put it. She a good-looking woman, bright skin, tall, "a real stallion" Mamma calls her, but she's not airish. You wouldn't know she the mother of four with the oldest one going on thirteen. But when she upset, she got a tongue on her that'll whip you flat as a May tornado.

"You don't have the sense the Lord gave a chicken."

"It got that, too. A chicken range," I say. She just look at me. Following a man who don't know where he's going would try even a sweet-tempered woman. Nannie the best woman in Kentucky, but she ain't sweet-tempered. "A good four-room house with garden and chicken range. Even got electricity," I say.

"Well, glory be. Electricity. In 1948, imagine that. It got colored? I bet you it got cracker."

"It like you say. 1948—things changing."

She just shake her head. She got a point. It's not like Lexington changing that much. Nannie use to be a nurse's aide over at Good Samaritan. Nurse's aide. That meant she had to wear a white uniform when she was cleaning—rooms, old folks, babies. And pay for that uniform herself. When she tries to fill out the application to train for the practical nursing, they ask her if she a troublemaker. Weren't more than a week after that they all of a sudden discover that they got too many nurse's aides. Ain't have nothing to do with her application for the training, they tell her. Just too many aides. Soon as they need her again, they be in touch.

She still waiting.

"That's how Lexington does it," Mamma says. I'm having to borrow grocery money from her, and I know she don't have two dollars to spare. But she find it when I ask. "They don't like to make any fuss," she say. "Don't want you to make a fuss, either. They figure you get the message when you don't hear from them."

"What about them calling her a troublemaker?" I ask. "That sounds like somebody fussing."

"That just a slip of the tongue. Usually, they don't say nothing. Of course, that's the way they feel, but they don't say nothing. No, not in Lexington."

"At least in Scott County," I tell Nannie, "that farmer won't be saying he get back to me. If he don't want colored, he'll say it right out."

Nannie glares at me. She glares at me when she thinks I'm right. But she right, too. If Lexington changing, it ain't change that much. She out of a job and me still looking.

Right now, mostly we looking for a place to live. We still crowded in with her mamma and sister in five small rooms off Georgetown Street. They didn't start out five rooms. The landlord put up those thin wall-boards, and what started out two nice-sized rooms end up five rooms you can hardly turn 'round in. Ain't nothing like a private conversation in that house.

Of course, the whole town crowded—even white people. We ain't caught up from the war, and, what with all the soldiers coming home and everybody having babies, we keep getting more and more jammed. The only ones with space to move 'round in are the horses on the big horse farms that ring all round Lexington. You got to be a horse to have any space in Fayette County. Or own one.

Nannie just come home from her cleaning job and found the usual mess. I do my best, but keeping four children quiet—Nannie's mamma was in the bedroom with one of her headaches—was about all I could do. I got some kind of supper on the table—the children weren't much happy—but getting the place picked up was beyond my powers.

I tell Nannie you don't have to be colored to be crowded.

"Did I say that? But I figure the six of us could move into old Mrs. Breckenridge's empty third floor, and it'd be six months before she even heard any footsteps. If I told her it was squirrels running around, we be living rent-free another six months."

Nannie's hard on white folks. 'Cause she got reason. We all got reason, but if you think about it too much, that's all you gonna think. Nannie's back to cleaning houses since Good Samaritan let her go, and she hate it. She worse than hate it. I see her saddening by the day. She always a sometimey girl, up one day, down the next. But now she almost always down. It weren't no bargain, that Good Samaritan job, I tell her and she agree—it weren't much. Didn't pay much more than cleaning private. But that white uniform she had to pay for made her feel like she was going places. Made her think she could make it one more step up that ladder. Maybe even further.

'Cept they always greasing the ladder. Or worse, taking out the rungs so when you step, ain't nothing there.

That my dream. My bad dream. I know some fellows got bad dreams about the war, but my war weren't much. But I get my climbing dream. Nannie says I get it two, three times a month. I don't always remember. Sometimes maybe six months go by and I think, *Thank you, Lord, I'm done with that dream.*

But it just hiding. Before I know it, I'm back trying to climb up some old ladder half-collapsed with wood rot. I'm grabbing for the rungs, but they keep disappearing. I'm hanging with my feet dangling till I can't hold on anymore and my shoulders start to ache like they being pulled out of their sockets, and I have to let go.

At first it feels good, letting go. Free. My arms flap like wings and I'm flying. But then I ain't flying. I'm falling, the ground coming up fast.

I know ain't none of it real. It's the same climbing dream I've had a hundred times. I know that dream so well one part of me is thinking, *Here come the flying part, here come the falling.* I know all that but I'm still scared. I try to ride it out. I say, *You in that dream again, Rudy. You gonna be fine.* But I'm scared. I got to wake up before I hit that ground, but I never remember how to do that.

I got to wake because I know that if I hit the ground, my neck gonna snap.

Nannie almost always shaking me awake by then. She always catch me in time. She don't even ask. She just strokes my head and makes some kind of sound that don't seem to need words. Sometime she move in, and before I know it, before I think it, she be inside me. Or I inside her. She say she think at least three of our babies climbing-dream children.

I hope not, I tell her. I hate to think our children have anything to do with that dream. I won't even let any of them go near a ladder.

"Maybe they don't need a ladder," Nannie answer. It the gentle time after we're awake. After we come together. "Maybe they're the ladder."

I just shake my head when she talk like that. Mamma told me to marry a smart woman—"Somebody got to have some brains," is the way she put it—and surely I did.

Nannie's the only one in the family to get her high school though it took a while. But it don't keep her from hurting. Maybe it make her hurting worse. She back to cleaning houses like she done since she thirteen year old. Cleaning that big old house on Second Street with just old Mrs. Breckinridge rambling around in it, not even seeing half the rooms she live in, while we squeeze into two rooms pretending to be five.

And Nannie be right. Housing worse for us. Colored got like six places in town we can move to, and they all so crowded it like that picture I seen once of Coney Island. That beach so full of people, sand just a rumor that their toes be spreading. I say six places but it really only three. Kinkeadtown, Speigle Heights, Smithtown. Some streets off them just the same places—Brucetown, Goodloetown. The others, Cadentown—so far out it might as well be in the country. Pralltown out by Red Mile is the country, far as I'm concerned. And Fort Springs just an army barracks for horse farm workers. I heard folks talk about Cadentown and Uttingertown, but I never could figure out where they are 'cept I know for sure Lexington Transit sure don't go there. If we gonna move to the country, we might as well have a job.

"I hear they opened up Ohio Street—the 300 block. Maybe even the 400 block." Nannie means opened up to colored. She looks down when she say it. Ohio Street's full of tiny bungalows—some so small it's like that house in Kinkeadtown my mamma and daddy still live in. Daddy say you could chew on the front porch and put your spit bucket on the back. Course Mamma says Daddy can't hit the bucket even when it right at his feet. Ohio would be like moving sideways.

"Ohio Street? Who decided that?"

Nannie just shrug. It a silly question.

"Who decides anything? The powers that be opened it up. They have to open up something if they don't want us living on the street. And I hear those blocks on Ohio Street already got colored—they just not official."

I think, *Well maybe Ohio Street would be OK then.* "You sure it got colored?" I say to her.

"Of course it got colored. Any place that's just about fallen down, got colored. Landlords probably can't find crackers poor enough or crazy enough to rent those houses. That would be the power that be, landlords needing rent money and not caring if it's colored hands that give it to them."

She looks mad like I'm the one doing the arguing. Sometime I just stand there and Nannie takes over both sides of the fight. Now she begins arguing for moving to the country.

"That Scott County place has four rooms. Mamma will get her couch back."

"And we might even get to sleep in the same bed again," I says. "Glory be."

Should'a let her continue the argument all by herself.

"That what this about? How you think we got so crowded in the first place? Sleeping in the same bed."

We just sit there for a while after that, not saying anything. We don't like each other's choices. Colored choices in Lexington, Kentucky. I thought the Army change things. It change things alright. Whites meaner than they were before the war. Nervous. Afraid we pushing things. What we pushing? Just trying to make a living. Just trying to find a place to live. Just trying to get the right foot moving the same direction as the left foot.

Sometimes I think things is going backwards. Or I'm going backward. Daddy was a farmer in Estill County. Owned his own place. I've asked him once—Mamma wasn't around—if we could go back and visit. He gave me a look like he don't know me.

"You was twelve years old when we left," he finally said. "Don't you remember nothing?"

I shook my head. It was a question they asked me all the time.

"I remember the river," I told him. "And a peach orchard. That's all. I remember we was happy," I said, but cut it off because I spotted Mamma coming in. It wasn't something we could talk about in front of Mamma.

"We can't ever go back," is what Daddy said quick.

Only I was going back—not to Estill County, but Scott County seemed about the same. Not to our own place but to a tenant farm. It weren't a direction I ever thought of going, but it was where we was headed.

I worry about how the children gonna get used to country living. They don't know nothing but the city. Nannie knows a little country, but not much. She left Wolfe County when she was seven. Bad as the colored schools be here, they was worse in Wolfe County. Couldn't really call them schools.

I'm the only one in the whole crowd who country raised. Soon as we had Harry, our youngest, we knew we was a crowd. Four children. Herbert, Franklin, Eleanor, and Harry. I tell people their names and always get a look. Some want to know where the Herbert come from.

We was still Republicans back when Herbert was born, two years into FDR's first term. All the colored was Republican in them days. We probably got the only two children in the country named for two presidents that hate each other. The WPA changed our minds about being Republican. It put me to work and paid me twice the going rate for colored. The going rate just helped you starve a little slower. Some of the white folks raised a fuss about that. I ain't saying FDR was a perfect man, but he kept us eating.

Eleanor was born three years later. My mamma said she ain't ever heard of a colored girl named Eleanor, but after Miz Roosevelt got Marian Anderson that singing place, Nannie wouldn't hear of no other name.

We took a break after Eleanor—or the army took it for us. We fought about Harry's name. "A cracker from Missouri," Nannie says. But when they start to give the president all that grief over integrating the army—folks say he gonna sign an order this summer—Nannie turned to me and said, "See. I was right."

"You sure were," I told her, "you sure were."

But then I mess up and say something about people changing—even crackers from Missouri.

"I know people change," she told me. Nannie hates it when she thinks she being preached at. "Did I say they didn't change?" White folks changing is one sermon she don't have no patience with.

"How long do you think it will be before those folks at Good Samaritan change?"

But *we* got to change. Even if we don't know what we're changing to. We can't live with Nannie's mamma no more. Four children, Nannie's mamma and sister. Just getting to use the toilet is like waiting in the unemployment line. Take a number and hold on. At least in the country, the boys and me could pee off the back porch. Can't do that on Georgetown Street. Besides, Franklin and Herbert are too old to be sharing their sister's room. And my back's too old and tired to be trying that couch. But Ohio Street. Well, it just make me tired thinking what kind of house be waiting for us on Ohio Street. I see Nannie thinking the same thing. I try again.

"Ain't gonna hurt to check it out."

Nannie don't say anything. When Nannie don't say anything right off, I know I won that skirmish. The only way I lose it is I open my mouth.

Nannie got used to doing things her own way the three years I was in the army—mostly down South, doing grunt work. When they finally did send us to France, the fighting was just about over. It weren't until that Bulge battle that Eisenhower let any colored get into it—after he started running out of white boys. Imagine that? Had to kill off a bunch of white boys before they let the colored fight. Not saying no colored got killed. Just didn't die like the white boys did.

Mamma says that's one time she didn't mind Jim Crow, but it hurt my feelings—all the boys' feelings.

But fighting or not, I was away. Nannie made most of the decisions before I went away, anyway, but she sure got used to deciding things without any argument. She had to keep a roof over everybody's heads with that sorry little money the army sent her and what she could scrape up on her own. Before Good Samaritan she was working that tobacco steam room down on Broadway. Make ten dollars a week if she lucky. Air to breathe go extra in them places.

I keep my mouth shut. I wait for Nannie. She ain't long in coming.

"This is Monday. The man said to come before Thursday. You better start figuring out how we're going to get there."

I better start figuring it out. It don't matter if I know where I'm going or not, ahead of time, I'm going to get there anyway. I got to turn my head to see where I've been to know where I'm going.

"You think white folks know where they going?" I ask Mamma.

"Some do," she say, and the way she look I know she thinking of somebody in particular. But then that look pass.

"Most don't."

CHAPTER 2

Rudy Johnson—March 1948, Lexington, Kentucky

The ad say not to call, which is good because we don't have no phone. Use a neighbor's phone and the whole neighborhood know your business. Course, they know your business anyway. The ad say not to write, either, which is another good thing because what would we say? "By the way, we colored"? Better just to show up and let them see for themselves. I studied the directions hard. 'Cept for the army, I ain't been out of Fayette County for years.

"Take old route 27 up near the county line. Turn left when you over the county line and keep going till you hit a church that sits in the middle of the road. That the end of the hard road. Then take the dirt road behind the church and keep going. You'll come to Lawson's place in a mile or two."

Nannie be studying the directions with me.

"Lawson's place. Just ask anyone," the ad say.

"Just ask anyone," she repeats. "They'll all tell you we crazy."

We borrow Uncle Zeb's pickup, pile all the kids but Harry in back, and head on out. Harry ain't three yet, and we don't want him bouncing out. Nannie keeps turning 'round and counting heads. I figure to show Mr. Lawson that we got the help part down.

"The ad say there plenty of work outside the crop. That will keep us busy."

"You sit back down and stop your fooling," Nannie's yelling at somebody. "We don't have time to be fixing broken bones." She look at me now. "You think I'm worrying that we not going to be busy? I didn't figure the man was offering us a vacation home."

"He ain't offered us nothing yet."

The church we looking for ain't in the middle of the road; it stop the road. Not that it look much like a church 'cept for the cross over the door. No steeple. Just a square gray building. More like a barn than anything. A side building made of yellow brick got a little dog-trot connecting to it. We follow the parking lot that curves 'round, and we find the other road sticking as straight as a telephone pole out the back end. We pass a few houses, but it like the road's just built for this church, which ain't like any church I ever seen.

The back road the other side ain't much more than a cow-path. Nannie keep her head turned to the children, but they sitting down, holding on as best as they can. Nannie got one arm wrapped tight around Harry and one holding onto the door handle. I'm trying to steer between the trees on one side and the rain ditch on the other. We don't got breath to talk even if we want to. We don't much want to. *What I got us into now?* I know Nannie thinking the same thing.

It take us twenty minutes traveling that road, and it ain't more than a mile if it's that. But it's gullied out half the time and full of branches and pebbles. I'm pretty sure it's more creek than road after one of our rain busters. Twice I stop the truck and move some sharp edged rocks that would have torn Uncle Zeb's tires to pieces.

Finally, the road smooth out the last quarter mile, like we passed some border. We almost slide down the last little bit. Some reason that make me more nervous than the rough road. The whole thing end at a gate. I stop, and Franklin jumps out and opens that gate like he raised up doing that, like he a country boy. Herbert start fussing at him that he the oldest and it his job.

But Franklin always first in everything, just not in birthing. I smile at that—fighting over chores—but Nannie's frowning. She think I favor Franklin.

I don't know why Scott County's always scared me. It ain't like Fayette County's some colored paradise. I see an old man coming out of his house as we pass through the gate. He a big old man. You can tell he used to be bigger—the way he hunched over some—but he still big. He's favoring one leg the way you do when one of your knees is giving you misery. But that don't slow him down any. He stride forward to meet us like one of them farm dogs that run right under your wheels, like they don't care we a two-ton truck and they ain't nothing but thirty pounds of mutt. I don't think the old man is gonna run under our wheels, but it startled me some. If anybody was gonna do some stopping, it weren't gonna be him.

Not on his land.

"Uhn, uhn," Nannie murmured. "He look like he trouble."

Can't know about that. I think maybe he just one of them big old men who don't know they old yet. Still, I watch his face close. If he gonna go for his shotgun, I want to be ready to curve on out of there as quick as I can. I pull up but leave the motor running.

"Mr. Lawson?" I ask, opening my door but keeping my seat. I feel Nannie ready to duck for cover beside me. Harry start to ask something, but she whisper a hush that would quiet a whole room of babies. Franklin, Herbert, and Eleanor don't need any hushing. I don't turn my head, but I know they frozen in place. "I read your ad in the *Statesman*. You say not to call, just to come out before Thursday."

He don't say nothing, just keeps staring.

"Well, I come out," I say, like he an idiot and can't see that. "Brought plenty of help," I nod behind me. Nannie takes her eyes off Mr. Lawson to turn and give me a look. I get ready to slam that pickup door and skedaddle on out.

"You're colored," is all the old man say. He's standing so stiff I'm thinking I'm back in the army and he's at attention. Only he ain't saluting. His face when he say colored is like he's saying we French. Ain't too many French people in Scott County, but there's plenty of colored.

"Yes, sir, I'm colored. So's my help. The ad didn't say one way or another. Hope that ain't a problem."

By this time a woman has joined him. She younger than he be. Maybe a decade. She one of those white ladies so skinny you wonder if they just visit at the dinner table. Nannie thin but she make two of this lady. She stares at us a second, too, but don't go to attention like he done. She turns to him, and then back to us. Just when I think I better be easing on back up the road, what I call her "Kentucky" kicked in.

"You folks survive that road? I tell everybody that if you didn't have back problems at the start of it, you surely will acquire them quick on that stretch of purgatory. Well, come on down now and take a breather. I bet you children could use some nice sweet tea."

I figure anyone offering us sweet tea ain't gonna shoot us. I shut the motor off. I slide myself out the door. The children look at me, and I nod. They jump out of that pickup like it the last day of school. It hot for March and that sweet tea a siren song to their ears. Mine, too. The lady's not gone inside more than two minutes—it's like she's racing; she move like that all the time it no wonder she so skinny. She comes back bringing a tray with a big pitcher and a half-dozen glasses.

Mr. Lawson ain't saying a word when she gone, just keep staring. Trying to take it all in, I guess. Colored. Like we the first colored this side of the Elkhorn. I thinking sweet tea or not, Nannie's right again. Scott County a foreign country, and we don't speak the language.

"I'm Mrs. Lawson and this silent man by my side is Mr. Lawson." She smile but don't reach out a hand to shake. He don't, either.

"I'm Rudy. Johnson. This my woman, Nannie. And these our children: Herbert, Franklin, Eleanor, and little Harry."

The names sink in a bit.

"You Democrat?" First words out of Mr. Lawson's mouth since he say we colored.

"Yes sir. Ever since a year or two after Herbert was born."

"Used to be all the colored were Republicans. Only Republicans I knowed."

"Yes sir. That's the truth. But FDR change all that. And Miz Eleanor."

He screw up his face at Miz Eleanor's name. People who think FDR walk on water still have a hard time with his missus. Nannie the opposite. She think Eleanor the one who walk on water.

We sit on the side of the porch sipping the sweet tea—even baby Herbert slurping it like it his mamma's milk. I waiting. I see we ain't what they wanting, but the only other vehicle I see is a sad-looking Chevy pickup and the remains of something—it could have been an old Model T, all rusted out—probably not running for twenty year. I found out later we was the only ones who had shown up for the want ad. And March was the time to start things going if you wanted a tobacco crop. Even corn ain't too far behind.

Gradually Mr. Lawson relax from attention—not going all the way to at ease but not looking like he in shock. He keep his eye on me.

"You a farmer?"

"Grew up one. Estill County. Ain't that different from here. My woman, Nannie, grew up over Wolfe County. Farm there, too."

"Wolfe County?" Mr. Lawson perked up at that. Or at least he moved his eyebrows some, which I'm thinking is about as much expression his face gets. He turn to Nannie. First time I think he look at her. "I have cousins there. Wilkinson. You know them?"

Nannie jump right in like she at a family reunion. "The county's full of Wilkinsons. I have cousins named that, too. Second cousins. Colored ones. I never knew the white ones except to nod to them at the post office. I reckon I'm cousins to them, too—maybe third or fourth. But then when cousins stretch out that distance, nobody knows for certain."

That speech just hang in the air like coal fire smoke in January. Nannie will do that—white folks don't know what to make of her. Mr. Lawson look even more surprised than when we first pulled up. Even Mrs. Lawson lose that polite-Kentucky-lady smile for a second. I don't know if Nannie claiming kinship or not, but I do know that white and colored cousins ain't a topic talked about much. I can tell Nannie pleased with herself, though she ain't smiling at least.

But after a moment they shake it off and go back to the county dance Nannie done started. Every time two Kentuckians from different counties meet, they try to figure out how they connected. Give them twenty minutes and they'll remember somebody who worked in the county you from—some uncle or granddad—or they did some business there themselves maybe twenty years before. Maybe—if you the same color—you might even find out you related. Maybe even if you not the same color. Every county does the dance—though we do it less in Fayette. Both Lawsons had lots of connections in Wolfe County. Took another ten minutes of county dancing for Powell County which is right next door.

"Pretty country," Nannie continue after we all pause a bit to catch our breath. "All those hills. Never have gotten used to all this flat land."

"Pretty hills?" Mr. Lawson straighten up, became army all over again, like Nannie had said something real foolish. "Nothing pretty about them. Hills like that will kill your mules. You with them."

"You have that right." Nannie looked him straight in the face. Nothing scared Nannie. "Daddy said he hoped heaven was flat as Kansas. He said he deserved an easy ride and so did his mules."

I don't know what the sound is at first—like some kind of gurgling but like something breaking, too. I jump until I figure out it Mr. Lawson laughing. He take a while, bent over like Nannie sucker-punched him in the gut. It don't seem like he enjoying that laughter much. I don't think he used to it. Miz Lawson look surprised like she ain't seen it before, herself. I don't know. It don't strike me as that funny, but I'm for anything that ease the mood.

Finally he stop as quick as he start. He sound a bit like he apologizing.

"I've just never heard anyone wishing to go to Kansas when they died. And taking his mules."

He look a moment like he might start that laughing again, but then he shake his head like he think better of it. He take a look at us again. He stop talking. We wait.

Miz Lawson finally take charge.

"Well, I guess you want to see the house."

I don't think it be that easy and it ain't. Mr. Lawson look surprised again. Like he forgot why we here in the first place. But he nod and walk towards the barn and I wonder if that's the house and think, *Well, Nannie ain't going to go for that. Ohio Street has to be better than a barn.* But then I see the house, almost hidden—maybe 30 yards past the barn. It was a square thing built on a little knoll. A good thing. It looked solid built. I could hear the Elkhorn though I couldn't see it yet. It just a creek but in spring it thinks it a river.

"It flood?" I ask Mr. Lawson.

"Not yet. The Elkhorn—it's over there behind those trees. Got kind of ornery a couple springs ago but it never reached the porch." He looked at the house hard. "Only been one family lived in it—family named Eliot. But they moved on. Got factory jobs in Cincinnati."

We pause before we climb the porch steps. Mr. Lawson look at his wife. She brush by him, but he grabs her arm.

"This is Jimmy's house," he said to her. That stop her for a second. Then she takes his hand off her arm.

"That's yesterday's news, James." She nod to the empty fields. "That's today's news."

The house got good ceilings and the walls is plastered. I walk in and I felt like I been there before. Mamma and Daddy always asking me if I remember anything about Estill County. They half wanting me to, half not wanting me to. But this house 'minds me somehow—the way the logs chinked in so tight, the way wooden shelves fit in and even curved the walls. It even got two quilting poles on two of the walls.

Suddenly I can see Mamma's crazy quilts hanging on them. She'd hang them on those poles, those she didn't pile on the beds, so there'd be an extra one or two there if it got chilly of a night. Not just crazy quilts, but all sorts.

"You don't remember the Double Wedding Ring?" Mamma ask me a dozen times. "That was my favorite," she said. Told me I liked the green she worked in from my uncle's army shirt. The way she described those colors, I felt like I could see them, but I never really could. But now they flashed in front of me like they was so close I could touch them.

Mamma had to leave them all behind. She won't say why. I ask her why she don't do some more, but she just shake her head. "That time done," is all she say.

"Quilting poles," I say, and I see Miz Lawson look surprised. Nannie just look puzzled.

That Estill County house had a second floor, Daddy told me. This house is smaller, with a ladder up to a loft—good sleeping space for the boys if it ain't too hot. There a sloping back porch for when it is.

The kitchen got a big cast-iron pot with long legs in the center of the room. It almost look new. A round solid table, look like walnut, by the window. A wood range rest by the window on the other side. Nannie and I quick-eye each other. She didn't grow up poor like me, but this is nicer than anything we expected. It don't feel like any colored tenant house. It don't feel like a tenant house.

Light pouring in between the two windows. It near noon now and you can see the dust beams floating about eye level. It so bright there ain't no need for the electric light overhead, but Mr. Lawson switch it on anyway. Two pie safes and what look like a flour barrel is off in the corners. One of the corners got a sink. I looked at Mr. Lawson.

"Yep. Running water." He say, proud.

The rest of the house look as solid built as the kitchen. Two big bedrooms and what they called a sitting room. "A sitting room," I whisper to Nannie. "See, it do feel like a vacation home." She just shake her head like I the fool she always thought I was, but she don't say nothing. I see her thinking. She be wondering who this house was built for.

The back door got a path to the privy which is just the right distance away—too close you smell it, too far you always worried you gonna meet critters on the way.

"Look like a good house," I say to Mr. Lawson and he nod like I just telling the truth everybody knows.

"Jimmy and I built it ourselves. A colored fellow helped us. Wood right off the land."

Miz Lawson don't say nothing. Nannie turn to her.

"Who's Jimmy?"

I thinking they tell us who Jimmy is if they want us to know, but that ain't Nannie's way. I see Miz Lawson take a breath before she answer.

"Jimmy's our boy. Killed someplace called Luzon. Philippines. Just a few months before the surrender."

Nannie nod. I make some kind of noise. I see Mr. Lawson pull himself up straight again.

"The house wasn't finished when he left home. James—Mr. Lawson—worked on it up until we got the news. The colored fellow came when he had the time. He was a good carpenter. Then the Eliots, they're the family that worked the land up until last year, worked on it some. But it's been empty now since September. Getting a little musty."

With that, she open a big window in the sitting room. A March wind almost blow us down, but it feel good.

"I thought colored were all moving North—getting them factory jobs in Pittsburgh and Cincinnati," Mr. Lawson say talking to me, ignoring Nannie. "Everybody moving off the farms these days, especially colored. You in any trouble?"

I nod. It a fair question. I in any trouble? I reckon I am but not the kind of trouble he thinking about.

"No trouble. 'Cept the kind of trouble too many children and not enough job to feed them bring. Guess that kind of trouble is pretty common these days."

He don't say nothing. He just walk up to that open window and let the breeze blow him. Looking at them empty fields. I don't judge ages too good. He maybe sixty. Maybe a few years more. She look younger, but then she probably ain't out in the fields like he is. Sun and wind age you quick.

I know we ain't what you looking for but we here, I'm thinking. *That's more than the Eliots can say. Or your boy, Jimmy.*

We walk over the fields next—me and the boys with Mr. Lawson. I almost got to skip to keep up with him, bad leg or not. Nannie and Eleanor stay back with Harry and Miz Lawson. They talking kitchen things. Well, Harry ain't. But I see him running around the chicken yard with Eleanor following, so I reckon he getting to feel at home. I'm half out of breath before we halfway across the fields. It not Wolfe County, but it ain't Kansas either. We talk seeding and planting and Mr. Lawson find out that I know some farming. What I know is a bit old. It's almost twenty-two years since I left Estill County—but it come back. And farming don't change that much. At least it don't in Kentucky.

It helps that I did tobacco as a boy. "Anybody can grow corn," my daddy used to say, "but tobacco is particular." I see Mr. Lawson feeling better after we talk, but he still don't say yes. The boys run off from us, find a high rock tree island in the middle of the field and start to scramble up and down it like it some amusement ride out at Joyland Park.

Not that they know that much about Joyland. They only let colored in Wednesday nights and either their mamma or me usually working—even if we did have the dime, which we usually didn't. And neither one of us crazy enough to run four children on our own in that zoo. But we managed to go two times. The children still talk about it. Like we showed them Europe.

I rather see Joyland Park than the Europe I seen from the back of an army truck.

Mr. Lawson jump back when they run off like he forgot they is there. Then he pause and watch them.

"That was Jimmy's favorite place when he was a boy. He built some tree house in that old poplar. Some of it might still be there." I could see Franklin scrambling up something. "Tell him to take care," Mr. Lawson said. "Boards must be rotten by now."

I yell at them, but they out of earshot. Or they pretending to be. I'm thinking they'll be climbing some old rotten ladder and breaking their necks. "Boys!" I yell again, but they still don't hear me. Mr. Lawson next to me probably wondering why I so upset about boys climbing some trees. I take a breath like Nannie is always telling me to. I turn to Mr. Lawson.

"Well, we gonna be your tenants, Mr. Lawson?"

He turn and look at me again. He keep on staring at me like he can't quite take me in. I swear I feel like he want to touch my face just to make sure I real. The boys yelling something made him startle back. They maybe can't hear us but we sure hear them.

"Mr. Lawson?" I ask again.

"Yes, yes." He say. "You folks move in as soon as you can. We need to get moving. We need to get moving." And he turn and near trot back to the house. I yell at them boys who hear me this time. I see them running to try and catch up with us.

"We got to get moving!" I holler at them, though I see that they running as fast as they can. We all running as fast as we can. I start fussing at them for climbing up that tree house but gotta leave off to catch up with Mr. Lawson.

He never look back until he gets to the house.

The one they call Jimmy's house, not the big one.

CHAPTER 3
Wilma Lawson—March 1948, Scott County

When I heard that truck coming, I thought, *Thank you, Lord. Somebody's answered that ad.* They'll be people filling up...Well, no, not filling up—no filling up, not since Jimmy—but there'll be somebody working the land, using that vacant house. The Eliots put people in that house at least—almost made me forget. Sometimes.

That sorry creek bed we call a road makes even the best cars grind gears, so I heard them a good half mile off and then some. I'm sure it was a full fifteen minutes before I saw the pickup making its way into the yard. I spotted a boy jump out of the back to open the gate. It was a distance and my eyes aren't as good as my hearing, especially squinting through the kitchen window, but I thought, *Is that boy...?* But my James was rushing out and I didn't have time to think. James had just become aware of the company. I don't think he's going deaf, he just doesn't much listen. I'll be talking to him five minutes at a time and he'll say something that makes me realize I should have saved my breath to cool my porridge, as mother used to tell us.

He used to think what I said was interesting. But then I used to think so, too. But without an audience, your words just sort of flap in the wind like those old quilts I set to airing on the summer clothesline. I can watch them for hours at a time. Reds and greens. Each bit of color patch a memory.

I sound like I'm nostalgic for the past. But not all those memories are sweet ones. Not even most of them. No hurry to get the quilts in if it doesn't rain. James and I don't seem to need much covering, except on the coldest nights. I've left them to swing on the lines for days though I know that the colors I love will fade in the sun. And the wind will tear that fabric, some of it so thin now a baby's breath would pass on through.

Good. Let the colors fade. Let the wind tear them.

No wonder James thinks my talking just pretty sounds he doesn't need to understand. Just noise he can ignore until he can't. Sort of like that old grinding pickup pulling into the yard.

"You're colored," are the first words I heard James say. My eyes hadn't deceived me. My breath just left my body for a second. I had to hold onto the kitchen chair for balance. It just never had occurred to me—to us—that colored would answer that ad. One thing I knew: they weren't from Scott County—no colored from Scott County would come to the Lawson place. Only that one colored man during the war and he was from Estill. And white families, young white families willing to work that hard, or willing to work that hard for so little money, seemed very hard to come by these days. That's why I told James to branch out some—put an ad in *The Lexington Statesman*. We didn't think to say "Whites only." We figured anyone who knew our place would know that.

I got my breath back and hurried on out. I didn't know what I was going to do, but I knew James would need help. I thought I'd explain things real quick and hurry them back on their way, but when I got out there...I don't know. Everybody just looked so scared. Even the man looked like he was ready to gun that truck back up that gulch of a road if we blinked at him twice. But it was the children in the back of the truck that pulled at me. It was like they were all staring down the wrong end of a shotgun barrel. I looked back at the man and saw for the first time the woman with the little one on her lap. She was sweating, as if it was August and not just an over-warm March. Why were they so frightened of us? Two old people who together wouldn't have a fighting chance against the average five-year-old?

Well, of course, I knew why they were scared. Oh, it pulled at me. *First things first, though*, I thought. *These folks need some sweet tea.*

I don't know how we settled things. I never would have thought it when they first drove into our yard. I know James would have committed me to Eastern State—when I was a bride they called it the School for the Feeble-minded—if I had told him last week or even this morning that we'd be tenanting to a colored family. That they'd be in Jimmy's house. I know it's not Jimmy's house. "That's yesterday's news," I said to James when he called it that. As if I don't think the same thing every time I see it out the back window. But he never even lived there.

Still, when I think that in a day or two this Rudy Johnson and his family will be moving in, it makes me wonder. "But it's just a house," I told James. And the land doesn't much care what color's behind the plow. It just needs somebody. We need somebody. Somebody reliable.

Listen to me. I'm preaching the sermon I preached to James all through that first night. He looked stunned. I felt the same way but had to hide it. If James saw I felt the same way, he would have called the whole thing off. The story would have got round and nobody—white or colored—would have risked ruining their vehicle on our road again. So I had to act like it was just normal that colored folk were going to be living fifty yards away, that little colored children would be swarming around my kitchen door, smiling at me like I was just a sweet old grannie. A sweet old white grannie. An Oma, like I used to call my German grannie. I had to act like it was normal and do my best to make James think so, too.

I preached those words and he stared at me like I've stared at those old quilts blowing in the wind. Sometimes the sun would shine on those old rags, and I could see right through them. James says I've gotten so thin, he can almost see through me.

"We're married so long we see through each other," I say to him.

I remember the pants and dresses and curtains I'd save to cut and sew for those quilts. I saved too many things. I learned early not to waste anything. I thought we were building a big future. We'd have a dozen children, just like my mother. James' mother stopped at two. The Lord stopped for them, she'd say. Just like He did with Jimmy. Our first and last.

I didn't need to save as much as I thought I did. I probably could even start wasting if I wanted. But saving's a hard habit to let go of.

I don't know what James was thinking when he stared at me. I only sometimes know what James is thinking. I can't really see through him. When I do, half the time I wish I didn't. I don't know if James sees right through my words to the memories behind them. I don't know if he thinks I'm still judging, still hurting. I've told him I wasn't. I told him that I understood, that those were the times we lived. That he was a different man in those years. That I was a different woman.

It's not something either one of us ever mentions out loud anymore. Not for twenty years. Not since Jimmy was of an age to listen and understand. You can't mention things like that out loud and go on living together.

To go on living.

It's hard enough thinking the thoughts without putting the words into the air. What kind of words could we use? I just choose any that come to mind these days—no wonder James puts my sounds out of mind. I put my sounds out of my mind, too, my words just as ragged as those old quilts hanging on the line.

Let them hang there, I sometimes think, *until they piece themselves back to the earth.*

Let all the stories that quilt through them fade away, too, Lord.

Lord, hear my prayer.

CHAPTER 4
Nannie Johnson—late March 1948

Mr. Lawson's a deacon at that strange church that blocks the road, Miz Lawson told me, though she don't go there. I waited for her to tell me where she went, but she didn't. She did tell us there was a colored church, not two miles away as the crow flies. "I think it's a bit more when the crow walks." She smiled when she said that. She wants me to think she's a nice woman, and maybe she is. But I hold judgment on people—especially white people. I've met white ladies who you think first off were angels who had just come around to brighten up your slum a bit. Later on, you find out their wings were borrowed. Stolen probably. So I'm not saying yet if she a nice woman.

"The pie's in the tasting, not the looking," Mamma's always saying.

We were in the house kitchen. Miz Lawson had brought over a whole bundle full of quilts.

"The nights don't know spring is just one week away," she said. "After dark, you'll think it's still January."

I nodded. "Nice of you," I murmur, but so low even I can't hear me.

"Still, it's not too much further walking." I'm blank for a bit until I realize she talking about the church again. "You just cut through the fields. Tell anyone you meet that you're our tenants. You won't have any trouble."

She got a strange look when she said that word "trouble" and that did trouble me some. But she smiled again. "No, you won't have any trouble."

We were going to be near neighbors. Not as near as ones we got on Georgetown Street, but shouting distance. I've been around a lot of white ladies—worked for more than a dozen of them since I've been thirteen. Work for a woman and you know her better than anyone—husbands, children. You hear her talk to a woman-friend and you think, "Lady, you don't know the person you talking to. Come 'round laundry day and find out who she is." Two of the women I worked for was just mean.

You want to know a woman? See how she treat her colored help.

Took a few years' break from white ladies when I worked the tobacco plant and then Good Samaritan. But I've never had any as neighbors. I don't count living in an attic room so you can fetch what they want quicker being a neighbor. That's just maid duty. This was cooking in my own kitchen twenty steps from her cooking in her kitchen. I worried how it was all going to work out.

She pointed to the south. "Zion Hill. You hear of it? It's where that colored church is." I knew something about it—real country colored. "Colored store there, too," she go on. "And a new elementary school, just a couple years old. Some folks claim the colored school is better than the white one." She laughed. "Well, it's a whole lot better than the one-room shack it replaced."

I didn't know where to look when she said that. I found myself nodding like I was some old Mose. But I'm happy to hear about the school. The one the children go to in Lexington sure ain't anything to brag about, though the teachers try their best. But how you gonna teach when the school is half falling down and the textbooks they hand out have been to the white schools first for a good ten years? Then when they're just raggedy sorry things, they send them over to our children. Sometimes the books are missing pages. In my tenth grade history class, the teacher had to tell us about the Great War. That chapter was missing. I reckon we should be grateful those books made it to the Civil War or we still be in slavery days.

Maybe we are.

But you can't think like that. Can't let your children think like that. When Eleanor discovered that the book she brought home from school was missing pages, I thought she'd be mad as all get out. Mad as I was. Mad as I stay. But she wasn't. She just nod her head like that's what she expected. *Little colored girls are lucky to get even that much*, her eyes told me.

I carried on like I was a crazy woman. Rudy really thought I'd gone over the deep end. But I wasn't crazy. I wasn't even mad. I just had to get that look out of Eleanor's eyes.

The school wouldn't do a thing. Said they gave out what they got. But they heard from me until the principal promised to talk to the powers that be.

"Yeah, you do that," I told him.

Meanwhile I made the bookstore over on South Lime order me a copy of the same book. *Little Elephant Visits the Farm* by a fellow named Heluiz Washburne. Cost me half a week's salary almost, but I didn't care. Eleanor's eyes almost popped out of her head when I handed it to her. Brand new. Almost shining.

"For me?" she asked. "It's not my birthday."

"For you," I told her. Made me feel mean her saying that. Like she needed a birthday to feel special. Loved.

"Don't have to be your birthday. Little colored girls deserve pretty books to read. Ones that go all the way to the end." And just so that look wouldn't ever come back, I put my finger in her face like she'd been the one who done something wrong. "And don't you forget it."

Oh, Lordy, we read that book over and over again. "I'm seeing little elephants everywhere," I'd tell Rudy. But as many times as we read it, it stay brand new. Eleanor makes sure of that. She lets her brothers sit close and look when she reads it to them, but they know it be worth their lives to even think of putting their grubby little fingers on that book.

"Even got a high school." Miz Lawson was going on. "The colored had to raise a ruckus till we finally built it." She said it like I wasn't colored and standing right beside her. But then I think maybe that same thought come to her because she looked startled again.

That's right, I almost told her. *I'm colored. You forget?*

"Mr. Lawson didn't know why we needed it. I said the colored needed high school just like everybody these days. But then, he never went to high school himself." She was back to being polite-Kentucky lady. "Lexington has a good colored high school, doesn't it?"

"If you're not too particular about your history books. But, yes ma'am, it mostly does. Went almost three years. Dunbar High School."

"You didn't graduate?"

"Not from Dunbar. Job opened up at the tobacco steam room plant. Couldn't pass that up."

Or rather Daddy wouldn't let me pass it up. Daddy was like Mr. Lawson—didn't much see the point of high school. Especially for colored. He walked me down to that plant himself—bobbing up and down to Mr. Douglas, the manager. Says, "Here's my girl, Nannie, who don't need to be wasting her time schooling anymore." And that old white man looked me up and down and asked me if I was a good girl—Daddy pretending he didn't notice.

Well, I know times was near desperate and we needed that ten dollars a week. Sometimes we needed it to eat. I try to remember that, when I get mad at Daddy. And Mamma for letting him do that. I try to remember.

Oh, that's not fair. Mamma did everything she could to keep me in school. But she had six others to feed. And nobody in the family ever made it as far as I did.

They showed me where I'd be working. Daddy and Mr. Douglas both had to cover their mouths for breathing in the dust when we passed that factory door. Skedaddled back outside as fast as they could. I guess they figured young girls could breathe anywhere.

Leastways, young colored girls.

"Yes sir," I told Mr. Douglas. "I am a *good* girl."

I said the "good girl" extra loud. He got the message.

"Jimmy did." Miz Lawson said. I looked puzzled. "Graduate from high school. Jimmy liked school. Even got to go to Georgetown College three terms before we ran out of money. Talked of going back after..." She paused. She laughed, but she didn't look like she felt it. "His daddy couldn't get over that. Kept saying a farmer needed college like he needed a top hat and tails. Like Fred Astaire. "

I asked, "Why don't a farmer need college?" She stopped then and looked at me. That kind of down-talk just riled me. People always deciding what other people needed. Colored don't need high school. Farmers don't need college. "A farmer likes to use his brain just like everybody. I guess he don't need that top hat you're talking about, but I guess his brains might come in handy anywhere."

She just stared at me for a second and I'm thinking, *Well this is a good start. She's gonna tell me I got a whole lot of opinion for a colored girl and I'm gonna tell her I sure do and maybe living thirty yards away from your kitchen door is not such a good idea after all. Rudy is gonna come*

*in and find us moving out before we much moved in. Well,
Miz Nice White Lady, sooner's better than later.*

Miz Lawson nodded. "That's right, Nannie. Some of
the smartest men I've known have been farmers." She
smiled. "Some of the dumbest, too."

She was spreading out a quilt, and I grabbed the other
end. It had deep purple squares fitted into a Log Cabin
pattern. I stroked one of them. It felt like silk. "This a dress?"
I asked. I couldn't picture Miz Lawson in a dress that color.
She startled when I asked that.

"Oh no," she waved her hand like she was brushing
away some fly. "A robe. An old robe."

She reached for another quilt. "That was Mr. Lawson's
idea anyway. Farming. Jimmy had other ideas. You said you
didn't graduate from Dunbar, Nannie. Did you graduate from
another school?"

"Got my GED," I said. She looked puzzled. "It's a high
school diploma they arranged for all the soldiers who got
in the military before they finished high school. Used to be
you had to be a soldier to take the test, but a couple years
ago they started letting other people take it, too. Studied
up and took the test. First colored woman they ever had to
take it. Drove them crazy trying to figure out if it was legal."

"If it was legal?"

"Law didn't say one way or another, so I guess it was.
Not like those white boys and me was studying together.
When we took the test, they put me in the back away from
the others. I didn't care. Went straight from there to Good
Samaritan nursing."

"You're a nurse?"

"Not anymore. But that's a whole other story."

We heard the men coming in from the field. Even far
away we could tell they was talking what they always talked.
Farming. Smart or not, that's what a farmer talks about.

"Mr. Lawson and Jimmy went round and round about
schooling. James doesn't much care for other ideas." Her
husband was walking in the door when she said that. It
made me a bit nervous, but if he heard her, he didn't mind
her. Or at least he didn't let on that he did. Just stared at
her a moment like married folk do with an old argument.

One thing I knew for certain: the argument sure
wasn't our business.

Our business was farming, and whatever Mr. Lawson thinks about colored living in Jimmy's cabin, he's offered us a good deal. Mr. Lawson was supplying all the seed, the mule team, the tools, and even the fertilizer. He wrote it all out, and I read it as carefully as if I was reading about little elephants coming to the farm. Except we were the little elephants. The best I could have hoped for was halfers. And I was worried about that. Even with the extra work he promised, I didn't see how we were going to make a living on half the crop. But he said forty percent was all he needed with everything else, including the house, thrown in. I was thinking maybe I had misjudged the man, like Rudy is always saying I'm doing, especially white folk. But I've been around old crackers all my life, and I didn't think so.

The back of my head was just crawling. This good a deal just didn't make sense. I would know how to handle a hard deal. A good deal made me almost crazy with nerves. I wasn't catching something and I wouldn't rest easy till I got it.

"Go ahead and sign," I told Rudy. He smiled so wide it was Eleanor all over again with the elephant book. I'm surprised he didn't ask me if it was his birthday. He smiled so wide I didn't feel the need to join in. I let my frown just stay where it was—"Where it's found a permanent home," Mamma would say. But that's OK.

My frown told Mr. Lawson that whatever he was up to, I'd find out. He and Miz Lawson could wrap themselves in smiles as big as Eleanor's baby elephants, could be sweeter than the sweetest sweet tea. My frown was a warning. Sooner or later, I'd find out what was going on.

CHAPTER 5

Nannie Johnson—late March 1948

We were in our new place within two days. Had to be if we wanted to get the crop in. Mamma thinks we crazy—she's acting like we moving to Mississippi instead of one county over. Rudy's folks are worse. His mamma cornered me in the kitchen. She almost begged me not to move to Scott County. Told me I was the smart one in the family. "Rudy don't have a lick of sense," is the way she put it. Told me we could move in with them. With them? She and Rudy's daddy, Simon, live in a tiny little shotgun in Kinkeadtown that makes Mamma's place off Georgetown look as big as old Mrs. Breckinridge's place.

I've always liked Mamma Sally. She's a big woman. You wouldn't know she lived in the country—Estill County—'til she was in her mid-thirties. She's an all-city gal now, loves Lexington the way only old country colored do. Way more than I do. I guess growing up here, I see what it isn't. I told her that and she say, "That's right. It isn't Estill County." Mamma Sally never interferes when Rudy and I are fussing except for the looks she gives him and the sounds she makes—little "hmn hmns" she puts in, folding her arms—all telling him he should be listening to his woman. I tell her private that Rudy's not dumb. He just didn't have the chance for the schooling I got.

"Oh, he not dumb," Mamma Sally agrees. "But his heart too soft for his brain to catch up. That's why he needs you."

"Because I'm a hard-hearted woman?" I asked her.

"Because you a colored woman with four little ones who see the world clear. Your heart ain't hard, it tough. Rudy a sweet man and you blessed to have him. We all blessed. But he blessed to have you, too. Sweet's nice for dessert. But it can't be the whole meal."

So it surprised me when she goes on about Scott County. Once we decide something—once I decide something—she don't ever say anything about it. She won't even give me a good reason and that worries me. Just keeps telling me city colored don't know how mean white folks can get out where they ain't even pretending the law will protect them. I tell them there's a whole lot of colored in Scott County somehow surviving all that lawlessness, but that don't seem to comfort her and Simon any.

Only one worse is my Mamma who won't let up.

"A whole lot of colored in Mississippi, too," Mamma says. "And a whole lot coming North. I don't see too many going South like you doing."

When I tell her Scott County is actually north of Lexington, she just look at me. But she finally gave it up, too. Both mammas know there ain't much use arguing with me once I'm decided on something. "Hard-headed," is what my mamma calls me. "Hard-headed and hard-hearted."

Well, I'm your daughter, I feel like saying—but you don't push Mamma too far.

The way the mammas carried on, I thought they'd never make the long trek out to Scott County. And they didn't for a month or so. But what's the Bible say about loadstone acting like a magnet, drawing out the iron? That loadstone ain't got nothing on the power of grandbabies. They teamed up on a Sunday, and both of them came out regular. Even drag Uncle Zeb with them when they can't get Simon, Rudy's daddy.

I told them all there was lots of colored in Scott County, but the first couple of weeks we didn't see any. That was OK. It was good not having neighbors for a change. I was enjoying the little bit of quiet four children are gonna let you have. Miz Lawson and I might chat two minutes here or there of a day—might need to do business together maybe twice or three times, but she keeps her distance. I don't know if it's because she can't get used to colored thirty yards from her door or because she wants to let me know that she not one to interfere in my business.

Either way, I'm grateful. Our neighbors over on Georgetown Street a bit too close for comfort sometime— those little houses almost sitting in each other's laps. Always minding your business and wanting you to mind theirs.

But you need neighbors. And white folks ain't neigh- bors, even quiet ones like Miz Lawson. Quiet don't mean nice. Might be brewing up some meanness to spring on you.

"White folks are neighbors like coyotes are neighbors to sheep," I tell Rudy when he's irritated me to death going on about how nice the Lawsons are.

"Girl," Rudy say when I tell him that, "you got yourself some bitter tongue."

I think of giving him the bad eye, but I keep my head down. Sometimes, I don't know why he's with me. I'm as chintzy as they come. Mamma keeps shaking her head when I give Rudy some of my mouth.

"Child," she asks, "how you get such a solid sender for a man and you so salty, a person needs a glass of ice water just to look you up and down?"

"Well," I tell her, "that one thing you never was with Daddy. You never dared say boo to Daddy. You let him turn you into a house-slave. Let him yank me out of school and jail me in that dustbin of a tobacco factory. But as long as you wasn't salty to your man, I guess it was worth my giving up breathing."

Mamma just look at me. Don't say boo to me either. Daddy's gone more than five years now. I got more words than my tongue can handle. She did the best she could. Had more life with Daddy than most women have with sweet-tongued lovers. And he never hit her, I give him that. Beat us half to death, but never touched Mamma.

"Rudy ain't your Daddy," is all she answered.

She sure right about that.

As long as we're determined on moving to the wilds of Scott County, Mamma says we have to find a church. Mamma has always been a church lady—not any Holy Roller, but she sure loves her Jesus. And she likes the children to have some Jesus, too.

"Jesus is the sweet man you don't have to put up with day to day." A Sunday Jesus, sometimes a Wednesday night Jesus if you're not working, seems just right.

If I lived with Daddy, I'd want that Jesus, too.

But I got my own reasons for wanting Jesus. I don't need to be worrying all the time about somebody taking advantage of his sweetness to do him harm.

He already crucified.

I need my Jesus, too. We all do. I promised Mamma we'd find that church Miz Lawson talked about.

But it was a couple weeks before we could manage it, before the weather seemed nice enough because we were going to have to trek our way out to Zion Hill Baptist since Rudy's Uncle Zeb needed his pickup back for a couple of weeks. It was more than the two miles Miz Lawson talked about, crow or no crow. Closer to three. Country people always thinking it's half the distance it really is. Maybe because they always walking and don't think anything about it.

Scott County got enough hills to keep me from missing Wolfe County. Not that I remember it much. The children carry on like we was torturing them, like we making them march that Bataan Death March people always talking about. Especially Harry, who we end up toting most of the way.

It mostly a straight line south just as if we *was* headed to Mississippi. I howdy the few people we meet— they're all white and they look at us like we're something from Mars: a family of six colored suddenly appearing at their land's end, asking to walk on through, must have seemed pretty strange. But they nodded when Rudy explained who we were and who we was working for. Though when we said the Lawson name, jaws dropped again.

I asked Rudy why it should be such a surprise the Lawsons took a tenant, especially since they've been advertising for one. He just shrugged his shoulders. Trouble has to shake his fist in Rudy's face before he sees it—or before he nods his head back to it. Even then his nod might just be Kentucky polite.

You shake your fist at me and you'll be waving at the sky, flat on your back.

After they do their double take, the farmers mostly smile and nod. A few don't look too happy. I figure a couple of times the little bit of walk around the man's land was the better way to go. But most folks were friendly. More than one pointed to an outdoor well in case we wanted water. Well water in Wolfe County half the time made you gag with the sulfur smell, but Scott County's is smooth and clear—with just a hint of that limestone taste. We take them up on their offer every chance we get.

One man, though, wasn't just grumbling. He wouldn't even let us through his gate. The path led around the edge of the field so it wasn't like we'd be hurting anything. Had one of those junkyards some farmers in Kentucky accumulate—every piece of rusted machinery Detroit ever thought of. A mean-looking dog, too, just aching to take a chunk out of us. We told him we was Lawson tenants and he gave a kind of snort.

"James Lawson taking you on as tenants? Ain't that something? Getting religion in his old age. Probably that woman of his, Wilma. Don't much matter to me. No colored on my land. I don't care if you tenant for the governor. Tell James Edom Wachs says hello."

I wanted to give him a piece of my mind. Wanted to tell him that if we had a mind to we'd march through his sorry looking place—with its trash heaps lumped just about everywhere, not placed neatly above the creek level till you could burn it—march through like Sherman ripped through Georgia and all the sorry-looking white trash that got in his way.

I was opening my mouth to let him have it when I saw Rudy's face. He wasn't scared—just waiting to clean up the mess I was about to get us into. Or die trying to. Then I saw the children's faces. They were scared. So I kept my mouth shut for once.

Mamma's never around when I bite my tongue, but I do. Sometimes I bite so hard, it bleeds.

The walk around his land might have added a good quarter mile, maybe more. Once we were out of earshot, I let Rudy have it. He nods like I'm right, which just makes me madder and I let him have some more. At least the children stopped their whining about walking. They know when I'm on a tear. Even Harry tries walking for a while until his little legs just buckle and Rudy swoops him up.

We just keep heading south.

Our Sunday-best was a bit sweat-stained when we finally made it. We was just in time, made us start out the crack of dawn. If it's one thing I can't stand, it people straggling in late. But like every colored church I've ever been to, there's a crowd of men who haven't made it inside yet. Could have been the same group of peckerwoods who lingered outside the church in Wolfe County when I was a girl. Some would sneak in half through the service. Some never made it inside. Daddy made it in about twice a year.

If the white folks we met trekking the countryside thought we were from Mars, I think maybe these people thought we came from a planet they hadn't heard of yet. Even the few boys snuck in among their men whose mammas hadn't rounded them up yet didn't say anything. They just stared at us.

"Lord have mercy," I whisper to Rudy. "Where have you got us to?"

He nodded again like this crowd of silent starers was his fault, too, but I waved him hush. I thought everyone in that crowd was stuck frozen—like that game we played as children where we couldn't move till the leader touched us—but someone broke free and darted inside to summon the minister to come take a look at us. He at least had a tongue. He was one of those big old men who don't seem to shrink much with age. Black face, white hair. He introduced himself as the Reverend William Price. I don't know why but somehow he reminded me of Mr. Lawson—though they weren't any two peas in a pod. I guess they both big old men, both of them looking like they used to having their own way.

"You folks lost?" He stood in front of his congregation—they clustered behind him as if they were waiting for his signal. I was thinking if it was the wrong signal, we be hustled on out of there pretty quick.

"No sir. Reverend," Rudy is all smiles again. "We the new tenants on the Lawson place. My wife heard about your church and we come to worship."

He stared at us like Rudy's not speaking English. Maybe he's not. Maybe this a foreign country we ain't ever heard of in Lexington.

"Lawson? James Lawson?" The rest of the crowd seemed as startled. "You on Lawson's place?"

"We farming the fourteen acres." Rudy acted like the minister was wanting the terms of our contract, "Seven tobacco now and seven corn later on. And helping on his land, too."

"Where you living?" the preacher continued, looking like he was trying to take it all in. The rest of them didn't say a word.

"He got a house out by the barn."

"You living in his son Jimmy's house?" I heard a woman whisper, "Oh, Lordy." The rest of the church had joined the ringers outside.

"Anything wrong with living on the Lawson place?"
I asked, and I can tell this isn't a place where women speak
any, especially when they got a man next to them who's
supposed to do the talking. They look at me like I'm another
wonder.

But it wouldn't have mattered if Rudy had done the
asking. I've lived in country enough to know that asking a
question out loud ain't the way to get information. At least
not in Kentucky. You can see their faces shut down, like
the way the old broken assembly curtain would drop at
Dunbar High School after a show. I swear I could almost
hear the clunk.

But strange folks or not, the Reverend was
remembering *his* Kentucky. "Oh, no, nothing wrong with
living on the Lawson place. Just surprised they have
colored to farm that land. It always be white folks." The
Reverend made a gesture for us to come in. "You folks walk?
You must be tuckered out. Come in. Child," he gestured to
a young girl, "go and rustle up some cold water. I expect
they just about parched."

Well, at least they noticed we were colored. That
was something. But something wasn't right and I gave Rudy
a look saying, *What have you got us into now?* Of course, I
know I got us into it, too, but if he's going to be the man—if
I'm to be the woman just following her man and keeping
her mouth shut—he's going to have to take the blame.

Sweet Jesus. I'm too tired to take it all on myself.

After the Reverend invited us in, it seemed to give
permission to everyone else to talk to us and they did—but
stiff, like we're applying for a job they're not about to give
us. They nod when we tell them we're from Lexington and
repeat it after us. Yes, Lexington. They met lots of people
from Lexington, as if it weren't less than twenty miles away
and it the biggest town in more than fifty.

But the way they talk, Lexington seemed a whole lot
farther away. "I been to Lexington," one old man told me, in
the same way Rudy might let on he's been to Paris. The France
one, not the Bourbon County one. If I told them we spoke
French in Lexington, they'd probably just smile and say they
weren't surprised. "Strange things do go 'round." That's how
they spoke. And if truth be told, they might have added we
was the strangest things they'd seen in a good while.

As soon as the minister made it to the pulpit, all the chatting stopped. I hadn't had a good impression of him outside—seemed too much like the big frog in the little pond. I'm not saying he was a false preacher—what we call a Mitt Man down home—only that he got on my nerves some. Mamma says the whole world gets on my nerves some. "You especially," I'd tell her if she weren't my mamma and taught me better. No, I knew he was real. Maybe just playing his role of minister too long. Maybe just too used to having an adoring congregation hang on every word. If he thought I was going to join the crowd of gazers, he had another thought coming.

But when he opened that Bible and started in to chanting, all that stuff outside the church just passed on by. I expected a big man like him to boom us out of our pews, but he spoke soft at first. The whole church leaned forward to hear him.

"My verse today is from the Old Testament, the book of Hebrews, Chapter 13, Verse 2. *Do not neglect to show hospitality to strangers, for thereby some have entertained strangers unawares.* Angels."

He looked directly at us and smiled. He waited until it seemed the whole congregation was looking at us and smiling. I wanted to drop in a well somewhere and hide, but Rudy sat there and took it in like the preacher's words was spring rain on a dry bed. He smiled back. The children—even Eleanor, who mostly shies from anyone new—smiled. I had to keep Harry firm on my lap—he looked like he was ready to join any lap that would have him and they all looked like they would.

All my children are like Rudy—thinking the world a welcoming place full of kind people just waiting to take them in. I'm the mean mamma, always chiming in with her "Wait a minute." "Hold back." "It's not all that it seems." Makes me tired sometimes. Sometimes I wish Rudy would take on some of the meanness—let me be the smiling mamma. But that's not his way.

Finally, after what seemed an hour but was probably only a minute or so, the minister continued. "Well, our new neighbors today don't look like angels. Maybe the children do, but then all children look like angels when they're not playing the devil. But the grownups sure don't look like angels—not like the angels we got in that window there," and he pointed and we all looked. Sure enough, there was an angel in the window. A blue-eyed blond angel. And we surely didn't look anything like him. Or her. It's hard to tell with angels. "But that don't mean they ain't angels," and he'd gotten louder.

I heard a few amens breaking ranks. The first few amens are like the first raindrops in what you just know is going to be a big downpour, a summer storm. Those first drops, those first amens, make a splatter of noise. Later on you won't be able to pick out one from another, later on it will be just a rain of noise, but those first ones make you hold your breath. *Oh, it's coming. A big storm is coming.*

"Look at your neighbor," the preacher was yelling now, and it was a clap of thunder, "look at your brother, look at your sister. Do they look like angels?" And people actually turned to each other like they hadn't seen each other five times a day all their lives. This was a small community. Shouts of "Yes, Yes," mingled with the amens scattering through the pews. "Look at yourself. You know you're a sinner. You know you've broken Jesus's heart time and again."

He paused then and we felt ourselves breaking that heart over and over. *Oh, why did we do it? Why?* I even felt myself wondering why. The man was a magician. Maybe just a very good preacher. He was back to whispering. We all leaned forward. The amens paused. "But does that mean you ain't an angel? Does that mean you ain't got the angel inside of you? Sisters, brothers, children, we all got that angel inside of us." He raised his voice and we raised our heads. "When we don't see that angel, it's because we ain't looking hard enough. Sisters, brothers, children, Jesus sees those angels. Jesus always sees those angels, even when we act the devil. Jesus sees those angels, and we got to see like Jesus. We got to see like Jesus."

The amens came back full force, but I didn't notice because I was amening with the rest of them. We were clapping and shouting. The children looked as fresh as if we hadn't made them trek almost three miles over fences and hills. Rudy was in full swing amening. Even little Harry was amening. It wasn't hard seeing the angel in Harry or Eleanor or Herbert or Franklin. I saw the angel in them even when I fussed at them. I saw the angel in Rudy.

The only angel I usually didn't see was the angel in my own mirror. I just hoped my family could see that angel sometime, even when I was being the mean mamma. Even when I fussed at them. Especially when I fussed at them.

What was hardest for me, though, was seeing the angel in the church window, that blue-eyed blond angel looking down at us. I've never seen a blue-eyed angel, not one outside a church window. I've never seen one walking about in the real world of Kentucky. That preacher might say I'm not looking hard enough. Rudy might say the same thing. *Keep on looking,* they might tell me. *Keep on looking.* "Amen," I say to that. "Amen."

I'll keep looking. But I'll keep an eye out for the devil, too. It's not always easy to tell who's an angel. Who's the devil. Sometimes, they all mixed up. It's kind of like figuring out if it's a man or woman angel. You'd think that would be easy—you'd think you could tell that much fifty feet off. But you don't know what to look for in an angel. Sometimes even the devil will surprise you. Even when they're smiling.

Especially when they're smiling.

CHAPTER 6
Rudy Johnson—late March 1948

Uncle Zeb finally sell me his old pickup, fifty dollars down and another hundred when I get it. I get it in dribs and drabs. Just hope I can drib and drab it all off before it joins the old Model T in Mr. Lawson's front yard. Uncle Zeb didn't want to sell it, but Mamma pressure him. Probably told her baby brother we can't survive in the wilds of Scott County without it. That's the way the whole family talks. Even when I told Mamma about the angel sermon, it didn't seem to make much difference.

"More devils than angels in Scott County," she grumbled.

"What you got against Scott County?" I ask her.

She look at me hard a second. Make me nervous the way she looking—like she expecting me to be remembering something. Like I suppose to know what she talking about. She turn away.

"I ain't got nothing against Scott County. I don't know Scott County. You know how I feel about country living. Your daddy and me bring you to the city, away from all that. Farming, especially tenant farming, is a way to break your back and empty your stomach. City is where all the jobs is."

"I already break my back on Nannie's mamma's couch. And not too many city jobs knocking on my door lately."

She just keep her back turned. Don't even answer back, which ain't like Mamma. She and Nannie are two of a kind. It's Estill County again. But Mamma ain't telling, and I'm done asking.

We haul the children down the two miles to that church stuck in the middle of the road. A school bus pick them up there. We thought to leave them behind in Lexington for the last couple of months—all except Harry, of course. But the new White Sulfur Elementary they just built in Zion Hill seemed a whole lot better than the crowded school off Upper in Lexington which they be going to. If Estill County had better schools, I too young to remember. White Sulfur replaced the one-room school they had for fifty years or more.

We promised Mr. Lawson plenty of help, so we needed the children with us. We got chickens to feed and three weanling pigs Miz Lawson found for us. The boys gonna have to help me build a pen for them. Right now, pigs so tiny they sharing the chicken coop. Chickens and pigs all getting along. "See," I tell the boys. "They don't make no fuss about the crowding."

Herbert and Franklin been grumbling 'cause Eleanor getting her own room and they sharing. Of course, when those piglets get a hundred pound on them the sharing might get a little rough.

I thought the children be bringing home stories from school—children usually get information way sooner than grownups. "Everybody nice," Eleanor say, though she miss her old school in Lexington. But they don't talk much. Herbert and Franklin say the same thing. Of course, boys never talk much. Still it's worrisome. Like the children been warned not to say anything.

Of course, might be nothing to tell, but Nannie don't think so. And Nannie usually right about these things.

I don't know what Mamma got against country living. A man can do just about anything without any neighbors or policeman saying no. Still can't pee off the back porch with Miz Lawson and Nannie around, but do just about everything else. Can't mosey over to Deweese Street for a quick beer or a haircut, but that's OK. I don't need the beer, and Nannie cut my hair just fine.

Of course, the work hard. And long. The days are stretching out in March, but that just mean the work day longer. But I don't mind. The boys don't even seem to mind. Don't even miss the no-accounts they hang out with over on Georgetown. It's peaceful here. Quiet. Don't have no roosters yet so we don't even have to listen to that. Just some birds chirping before light telling me it's another day. I wake even before Nannie most mornings in that gray half-light before the sun full up. I like that time better than any, like to wake up gradual. Even when I was a boy, Mamma let me be late rather than rouse me rough. Nannie the same way. Only time she wake me is with the climbing-ladder dream. And then she do it soft.

I love that ten minutes just laying there. It the sweetest ten minutes of the day. I ain't what you call a real church man. Don't want to be any deacon or usher. Don't want to join any Bible-study group. But that ten minutes in the morning, I lay there thinking about all I got. Not thinking. Just feeling it. It start with Nannie, who pushes herself up to my side so hard sometimes she almost push me out the bed. Don't matter if the bed big or small, I get the same little corner. And Harry on a trundle right beside us, snoring like he as big as Eleanor's baby elephant and not just a few pounds more than them weanlings.

Mamma come in on us one time and wonder how any of us get any sleep with him "snorting like a little pig."

"Wouldn't know how to get to sleep without it," I tell her. Same with my big-grumbling little boys overhead. "Ain't fair sharing," they say. It don't matter them pushing and shoving each other so rough some nights Nannie and me think the roof gonna tumble down on us. They'd miss that pushing when it gone. So will we. Just like I can't sleep without Nannie's elbow pushing in my ribs as if she Eve trying to get back in. Sometimes Eleanor get lonely in her own room next door. She push herself into our bed and I squeezed both ways like a grilled cheese sandwich. That OK. Once that pushing gone, you on your own.

Once that pushing gone, it all gone.

I lay there thinking how I gonna get past Eleanor without her waking? How I can slip on out and give Nannie a bit more rest. I lay there that ten minutes thinking of all I got to do, of the hard day's work ahead. But that ten minutes is like a full night's rest. I mind a full day's work? Jesus, sweet Jesus, if this ain't what you meant by heaven, it will do alright until we get there.

I don't know what Mamma has against all this peace and quiet.

When I heard the piglets squealing, I thought maybe a fox or a raccoon was trying to get in the chicken coop. It was pitch black outside and I weren't thinking straight. I was hardly thinking at all. That coop was shut tight, but I'm half wondered if one of the children left a latch open. I pulled myself away from Nannie, who barely stirring. I didn't bother with my overalls—just leap over Harry, grab a broom handle, and head for the pigs. It a shame if something got those pigs—going to be the children's chore this summer, though I didn't want them making pets of them. Hard to eat a pet.

The chicken coop a good two hundred yards from the house. I thought it too far but Nannie grew up with chickens and she ain't that fond of them. "The rooster don't just crow at sunbreak," she say. "It crow all day long. And you can clean all day long, chickens ain't the best house-guests." Two hundred yards is a good hike, but almost too close for Nannie. It quiet by the time I get outside. That mean the fox already gone and done his damage, or else it a false alarm. Maybe pigs get bad dreams, too. They ain't four days away from their mamma. Maybe they missing her. Miz Lawson saw a sign down at the grocery store. Thought three piglets just the right number for us: one for each child. Any more and we'd be running a pig farm. Three is a pretty small number for a litter. But the boar had killed the others and the farmer afraid he'd get these, too.

Miz Lawson real happy when she brought us to the truck to show us the tiny piglets. Smiling, even.

"I caused quite a stir when I said I wanted them. Mr. Thompson, the grocer, couldn't believe I was in the business of raising pigs again. Jimmy used to raise at least three every summer. One year he brought home seven, but I told him never again. Seven pigs in the vicinity is not the way to gracious Southern living. No, I told Mr.Thompson. These three pigs are for my tenant's children."

She stopped talking like she a car that slammed on the brakes. She does that sometime. She stopped smiling, too. Nannie looked at her.

"He say something about that?"

Miz Lawson wave her hand. She always wave that hand.

"Oh, people say things all the time. I don't pay them any concern."

The children was all squealing over them piglets by then. Eleanor already got one cradled in her arms like a baby doll.

"That ain't no baby doll," I tell her. "That's a baby pig you're gonna raise and we gonna eat." She look at me like I'm saying we gonna eat Harry, but she got to learn. She a farmer's daughter, now, and this what farmers do. She put

JOSEPH G. ANTHONY

him down and he run to his brothers. Or his sisters. We ain't looked that close yet.

What with all that we never did get a chance to ask Miz Lawson what that man say to upset her. I'm thinking if she wanted us to know, she'd tell us, but Nannie ain't satisfied.

"Something going on," she say.

I'm still about a hundred yards away when I see the horses. Two of them. I'm trying to take it in—I know Mr. Lawson ain't got any horses, and I can't think of any near neighbors who got them. Horses is for rich people. This the Bluegrass, but you wouldn't know it sometimes. I'm still standing there like I'm frozen when first one fellow and then another come running out of the coop, pull those horses up, and jump on them.

"Whoa," I yelled, and they both turn and look at me a second. I wondered if they gonna charge right at me, but they let out a yell—it a yell that curdle your blood, but I can't make out no words—yank their horses' heads and gallop the other way. They still yelling. I hear Nannie opening the door behind me. "You get on back," I shout to her, but I see her coming anyway. This ain't making no sense. Chicken thieves? Pig thieves? Them chickens and pigs ain't worth a thin dime. Come back after a summer's fattening and maybe you get something, but nothing now.

Those piglets ain't ever gonna see a summer or get a summer's fattening. One good come out of it: they done with missing their mamma. Somebody had slit each of their throats, then slit them lengthwise so their little guts was hanging out their bodies. One piglet was stuck to the wall with a pitchfork. Blood was everywhere. Pigs do bleed. I remember that from pig-slaughtering times.

That blood was precious. Mamma and the other women used to catch every drop they could to make blood pudding. Daddy sure loved his blood pudding. I never cared for it myself. You'd think these piglets were grown up hogs as much blood as was spread around.

The chickens seemed OK. They strutting around like they ain't just witness a mass killing. Chickens are like that. They forget real quick. A good thing. If you a chicken.

Nannie beside me before I know it, holding a lantern. I'd run out without no light. Didn't think I'd need one for a little ol' fox.

"Jesus," is all she say at first. She let that lantern ghost its way up the wall. Looked liked something was written on it. Somebody had taken a bundle of straw and dipped it in some of that piglet blood. Used it like a pen:
THIS IS WHITE LAND NIGERS
"Jesus," Nannie said again.

I heard the kitchen door slam again. One of the boys—I couldn't tell which—was headed towards us. "You get back to bed now!" Nannie yelled. He stopped. It was Franklin, I could tell now. Herbert would sleep through an air raid. "Now!" Nannie yelled again but he still stood there.

"Son," I shouted. "You go on like your mamma said. Your mamma and I are just fine. We be in in a minute."

He nodded and turned around at that.

All that yelling finally turned on the lights in the big house. Both the Lawson were on the back porch. It was getting to be that half-gray time. But ain't much hope for that ten-minute peace today.

We stared at the writing like it was going to say something different if we looked at it long enough.

"That how you spell nigger?" I ask Nannie.

She turned to look at me. "How did I marry a man who don't know how to spell better than a third grader? Eleanor spells better than you. Harry, maybe. Of course that's not how to spell nigger. Those crackers aren't just mean crazy, they're stupid."

I just shake my head. Mamma was right. It a good thing I married a smart woman.

CHAPTER 7
Jimmy Lawson—June 1928, Scott County

Mamma says if any of my pigs get into her garden one more time, she's going to get Daddy to nail us all up by our ears—pigs and boy included, she threatens. I never saw her so mad. I told Mamma I thought they were safe inside the pen I built, but pigs can snout up anything. Mamma said I built them for what they weighed last month. They're getting to be hogs. I bet they gain two pounds a day. Mamma was right. Seven is too many. All I do is run pigs. I've hardly been swimming in the Elkhorn all summer, and it's running hard. Last year was so dry you almost had to lie face down in it to get wet, but the rain's been steady this spring. Mamma tells me to take a dip in it before I even think of coming inside—especially after I've been with the pigs. I only have time to jump in and out.

I asked Mamma if she always hated pigs.

"Not always," she said. "I was an agnostic on the subject of pigs. But you and your seven have made me see the light. I now believe pigs are the blight of the earth."

When Mamma talks like that, I just bend over laughing if Daddy's not around. He hates it when Mamma throws around Bible words like "seeing the light." Mamma's not a church lady. Aunt Alice says that Mamma was raised Catholic as a girl, but she never talks about it. I think it's a sore subject with Daddy. There's a Catholic church in Georgetown, but she's never been as far as I know. She almost never goes to our church, either, even though Daddy's one of the deacons. He even preaches sometimes when the minister's away. She might go then.

"What's the Bible verse," she'll ask. If it's Old Testament, she mostly stays home. I stay home, too, if I can get around Daddy.

"What's an agnostic?" I asked her when I stopped laughing.

"Someone who neither believes nor doesn't not believe," she answered. When I shook my head, she tried again.

"Somebody in the middle. On the one side are the believers, on the other side the non-believers. In the middle are the agnostics."

I still looked puzzled.

She smiled. She likes it when I question things. "When you're not joining either group. You're off by yourself. Sometimes that's the only place to be. "

I thought about that a moment. "I don't think I like agnostics. Seems chicken. You should pick a side."

Mamma didn't say anything for a moment. "You're probably right. But it's not always easy—especially when you see both sides." She waved her hand—that meant she was done with talking. "But I know the side I'm on concerning pigs in my garden. And you'll be feeling your sides if it happens one more time."

I went out and worked on the pig fence. I don't know how they pushed through—they weren't that big yet. I reckon at least two pigs had joined forces together, maybe three. Pigs are smart. I cussed those pigs a right blue streak. But I kept my voice low. Mamma was mostly joking about me feeling my sides—even Daddy hardly ever licks me— but neither one of them go for cursing, even at pigs.

One of those pigs came up to nuzzle me—like she was my black bitch dog, Haggy. Pigs are like that. I pushed her away.

"They ain't pets," Daddy warned me. First pig I had I named. Come slaughter time, that hog's eyes searched me out. Daddy looked at me, shook his head, and looked away, he was so disgusted.

Mamma found me hiding in my room later. Told me a soft heart was a hard thing in this world. I never named no more pigs.

I think I only named that pig because I felt like I needed to be naming something. Mamma had named my bitch Hagar. It's a Bible name, which Daddy says is sinful naming a dog for someone in the Bible, so I mostly call her Haggy. But when Mamma calls her, she always says Hagar. She'll shout out the back porch, "Hagar, Hagar," and Haggy will knock me down to get to Mamma. She loves Mamma more than me. Sometimes Daddy looks like Mamma's hitting him in the head each time she yells out Hagar, but he don't say nothing.

First chance I got, I went and wrote that word down in the notebook Mamma bought me. Agnostic. Looked it up in the big dictionary Mamma has on its own stand smack center in the sitting room. Should be a Bible on that stand instead of a dictionary, Daddy says, but he don't interfere. The sitting room is Mamma's.

A person who claims neither faith nor disbelief in God. I thought hard about that. "You believe or you don't." That's what Daddy says. And the ones who don't believe are damned. A whole lot of people are damned. Sometimes even before they're born. I don't understand that, but it'd be like cussing to ask Daddy. He'd pull that strap out so quick I'd be spinning faster than Mamma's egg whisk when she's beating egg whites. But I still think it. *Why would God make people just to damn them?*

Sometimes, I worry about Mamma not going to church regular. I lie awake at night wondering if she's going to hell just like Aunt Alice, Daddy's sister. It's two, three years now, and sometimes I have to think hard on Aunt Alice to get her face. I remember her smell better. Mamma has a row of lilac bushes pushing up the walk to the house. When they're in full bloom come May, it's like the smell hits you smack in your face. Daddy says it's like running the lilac gauntlet. Aunt Alice smelled like that, only not so strong. Even still, sometimes the smell was so thick it lingered when she was gone. Got into your shirt or sweater so when you sniffed at a sleeve of yours—even days later— you thought Aunt Alice.

Aunt Alice was the only lady I knew who cut her hair, though Mamma threatens to cut hers every now and then. Said it would be so much easier only Daddy would have a fit. And one time Aunt Alice left red lipstick marks on my cheek when she kissed me. Mamma didn't say anything when she wiped them off, but she looked surprised.

Aunt Alice sometimes would bring a soldier along with her when she came out to the farm. She lived alone in Georgetown. Worked in the poultry place on Water Street. "This is Uncle Tommy," she said to me one visit, but Daddy got mad. Said the fellow wasn't anybody's Uncle Tommy as long as there weren't any marrying. Aunt Alice just laughed. She leaned down and whispered in my ear, "You just think Uncle Tommy in your mind."

Then Uncle Tommy picked me up and threw me up so high I thought I'd hit the ceiling. He smelled nice, too, only his smell was tobacco and whiskey. A lot of fellows smelled like that.

Aunt Alice hated that poultry place. Hated living with her old maid cousin, Sarah, who fussed at her about just about everything, but especially about Uncle Tommy. She had to live with cousin Sarah. Talked about living alone, but Daddy said a young woman couldn't do that in Georgetown, Kentucky. Even Mamma told her that.

Aunt Alice didn't have any parents, and we lived too far in the country, so she had to do with old Cousin Sarah. My grandmamma and papaw died in the flu sickness back in '19 when I was just two. Don't remember them none. And Mama's folks died before she was barely grown, so I'm out of luck for grandparents is the way Mamma puts it. Her daddy and mamma had married her to Daddy and then just "gave up the ghost."

"What's that mean, Mamma? 'Gave up the ghost.'"

"I think it means they thought the Holy Ghost didn't have much say-so in die-hard Protestant Scott County." When she sees I don't know what she's talking about, she tries again. "Your grandparents just were waiting to see if I was safe before they passed on."

I still didn't understand that, but I knew Mamma was done being questioned. Mamma gets that strange look in her eye when she tells that story. Safe. Like maybe she don't believe it yet.

Mamma was an only child—just like me. And Aunt Alice was Daddy's only sister—no brothers, either. So I'm out of luck for aunts and uncles—even cousins, if you don't count the old ones like cousin Sarah.

I lost the only aunt I had when Aunt Alice ran off to Chicago with Uncle Tommy. I guess she couldn't stand it anymore. People talked about her terrible. I even heard some of the talk, though most people were shy of talking bad about her when I was around. It's because she sometimes saw more fellows than Uncle Tommy. Edom, a fellow who stripped tobacco for us, was telling me that. I didn't see anything wrong with seeing other fellas I was going to tell him when he shut up quick and walked away. He saw Daddy coming. Daddy would pounce on anybody talking about his sister, though that don't mean he didn't say plenty to Mamma. Mamma told him people would talk about any woman living alone—or practically alone. Half-blind cousin Sarah couldn't keep much tabs on Aunt Alice.

I half-heard that kind of talk all my life, but something more must have happened before she left with Uncle Tommy—some story going round that made everybody jumpy. I don't know what it was—even that tobacco stripper, Edom, wouldn't give me a hint. Got real red in the face when I asked him why everybody was real upset with Aunt Alice. Just shook his head and walked away. I heard Daddy shouting at Mamma. He weren't shouting at her—just shouting while she was there in front of him, and I knew it had something to do with Aunt Alice. I lay my head down on my bed floor and listened as close as I could, but what I heard didn't make much sense. I heard the word "nigger" and then Mamma shushed him. That surprised me because Daddy never uses that word—says it's common. Won't let me use it neither. Even when the farm hands use it, he looks at them hard.

When Aunt Alice finally left, that was another ruckus. Daddy wanted to hunt her down, but Mamma said what good would that do? "She's free, white, and twenty-one." I thought that was funny the way Mamma said that. I ain't ever heard that expression before.

"Maybe they married in Chicago," I heard Mamma telling Daddy. Daddy turned his head at that.

"Tommy?" he asked her.

"Who else? That's who she ran off with, didn't she?"

"We don't know who she ran off with," Daddy said. "Nobody saw her leave."

"Well Alice is gone and Tommy is gone," Mamma finished. "I'm just putting two and two together. It doesn't make five."

That was one of Mamma's expressions when she tried to explain something simple. "Two and two don't make five." But this wasn't simple. *It don't make five*, I thought, but felt real bad. I couldn't understand any of it. I didn't know why she couldn't have married Uncle Tommy here and stayed close. Everybody I knew had more aunts and uncles than they could name. She was my only one.

I don't know if Daddy believed Mamma or not, but he didn't go after Aunt Alice. "She was damned from the beginning, I reckon," is all he said. That made me feel real bad, but Mamma came and found me, just like she did after Betsy—my sweet old hog—got slaughtered.

"Your Daddy doesn't know who's damned or not," she said to me. "The Lord hasn't given anybody that know-ledge—especially not your daddy. Aunt Alice is finding her own way. It might not be our way but that doesn't mean it's wrong. I expect she'll have a very good life."

I remembered feeling real surprised that Mamma didn't think Daddy knew who was damned or not. I was pretty sure he did. But I felt better. Maybe Aunt Alice would be OK, though I figured we wouldn't be seeing her for a good spell, maybe never, and that made me feel lonesome. "You can't say never," Mamma said. We don't know that—but she allowed it might be a while.

It wasn't a year after she left that we heard Aunt Alice got killed in some fight. She wasn't doing the fighting, was just in the wrong place at the wrong time. Stabbed or shot—never did hear it straight. Wasn't supposed to hear any of it but I questioned Edom and the others and they told me bits and pieces till I heard most of it. And Mamma told me what she knew when I questioned her.

Aunt Alice didn't die right off. Lingered maybe three days. Time enough to tell the hospital people our names, Mamma said. But we didn't get the news until she was gone a couple of days. They called the sheriff in Georgetown but he took a day or so to drive on out to us.

For weeks, Mamma would cry of a moment at the thought of Aunt Alice dying alone. "Poor Alice," she'd say real low. Daddy would pull himself up when Mamma cried—like he was standing at attention. Uncle Tommy used to play that with me.

"What happened to Uncle Tommy?" I asked Daddy. He didn't even fuss at me about calling him uncle.

"Long gone," is all Daddy said.

The Chicago people wanted to know if we were going to bring her back home or pay for her burying there. If we didn't they'd have to put her in a pauper's grave. Daddy told the sheriff to go and put her in that pauper's grave, but Mamma raised a fuss—Mamma almost never raises her voice about anything unless she's yelling for Hagar. She told Daddy she'd pay for the grave herself if she had to. She'd sell her jewelry, though I don't think she had much more than her wedding ring.

I ain't seen anybody tell Daddy he's wrong right to his face. He's just a deacon down at the church, but as far as anybody can tell, he runs the place. The minister is always nodding yes sir to anything Daddy says. Like everybody else. One time a farm hand gave Daddy some back talk, but Daddy just looked at him hard. That man stopped talking except trying to explain himself, but it was too late. Daddy just threw a few dollars at the man and told him he had ten minutes to clear out. And that was in the middle of tobacco stripping time when help is scarce.

But when Mamma told Daddy she'd sell her wedding ring, Daddy didn't have a word to say. The sheriff kept his head down like he thought our old pine floor real interesting all of a sudden. Finally, Daddy told the sheriff that he'd pay for a decent burial in Chicago, but not to bring her home. And not to wait any longer. None of the family would be attending.

"She left home a long time ago. Chicago's her home now," is what he said.

Mamma calmed down. "Poor Alice" is all she kept saying. Daddy wouldn't let Mamma name Aunt Alice in church—or ask the church people to pray for her.

"We're not Catholic," Daddy said. "We're not going to pray her out of hell."

"Catholics don't pray people out of hell," Mamma said. "We help them out of purgatory."

"Same difference," Daddy said.

"No," Mamma answered, and she got that look in her eyes again. "Purgatory ends. Hell doesn't."

I never heard Daddy say Aunt Alice's name again after the sheriff left, though sometimes Mamma would tell me stories when Daddy weren't around. Stories about when they'd been girls together. Scott County ain't so big you know just about everybody.

"Were you friends?" I asked Mamma, and she'd nod.

"We tried to be," is what she said, which I don't understand. *You're friends or not,* I thought, but that's all Mamma would say about it. She's like Daddy there. If she don't want to talk about it, it don't get said.

It'd been maybe two years since I had seen Aunt Alice when we heard about her killing, but I ran to the chest where Mamma kept the winter sweaters. I got out the big wool one Mamma had knit for me. I hadn't worn it for a good couple years since it had got too small for me, but Mamma kept all that stuff. "You never know," she'd say. I'd been wearing the sweater the last time Aunt Alice visited. I remember because she went on and on about how tight the stiches were and kept nuzzling me till I thought I was going to fall right over with that lilac smell. I found that sweater and nuzzled it myself like I was one of the pigs trying to snout my way to freedom.

But I couldn't smell anything. Leastways no lilacs. Mamma had stuffed some moth balls in with the sweaters. Their smell crowded out Aunt Alice. I cried a little then, but nobody heard me. Not even Mamma.

I think it was maybe then that Mamma stopped going to church so regular. I worry about her. I keep thinking *Mamma's a good woman. She might not be a church lady, but she didn't run off with any soldier. And she ain't ever wore any rouge or lipstick.*

"It don't matter," Daddy says, "if you're good or bad. If you're not a believer, you're damned." I wanted to ask him if babies born damned were believers or not, but I didn't dare to. I'd felt that strap. It weren't worth it.

Maybe Mamma's an agnostic, I'd think, worrying at night. *Maybe she'll just go to Purgatory.*

Whatever that is.

CHAPTER 8

Jimmy Lawson—June 1928, Scott County

When I heard the commotion, I thought at first, *Oh the pigs have got out again and I'm in for it.* Mamma's not like Daddy. She's not reaching for the strap for every little disagreement you might have with her. But if you try her patience "one nerve too many," as she puts it, she'll find some branch to wrap your legs around. I was thinking, *How in tarnation could those pigs get out again,* when I realized it weren't pigs I was hearing. Some men were shouting words I couldn't make out and horses were making that kind of high whine they make when they're upset over something. I ran to the window. I weren't half-awake, and first I thought I was looking at a crowd of ladies on horseback because all I could see were a bunch of people in what looked like dresses. But then even in the half-moon dim light, I made out two fellows with beards.

Why are those fellows wearing dresses? I thought, knowing I wasn't making no sense but neither was what I was seeing. Then I saw Mamma outside, too, and she was in her nightgown—in front of grown men, which maybe surprised me more than anything I seen. Two or three of the men jumped off their horses and were reaching for a fellow who'd been riding double just in front of another fellow. The man in back was holding the first fellow up.

That man's hurt, I thought just as Mamma yelled out, "James!"

I ran down the steps as fast as I could with Haggy barking and in and out of my feet so close it was like we were six legs running. Everybody, those men in dresses, Mamma in her night clothes, looked up startled like I was one of the horsemen Daddy's always talking about—"the Apocalypse made flesh" is how Mamma put it later. Even Daddy paused in his groaning to look at me. He was dressed in this deep green dress I ain't seen before. He looked hurt bad. Mamma was shouting at one of the men.

"Why did you bring him here? Why didn't you bring him to Doc Klein?"

"Can't bring him to no doctor," the man said. I knew him, but I couldn't think of his name. He worked for us sometimes during harvest time. He wore a white dress. All the men were wearing white dresses except for Daddy. Daddy's green dress was darker where he was bleeding. "Especially no Jew doctor. He just needs nursing. That's why we brought him here."

Mamma ripped the dress away from Daddy and I saw my daddy'd been shot. Daddy'd been shot *bad.*

"Whoa, Lady," said Edom—I remembered his name now—"that's a sacred robe."

Mamma didn't even look at him. "Jimmy," she said, and I could tell she was through with yelling, and it calmed me. "Get me some bandages. Quick. You," she pointed to another fellow—not Edom—"get me some clean water. Put it on the coal stove to warm up. You," she pointed to two other fellows, "help me get his pants off. Easy."

Everybody Mamma pointed to jumped to it. The rest just stood quiet, and tried to calm their horses some. Nobody said anything more about Mamma ripping up that green dress. I don't know that Dr. Klein could have done better than Mamma, though everybody claimed he was the best doctor this side of Lexington. Mamma took her time. I sat right next to her on the porch floor. I could see where Daddy'd been shot in the right arm, but the bullet had passed right on through. His left knee was bloody, too. Mamma cut the pants off. He lay there mostly naked. I knew it weren't proper— Ham saw his father naked and was cursed—but I couldn't take my eyes off him. Mamma pointed to a groove in his left ribs, and it was like I could follow that bullet in my mind's eye. I saw it tear through Daddy and come out through. Must have, for Mamma never did find it for all her poking about.

Daddy just lay there while she poked and cleaned. He even stopped groaning, though Mamma didn't seem too gentle in her prodding. The men had carried him to the back porch. One fellow asked if they should carry him up to the bedroom, but Mamma shook her head. Didn't want to move Daddy more than she had to. Told me to drag the mattress down with the bedding. She set him up on the porch. I sleep there hot nights if the mosquitos ain't too bad.

They were bad that night. All that rain we'd been
having that spring, though that night it was clear as it could
get with just a half-moon. And hot. That wet hot we get in
Scott County which makes you feel like somebody's pulled
a wet blanket over your head. Weren't no breeze. "The kind
of weather," Mamma says, "where the air's so thick, you got
to share your breathing with your neighbor."

Only nobody seemed very neighborly that night. We
just sweat on our own and listened to Daddy groaning while
Mamma poked away at him. Edom and the other fellows
got some water from the well and offered it to Mamma. She
didn't want none for herself but dipped some into Daddy's
mouth. Mamma kept her eyes steady on Daddy's face—like
there weren't maybe a dozen men on our little porch and
she dressed in that thin white cotton gown she wears on
hot nights. Of course, nobody looked at her. I know because
I was looking at them, making sure they didn't. They looked
every which way but at Mamma, and she sure didn't look at
them. Didn't say anything, either. Or ask any questions. I
wanted to ask a million, but I didn't dare.

When things calmed down a bit, she noticed me. Told
me to take Hagar up to my room and go back to bed.

"Is Daddy alright?" I asked her, and she looked at
me hard like I had done the shooting.

"Your father is not going to die from this wound," she
said to me. Like she was some nurse in a hospital and I was a
stranger. I felt like a stranger. I didn't feel like I knew anybody.
Or maybe I remembered them, but distant—like the fellow,
Edom. I saw that I knew a whole bunch of the other fellows,
too, but none of them caught my eye. Nobody said howdy.

"How you know?" I asked. "Aunt Alice died of a gun
wound. Maybe just like this."

Mamma didn't say anything for a second, and I began
to worry real hard. "I don't know what your Aunt Alice died
of, but if it was a shooting, it was a lot more serious than
this one is."

She looked at me like she just remembered who I
was. "Your daddy is going to be OK," she said, and it was
Mamma's voice again. Just to have Mamma's voice back was
like when she rubbed the side of my head when I got one of
my headaches. The pain didn't go away all at once, but it
weren't as bad. "You go to bed now. Take Hagar with you."

I had to call Haggy twice. I don't think she wanted to leave Mamma alone with all those men in white dresses. Mamma finally had to tell her to go with me. I lay in my bed and listened as the men rode off. Daddy stopped groaning after a bit. I heard Mamma saying something, but I couldn't make it out. I got out of bed and put my head to the floor, but even then it took me a while to figure out the words. They were real soft—so soft I thought maybe I was dreaming them. They were the same words over and over again.

"James, James. What you have you done?"

CHAPTER 9
Nannie Johnson—April 1948

I'm still afraid to let the children walk them two miles alone to Mr. Lawson's church where the school bus picks them up. Herbert complains mightily about that. "I'm almost thirteen; I don't need my mamma walking me to school." "I like to walk," I tell him. "Anyway, I miss you all away at school all day." He look at me like he don't know what to think. That not the mamma he knows, the one yelling at him half the day about something. I don't know what to think, either. I'm there waiting when the school bus brings them back.

To tell the truth, the walk does seem to calm my nerves. Mamma says, "If April in Kentucky can't feel a blessing, you closed yourself off from the Lord." The children sense it, though I don't see the boys stopping to look at any wildflowers. Even Eleanor don't seem very interested when I point at a Virginia bluebell—they just about my favorite—the way they poke their blue out from dead scrub. She nod politely and then run to see what her brothers have discovered. Something left over from winter, probably—an empty tortoise shell or a possum who's not just playing dead. Harry's pulling at my arm all the way, mad I won't let him go free range over the hills. I catch the wildflowers on the run, mostly.

But coming back with just Harry, who's tuckered out by then, I get to mosey. Rudy says I never slow down, but I slow down those walks. It always surprises me how quickly everything gets green—that soft green that makes it seem like there's a haze over everything. I point it out to Rudy and he just smile at me. Might as well be talking to Harry. That green just mean he's behind time in his planting to Rudy. Oh, that's not fair. I've seen him gazing at the fields five minutes at a time. He's not just thinking chores when he look like that.

"Harry, Harry, come look!" He scrambles back to me, and I pull away the dead fern that was hiding a blue gray trillium. It folded its three leaves in with the dew. "It the Easter flower," I tell Harry, who looks a little disappointed. I think he was hoping for a dead shrew—or a live one. But all my children are polite, even Harry. He touches the petals gently.

I wish the trilliums was the only things hiding. I know that the serpent slides through this green paradise. Or rides the hills at night. Such a beautiful place. You wouldn't think it. But evil's there. Evil's here. I can feel it.

The children still don't know what happened—not all of it at least. Rudy and I cleaned up as best we could— spent half the morning scrubbing up pig blood. The Lawsons were out there with us. I told Miz Lawson there was no need for that, but she wouldn't hear of it. I thought to myself it was the Lord telling me not to give up on all white people because I was just that close to doing that.

Rudy says I shouldn't judge all white people the same. "Why not?" I ask him. "That's what they do with us."

Rudy said he'd walk the children—give me a break. But the man's already been up almost two hours and in the field by the time the children be ready to go. And he's in the middle of the fields when they come back. He can't be interrupting his work, though Mr. Lawson said he could take all the time he needed, he'd cover for him. Both the Lawsons have been tumbling themselves over backwards trying to make things right since the night of the pig killing. They keep telling us how sorry they are that this happened.

I told Miz Lawson, "Neither you or your husband has anything to be sorry about." It be like me apologizing for some fool colored man robbing a grocery store. I'm not responsible just because we both colored.

"We're not blaming you because the fools who made our poor chicken coop some kind of butchery was white. It's not like you the KKK," I said to her, and she step back sudden.

Rudy's nodding beside me, glad to hear me talking like that. I'm trying not to blame all white people. Still, she made me feel bad, the woman was so upset.

Of course the children wanted to know what happened to their pigs. "Probably foxes," we said. We weren't sure. Eleanor let out a wail. Of course, she already named her pig. She took it personally.

"They killed Porky?"

"Porky?" Rudy looked at me.

"For the cartoon character," I told him. Rudy hasn't been to the movies in the fifteen years I've known him except for going to see Joe Louis at the Strand, but even he should know Porky Pig.

He turned to Eleanor. "I told you not to make a pet of him." He was as close to scolding Eleanor as he ever get. Hardly even scolds the boys. Only scolds them when he's fearful for them. If there's any scolding to be done, I'm the one who does it. "You don't eat pets."

"You told me I could take care of him all summer. That we wouldn't eat him until next winter maybe."

Eleanor wasn't one for sassing either of us, and it took us both back a bit. Rudy looked at me like I knew what to tell her. Finally, he just patted her. "I guess the fox had other plans." She just hugged her daddy 'round the waist and wouldn't let go for a good two minutes.

The boys looked like they'd like to be hugging their daddy, too, but being boys they weren't allowed to. Little Harry did his best by hugging Eleanor from behind. He didn't know what was going on, but he knew his sister was upset.

The sight of those three—Eleanor hugging Rudy, Harry squeezing Eleanor—just about wore me out.

I don't know that Franklin was buying the fox story.

"How the foxes get all three of them? Why they just kill them and not drag them away to eat?"

That was my fault. I told Rudy to leave off digging the graves for the pigs. If we had to give those pigs a proper burial, neither one of us would have gotten any work done that day. He dug just a little hole for all three and darn if some critter hadn't dug them up for Franklin and Herbert to discover. Their yelling brought Eleanor over. She said she recognized Porky, though I don't see how. Those piglets was just about all torn to shreds.

"Didn't have time to drag them off. Your daddy and I scared him off."

Franklin nodded, but I could tell he was still skep-tical. Half the time I like that he's questioning. The other half it about aggravates me to death.

I think if the Lawsons hadn't been so nice, we had taken Uncle Zeb's pickup back to Lexington the very next day. Those little shotgun houses on Ohio Street maybe ain't much, but they don't come with Night Riders at least. But it didn't seem right to leave the Lawsons in the lurch—be next to impossible to get a farmer this late in the season. And besides, the idea of some white trashy rednecks slaughtering our piglets and sending us scurrying back to my Mamma's couch just about made my teeth grind.

"You can just forget that idea," I told Rudy. "What kind of a man are you, anyway? Don't you have the gumption the Lord gave chickens? You see how they just went about their business? And besides that, what will the boys think of you? Don't you want your boys to be proud of their daddy?"

All that because Rudy asked me if I wanted to pack up, considering I hadn't exactly been sold on the whole idea of Scott County in the first place. I knew Rudy didn't want to go. He'd go if I was set on it, of course. Sometimes a hard down man can get on your nerves as bad as some mackman. Especially somebody like Rudy, who's so good. It makes me feel that much meaner. He nodded after I lit into him like he always does—like he's grateful that I've shown him the errors of his ways.

Mamma says she don't know how in the world the Lord blessed me with Rudy—that she don't know another man in all creation who would put up with my tongue.

"He's blessed to have me, too," I tell her because she's always seeing Rudy's side in everything.

But I know she right. Sometimes I look for the bad in Rudy kind of like I look for the serpent in the garden— like I know that April in Kentucky is a pretty picture but not the whole deal. It's taken me a long time to figure out that Rudy's just what he seems to be.

I wish I could get my nerves calm. The boys out of my sight for a minute, out helping their daddy or playing in that tree grove—probably going to break their necks in that tree fort someday—and I out there calling. They come running when they hear me, and I don't know why I called them half the time. I can't be saying that I was just checking to see if the Night Riders had got them. I send them off, telling them I don't have time to be fooling with them, and they look at me like I crazy—like I hadn't done the calling in the first place. But I'm their mamma. They might backtalk their daddy, but they know better with me. An hour later I'm calling them again, and we go through the whole thing one more time.

The boys ain't wrong. I *am* crazy.

I don't need to be calling Eleanor. She the opposite. I think she sense something because I can't turn for tripping over her. I tell her to take Harry out to the yard and play with him. I tell her to go feed the chickens—we added some more chickens now that we not doing pigs—and she go away for ten minutes and she back by my side. "I'm afraid of foxes," she says.

"Foxes ain't going to come in the middle of the day," I say to her. "And besides, foxes are scared of human beings a lot more than you scared of them."

She nods. Maybe none of my children backtalk me, but I can't keep them from thinking. I can't keep Eleanor from seeing again in her mind's eye the way Porky was slashed and cut. I can't convince her that a fox that can do that kind of damage to another living creature is a scared, timid creature. I can't convince her that little girls are safe from foxes as mean as that.

I can't convince myself.

Miz Lawson sometimes takes her off my hands so I don't go completely crazy. She teaching Eleanor how to quilt—something I never had the patience for. At first, I thought Miz Lawson wanted her over to help clean or something, and I wasn't about to have my little girl do maid work and she not even nine years old yet.

But I should have known better. Eleanor does help with some kitchen things, but it's only because she want to. She like kitchen things more than I do. Miz Lawson teach her that, too. We trail back and forth between our kitchens so much, we already worn a path. Miz Lawson says she glad for the company. Seems that Eliot family kept to themselves the year they were here.

I was sitting peeling potatoes, watching them piece together a quilt, when Mr. Lawson came in from the field. He work his own acres, though he's wearing down. Rudy spends almost as much time helping him as he does on ours. That's the extra work. I don't mind. We need the money. He just froze still when he saw Eleanor with some piece of green silk in her hands, cutting a diamond shape—she had already made a dozen or so diamonds from the cloth. She had that dreamy look she gets when she forget all her fears, when she can lose herself in some little bitty task that would just about tear my last nerve. I was feeling peaceful myself, grateful to Miz Lawson for finding Eleanor something she loved to do, grateful not to have to be doing it myself.

"What's that child doing with that cloth?"

He turned to look at Miz Lawson who kept her head down. I thought, *Oh Lordy, Eleanor's cut up something expensive she wasn't supposed to.* But I was confused, too. Hadn't I seen Miz Eleanor give her the cloth and show her how to shape the diamonds?

Eleanor looked up from her cutting slowly, like she been swimming underwater and just broke surface. Eleanor can sense any change. Just then she was thinking something strange was in the air. She stop cutting for a moment.

"That's OK, dear," Miz Lawson told her. "You keep cutting." She turned to her husband, "We're making a quilt, James. Something useful. That cloth's been sitting in a trunk for twenty years. I'm surprised it's not dry rot."

"I thought you had thrown it away."

Miz Lawson didn't answer for a moment—kept her eyes down to her own cutting. She was doing circles of green. Finally, she picked her head up.

"Throw it away, James? We don't throw anything away on this farm. Especially not something that costs us as dear as this cloth. We paid a pretty penny for this cloth, don't you remember, James?"

She smiled over at me as if she had just remembered she had company. I was pulling apart a couple heads of early lettuce, all from Miz Lawson's garden. We come too late to plant our own. She had a slew of radishes, too. They mostly a cover crop, but she saved a whole bunch from being plowed under. I was trying to figure out how to blend the radishes into something—neither the boys nor Rudy cared much for them, though Eleanor and me love them. Dab a little salt on them, and they're like popcorn.

I smiled back, though mostly I was thinking how we could skedaddle out of there. Neither one of the Lawsons was raising their voice, but I know a married fight when I see one. Something was going on. Eleanor had lost that dreamy look completely.

"Time to go, Eleanor." I started to scold her like she hadn't been doing exactly what I wanted her to be doing. "You clean up that mess, now, and thank Miz Lawson. The boys and your daddy will be wanting supper, and I got to figure out something more than lettuce and radishes."

We were out of that kitchen in less than thirty seconds. Miz Lawson didn't try to stop us, and Mr. Lawson hadn't got over that surprised look he'd been wearing since he came in and spotted Eleanor cutting that green cloth. I was wondering if that had been some fancy shirt of his, though I can't imagine him wearing that color. None of it made sense. Mr. Lawson didn't look like the kind of man who interfered with his wife's sewing—or quilting. But what did I know? White folks was strange folks. Even Rudy would agree with me on that.

April was waiting for us out that door. A peach tree stood halfway between our two houses. We could see it from both our kitchens. It was an early peach in full blossom. Miz Lawson said half the time some freeze would kill the blooms before they peached. She bought the tree in some nursery in Lexington, she told me.

"Should have known better," she said. "If a tree isn't from Scott County, it doesn't usually put down good roots."

I nodded. *She might be right,* I thought. *Scott County soil is peculiar.*

"But when the tree does escape the frost," she went on, "it gives the sweetest peaches you could imagine. Round and juicy—and so many I have to prop the limbs for fear of them breaking."

I stopped to smell the pink branches. Made Eleanor stop to smell, too. She ask if we could break off a branch to bring inside. I started to scold again. "If we break a branch there won't be any peaches from that branch. That just wasteful, and we don't waste in this family."

I was in mid-scold when I stopped. Seemed to me Eleanor had the same look on her face she did when she got to the end of that torn-up school book, like I was telling her she wasn't worth a peach branch. Even a peach branch that might freeze over that night because nothing was safe from freezing the wrong side of Derby day. Not even then, some years.

I stopped my scolding mid-sentence. Mamma don't think I can stop once I start rolling, but I can if I've a mind to. I told Eleanor to go get the big kitchen knife and not to run. We'd cut that limb clean. That way we'd have pink blossoms on our kitchen table even if it did freeze.

April's not all promise. April's the Lord's blessing right now. April's the Lord's blessing even with the serpent in the garden.

Even in Scott County.

CHAPTER 10
Wilma Lawson—April 1948

I thought James might keel over when he saw the child, Eleanor, cutting up his old robe. Of course I hadn't thrown it away. If we don't get to throw away the memories, too, I don't see the use of discarding a piece of cloth for which we paid more money than we could afford. I kept my head down—waiting. Nannie started to scold the child. Nannie scolds when she gets frightened. I grow silent. I wish I could scold. It might make things better. James finally found his voice.

"You've been saving that robe all these years? Hiding it."

Have I? I don't know.

"It's been in the same chest for twenty years. You just never looked."

He just kept staring. "Why?" is all he said.

Oh, that made me mad. Suddenly I felt I could have shouted, only I didn't want to frighten Nannie or the child. Nannie already knew something was up. That's why she scurried out so. And Eleanor doesn't miss a thing. Such a sweet little girl. How I would have loved to have a little girl.

God's punishment. One child. No. The one child was a blessing. Still, even gone, a blessing. I know that. But to have had another child. Another little boy—like their boy, Franklin. I don't know why I favor Franklin. Harry and Herbert are just fine, but there's something special about Franklin. What a fine brother he would have been to Jimmy. When I said that to James, he looked at me as if he was going to drive me down to Eastern State right then and there. "He's a colored boy," is all he finally said. *He is?* I wanted to say. But I didn't. So much I don't say.

"I meant a little white boy like Franklin," I told him, "or a little white girl like Eleanor."

He just kept staring at me like I wasn't making any sense. Which I wasn't. I don't know any white children like them. So strong. So fragile. Maybe there are children like them. Maybe it's that I just don't see children up close any-more and haven't for a long time. The Eliots didn't have any. James says the church school is busting with children. Everyone making up for missed time during the war.

But I haven't been to church for a long time. It's twenty years. One year—I was twelve I think—I went to Mass almost daily. All that sweet twelve-year-old piety. I wonder what my parents thought. They were baptized Catholics but not much else.

I wouldn't mind a picnic on the land for the church-children. Just as long as I didn't have to go there.

But that's not the truth, really. I don't think I want any other children—white or colored—scattering around the farm. I'm happy with these children. I want them here, fifty feet from my kitchen door. I want them safe.

Isn't this something? All those years when we were out here by ourselves, and I didn't once think of shouting. Now I close my eyes and just see myself shouting. But I can't. It would scare the children.

"Why?" I managed to keep my voice low, though we both knew I might as well have been shouting. "You really want me to answer that?"

"You've never forgiven me," is what he said. If I were to forgive him, I might for the look he wore at that moment. "All these years and you've never forgiven me."

"I'm not the one who should be forgiving you, James. Besides," I lied, "I have, James."

"You blame me for Jimmy."

"Jimmy?" And my voice did raise now. "Jimmy was killed by the Japanese in the Philippines. How could I blame you for that?"

"He was killed by a Jap. A colored Jap. It's retribu-tion. The Lord's retribution. You blame me."

I gave up pretending to quilt. *Who is this man,* I wondered for maybe the thousandth time. This man my parents thought I'd be safe in this world with? A good man, they told me, a religious man. A righteous man. His face was twisted in pain. In guilt.

"That's your God, James. Not mine." His Baptist God. The one I'd given up my childhood Catholic God for.

"Oh, Wilma," and his words were low, harsh. "You need to forgive me. I need you to forgive me."

"I do, James," I said again, and maybe I was beginning to. "I just can't forget."

He let out a sound then, and I looked over to Jimmy's house—the Johnson house—but I don't think the sound carried that far. It only pierced through me—cut me again with an old grief.

"My God, Wilma. Do you think I can?"

CHAPTER 11
James Lawson—June 1928

I did not want to be the Grand Dragon. A foolish title. A pagan, almost heathen name I told the men who came to me time and time again, begging me to lead them. "Lead who?" I said to the hemp merchant—he came in wet right from his fields, smelling like old ropes, carting two gaudy robes—one in a purple so deep it reminded me of the dried pig blood on our aprons when we finished the slaughtering. "The purple's not really proper for you," the hemp merchant said, as if I cared of such things, "but we want you to have it anyways." The other robe was a sharp green that almost hurt one's eyes. I have never seen that color in nature. "Wizard's robes," I told him. "Costumes meant for children. Not for a Christian man."

The hemp merchant went away—the men he brought with him mumbling about disrespect and blasphemy. Blasphemy! What did they know about blasphemy? I have studied the Bible daily since I was a boy of ten. A damned race—a race of degenerates and desperate men.

They sent the minister to speak to me the next time. He came alone.

"Reverend," I greeted him. It was six months back. The news of Alice was just a few weeks old, still churning in my soul. The Reverend Jeremiah Edwards was one of the few who knew the whole truth—he and the sheriff who brought me the news. Even Wilma don't know how Alice died—the black demon pimp who stabbed her and left her bleeding on a barroom floor and then abandoned her.

Oh, she was a fallen woman—a scarlet woman, the Bible would call her—but she did not deserve to be abandoned. She did not deserve to die alone.

I have spared Wilma what I could not spare myself—the image of my sister on that floor. Rumors have spread like mud through a wattle dam, though nobody dares whisper them in my hearing. I don't think they have dared approach

Wilma or the boy, either. But I told the whole story or all that I knew to the Reverend. Wilma had asked for prayers to be said aloud in the church. I told him what I could not tell her. My sister's name—Alice, Alice—was not fit to be mentioned in the church. The very church our father had helped build.

The Reverend Jeremiah Edwards came bearing the two robes. He had come out to the barn, away from Wilma. He lay the two robes in front of me as if he was covering an altar.

"We need you, James."

I was surprised. I had heard that he was a member, but a silent one. Not one who did the riding. One of those who counseled—who urged others to action. But he had never approached me before. He took out the Bible he always carried with him.

"A sinful nation, a people laden with iniquity, a seed of evildoers, children that are corrupters: they have forsaken the LORD, they have provoked the Holy One of Israel unto anger, they are gone away backward."

"Isaiah, 1, verses 3 and 4. We need you, James," he said again.

"You need me to dress up like a carnival wizard and lead a bunch of hooligans, Reverend?" I resented his quoting the Bible at me—as if I was a boy to have Bible verses drummed at me. "You're not such an old man. Not ten years on me. Why don't you lead them, Reverend?"

"You're the leader, James. Even in the church, they all listen to you. I just have the title. If they listen to me, it's because I have the title. They listen to you because of the man you are. We need you, James."

I poked at the clothes. The colors almost hurt the eyes.

"The clothes are just a symbol, James. Of order. Of a hidden strength in all this disorder. The nation is coming apart. We passed the law of the land prohibiting rum and whiskey, but drinking runs rampant—right in this county. Throughout the land. Adulterers and fornicators stare brazenly at me from my very own pews, passing as respectable men and women. The women cut their hair and raise their skirts. Not just the girls, grown women—women of years, wives and mothers. And the young follow where the worst lead."

He paused. He stroked the deep purple robe. His face, enraged, had taken on some of the hue of its color, but he spoke softly.

"And the colored? They are the worst. It was a mistake to let them fight in the war. They came back full of arrogance. Forgetting who they are. Who we are. The good ones try to keep the old respect, but they are urged forward by the savage among them. The jungle has come back into their blood. Africa is here in Kentucky. In Scott County. The worst are respecters of no one. Nobody. Nothing."

He took a breath and stared me straight in the eye. "They think our women, their women."

Neither of us said anything for a few minutes.

"These men you call hooligans are good Christians. Or they could be. They want to be. Without you, James, they will be a mob. They will be part of the chaos they want to fight against. Without you, the good colored will become more and more like the most savage of their race. Don these silly garments, James. Be the Christian leader we need you to be."

I didn't answer right away. Though he hadn't mentioned Alice's name, I felt myself jolt with anger. Anger and shame. They mixed in my blood like the whiskey I had not put to my lips since my mother shamed me into renouncing it when I was a boy of seventeen. But when I calmed, I appreciated him not mentioning Alice by name. For he had reminded me by that omission that it was not just my particular shame, not just Alice's sin. Women all over the country were falling prey to the devil of chaos, the Satan of newness.

The colored were victims, too. They had less strength to fight the demons in their blood. They needed like wayward children the lash of the whip. The whip would save them. The whip would save us all.

I did not tell Wilma my decision. I do not know that she would have opposed me—especially if I had told her the whole story of Alice. But she is a woman—with the dangerous softness that cannot stand against the terrors we face. I do not mean that she is weak—she has always had the strength of a woman, the forbearance that sometimes awes me with its resilience. She handles the boy with a grace I can't approach. But she wouldn't be able to do the violence I know is necessary—the cleansing violence that will bring us back to the purity we need.

Alice, oh Alice. If I had known how to scrape from you all the blackness of your soul, I would not have spared your back from the lash. I would not have sought to gentle you softly into hell.

It was not a month after that we heard the sound of a vehicle approaching. We were always startled at anyone braving our road. We had very few visitors. We liked it like that, though the boy sometimes complained. He should have had brothers to tumble with, but it wasn't meant to be. Wilma looked at me questioning when she saw it was the sheriff. We both remembered his last—his only—visit, when he had come to tell us about Alice. "Must be church business," I said to her, and she escaped into the back garden before he arrived.

Church business, I had said, but I knew better. In the month since I had agreed to be the leader, the sheriff and I had often met. But we had met in town. Something must have been very important for him to brave Wilma. I felt a chill. I knew. The whole county knew. Only Wilma and Jimmy—isolated, set off like an island in a raging river, protected by our bad road—did not know.

"They've taken him by train to Cincinnati—getting him out of state. Headed to Chicago." The sheriff had looked around quickly. I could see he was relieved Wilma had left. "The girl isn't more than fourteen."

"Rape?" I asked him.

He paused a second. "What else?" he answered.

He was sitting at the kitchen table. We were both keeping an eye on Wilma in the yard with Jimmy. We could hear her fussing at him about the pigs—they had gotten into her garden again. Between the sheriff's unwelcome visit and the pigs pushing their snouts into her vegetables, she sounded about as mad as she ever got. I heard the surprise in Jimmy's voice. His gentle mother did not usually rage at him.

I was often ready to help him steady his attention span with a lick or two, but she'd tell me she would handle it.

"You're too easy on the boy."

"And you're too hard. So together we're just about right."

"It's a hard world," I told her. "A soft heart will just get you run over."

She just looks at me when I tell her truths like that. I don't know what she is thinking half the time. I know, though, that she would be opposed to what I have to do now. The hard task the Lord has given me. She would rage at me harder than she does at the pigs in her garden. It's better that she not know until she has to. If she ever has to.

"Will you be joining us?" I asked the sheriff.

He shook his head. "I'm already in trouble with the governor for letting you take that fellow out of the jail and giving him the whipping he deserved." We had whipped a man—ten lashes—for adultery. A white man. We didn't only chastise the colored.

"The governor's even threatening to remove me from office. I said, 'Governor, the people of Scott County have duly elected me.' I thought once we got a Democrat in there, we wouldn't have to worry about stuff like this."

"The governor is a politician," I said, knowing I was looking at another politician. "He should know, though, that whatever it takes, we will strongly urge any man—white or colored—back onto the pathway, of the Lord."

Or woman. Although I will not let a woman be touched by any man. But we have posted notices about those women who have stooped, who have disgraced themselves and their families. We have spoken to their menfolk. Strongly. Most of the women needed only these reminders. Three have left the county. Two others haven't taken our warnings. We are considering what to do.

But that is a problem that can wait a while. The colored rising is what we must deal with immediately. It is not that they are evil. They are children easily led astray by evil men and evil times. These times have challenged even strong men. Women and children and weak men have lost the inner compass the Lord provides to the elect. We cannot let the weak sink into the muck of chaos that surrounds us. We must help the colored find their way back to the order they have lost.

We had tried to be gentle. We had tried to give fair warning.

We have had whippings for adultery. White men all. We corrected some young colored hooligans—they had been drinking on Main Street in Georgetown away from colored town and had frightened some women. We made them take us to the still that had corrupted them, which we knocked down though it belonged to a white man. We gave them all a public whipping, and would have whipped the white owner of the still, too, if he hadn't run off. Some of them feared worse than whipping. One of them begged us not to hang him. As if we were outlaws—hanging men for drunkenness.

It is true that some of our men urged us to more violence than was called for; that is the nature of these kinds of gatherings. But if I have a mission, it is to make sure that the Lord's justice is measured. "We are not murderers," I tell the men. "We are the Lord's arms. If the law was what it should be, we would not be needed. We will act with the Lord's measured calm."

A group who gathers around Edom does not care for my restraint—Edom, a sometime farmhand of mine who squeals and grunts like a piglet and would defy me if he dared. So many of the men are but a hair's breadth this side of righteousness. The lightest of winds would blow them to the edge of destruction.

It is as Revelations reveals: The fearful and unbelieving, the abominable, the murderers and whoremongers, the liars and the idolaters, all shall sink into the lake of fire and brimstone, the second death.

Their hell is ever at their lips. It rises like sulfur from their groins. Their wild passions are held back only by the thinnest of ropes. They are not the men I would choose for this mission. But we do not get to choose the army of the Lord. We must make do with the instruments He provides. The men may grumble, but they and the Lord have chosen me as their leader, and they do what I say.

Sometimes I must temper their zeal; sometimes I must let them express it in actions I do not approve. A general does not choose every battle.

Three weeks earlier I had let them burn three crosses out in New Zion, the colored village. The minister in the colored church there had been a sergeant of a colored troop in the War. He had learned things in the war that ill-suited him for Scott County. He had begun to gather his parishioners into a political grouping—the Lincoln Republicans they called themselves.

The colored are all Republicans, which doesn't matter. The sheriff—the politician—thinks each colored vote a threat to them, but I tell him that their numbers are

WANTED: GOOD FAMILY

too small to matter. Half the colored do not vote. Those who worry about such things need only to round up workers on primary day. Times are not so good for the colored that many can forgo a day's wages just to vote.

Still, this colored minister has troubled the sheriff and others, too. He has tried to make sure all the colored—all his congregation at least—voted in a group. He pressured those who valued their relationships with us, who valued the order of the community more than they did one man's ambitions.

He didn't have enough colored over there to threaten the way things run in the county—or who ran them—but his efforts alone threatened our way of life. Or so the sheriff felt. And so did our minister. They said that some of the less intelligent colored were beginning to have ideas, to act in ways we could not tolerate. Our men grew increasingly agitated. They looked to me for action. We had heard that the colored minister would be urging his flock—men and women—to vote united on primary day less than a week away.

I prayed about it. Politics was a dirty business—I did not see it at first as my mission. And yet I knew that if I did not lead, chaos might lead instead. This colored minister was threatening the order of the county. Our way of life. This is what they told me. This is what I told myself. This is what I believed.

We rode out there on a Wednesday night in late April when we knew the church would be full. We were thirty men—the largest group we have ever assembled. The sheriff rode with us that night, though he rode in the rear with a borrowed horse. A three-quarter-moon shone off the white robes of the men, florescent in the night. I could feel the rising excitement of man and beast. My horse pulled me forward faster than his normal gait. I yanked the reins sharply, and he slowed. The men slowed behind me, pulling their hoods down as we approached the church, masking their faces. I was the only one with no visor on my face. I dressed in the dark green robes of the Grand Dragon. I no longer felt the colors foolish; they were the colors of my rank.

The minister came out when he heard our horses—his people spread behind and around him as if they formed a giant fan. I heard some of the children crying, but I did not see them; they were hidden behind the crowd. I heard the women shushing them.

The minister stepped in front of the crowd, though two of his men tried to hold him back. He shucked them off. He was a big man—as big as me. But older. I could see the sergeant in him, but he bellowed at us like the preacher he was.

"What do you men want here? This is a church of God. You have no business here."

"The goddamn black..." Edom's words strangled through the white gauze of his mask. "We need to grab that black bastard up by his feet. String him upside down and let him hang there till his legs pull off his body."

Some of the men were inching their horses towards the crowd. Some of the women shouted out. "Help us, Lord! Help us!"

I raised my hand and the men pulled their horses up. I looked at the minister. He was a brave man but a foolish one. *The Lord will help you*, I thought. *The Lord will help you see the light.* I let the silence settle before I spoke.

"We've come to give you fair warning, minister. Take your people back into the church. Pray to the God you say you pray to. Keep your prayers inside the church and away from the polling place. Render unto God the things that are God's and unto Caesar those that are Caesar's. Do not mix the two."

With that I waved my hand and the three crosses were staked into the ground on a knoll about twenty yards from the church. They were coated in tar. I signaled Edom, and they blazed with a heat that made some of the horses shy. I held my own mount tight. I looked at the crowd. No one made a sound. Someone had even stilled the children. The minister turned his gaze to me.

"You're James Lawson, aren't you? Why aren't you wearing a mask like the rest of your mob?"

"The black sonofabitch," Edom was yelling now. "I say we rip his black tongue out of his mouth."

He was already five feet ahead of me when I yelled, "Stop!" Edom pulled his horse up but stayed in front of us.

"You gonna let that black heathen talk to you like that? Talk to all of us? He needs to learn how to speak to a white man or he ain't going to be speaking at all."

"I said *stop*. We didn't come here to do violence. Rejoin the ranks."

A moment passed when I wondered if he and the four others who had followed him would obey me, but they did. They urged their horses slowly back. The crosses were in full blaze now. We did not need the three-quarter moon to see each other clearly.

My men retreated ten feet behind me, leaving me alone. The minister had outpaced his congregation by the same length. Alone, too. We stared at each other. *A colored man,* I thought, *standing there in front of me as if he were my equal.* I felt a strange dizziness. I steadied myself. *Here was the test of the Lord. I will not fail Him.*

"My name is James Lawson, Minister," I shouted to the man, "and I lead no mob." He did not flinch, though, with one wave of my hand, Edom and the others would have dragged him from his place and hung him from the nearest elm. "I hide from no man. I am the Lord's minister, and this is my warning."

With that, I turned my horse and rode off. I did not glance to see if the men followed me. I knew that they would. I did not glance again at the minister. I knew he still stood there. *The Lord's ways are mysterious,* I thought, as I listened to Edom murmur obscenities, murmur too low for me to notice, though I did—as did all of us. *Our way should be clear*, I thought. *Why do I still see as through a glass darkly?*

But this mission was clear—our duty clear.

"Where do you think we can intercept him?" I asked the sheriff.

"I'm thinking the Maysville Station. They stop to pick up the mail there. Just two deputies escorting him. They won't give you any trouble. Fellow who called me said they would hand him over in a second if they could do it without getting into trouble with the governor."

"Why just two?"

"Don't want to attract any attention. Figure to get him out of state before anyone's the wiser."

If they thought to keep us calm by keeping us ignorant, it was too late. The countryside was ablaze. Not just Scott County. Woodford, Fayette, Madison. Two other ministers had come to me already, urging me to do something. Now the sheriff. Without me, small bands of riders not under my control had already burned two black homesteads. Rumors were abounding that the colored were arming themselves, ready to march on Georgetown. I knew for a fact that the minister of New Zion—that big black bear who had stared at me so calmly, boldly—had placed armed men in front of his church, twenty-four hours a day.

He sent word to me directly through the farrier we use, a colored man named Jesse. I was surprised he braved the trip to the farm. Not many colored make it to my door since the cross burning. With this latest trouble, most colored stay indoors or as close to indoors as they can. The man diddled over my mare's feet so long I thought he was going to tell me she had to be put down. But he was just waiting to catch me alone.

"If you're going to tell me the horse is lame or worse, spit it out, man."

He looked surprised. "No, sir, the horse is fine. Only I promised the reverend I'd deliver a message to you in person." He waited. He looked straight at me. Twenty years of shoeing our horses, I had never seen him look at me like that. I nodded.

"Reverend Crenshaw says there's stories going round about burning our church. He wants you to know that anyone trying to fire our church is likely to get shot, seeing as how we got men with rifles posted twenty-four hours a day. He's hoping you be the person to get the word out—keep them fellows safe. He says it's your duty as a Christian. His, too."

He left then. A colored man telling me my duty as a Christian. I knew my duty. It was to keep my country safe. The people were angry. They were right to be angry. But a colored church burning or not burning was not my chief concern.

But a man who raped a child could not be left unpunished. She was a white child, true. But the minister should not have cared about her color. If this man escaped justice, the whole region would go up in flames.

"Where is the girl?"

The sheriff shrugged.

"Hiding with her family, I reckon. They may have taken her out of the county for all I know. You know how a family like that must feel."

He did not say the words, "You of all people must know how a family like that feels." *But Alice hadn't been raped. Alice had...*I shook the thought away. This was not Alice we were talking about.

"Why are the authorities taking him out of state?"

"Want to keep him away from us, what do you think? Want to keep him away from justice. I don't know what men like that are thinking. I just know that if we don't see action soon, we're gonna have a race riot on our hands. It's gonna be a bloody mess. You got to do something, and you got to do it quick."

I didn't want thirty men like we had with the cross burnings. I needed less than a dozen, and I wanted to pick them carefully, men who were steady, resolved. Who would treat what we had to do as justice, not vigilante violence. If we did it right—if we carried out the Lord's judgment in quiet firmness—then calm and order would be restored to our county. To our whole region. Then colored churches—even colored churches such as the Reverend Crenshaw's, who brought the stink of politics into sacred spaces—even those churches would be safe from the anger of an aggrieved people.

A crowd of more than fifty men awaited me as I rode my mare up to the church of my childhood. Only our minister seemed missing. The Reverend Jeremiah Edwards didn't think it seemly for a man of the cloth to openly support what was about to take place. Almost a dozen women were bustling about preparing food and hot coffee. They gave a cheer when they saw me ride up. They'd been waiting. One of the women asked me about Wilma. I shook my head. Wilma didn't know. I didn't tell the woman that Wilma would have tried to keep me home if she had known, but something in the pitying look she gave me told me that she knew. They all knew I rode alone in this.

I tried hard to get most of the men to stay behind— such a large group would be a hindrance, a danger. Only when I told them the rumors of the danger of our churches being burned did I persuade some of them to stay behind. Even still, we set out to Maysville with more than twenty men, among them men I would have never brought with me if I could have left them—Edom and Jacob, men covered with the stench of violence like hogs coated in filth. Each of them had a cluster of followers around them, listening more to them than to me. If I had forbidden them to come, they would have taken off on their own. Better to keep them with me and under my control than off sowing the whirlwinds of chaos.

It was a hard ride to the Maysville Station. It was more than fifty miles—closer to sixty, though we cut through fields, trampling corn and tobacco ready to be stripped, leaving open gashes in fences when no gate could be found. If they weren't closed quickly, the cattle would trample what we had missed. Some—men and women, children—knotted together on their porches as we passed. Some shouted greetings. Most stayed silent. A darkness surrounded the poor cabins as if they had been long deserted. Colored cabins. I heard some of the men about Edom murmuring that it would not take long to torch them as we rode through. I didn't answer, but I kept a steady march and they kept their horses at my pace. We were not Sherman's army, burning destruction through a peaceful people.

It was first dawn when we arrived at the station, our horses panting. They were farm horses and not used to such hard use. The train wasn't due for another hour. We had rounded a bend and caught the stationmaster unaware. He stared at us, astonished, as if we had been a band of Morgan's raiders lost for sixty years. We made sure he did not signal ahead to the train. Three people, two men and a woman, were in his small office, on their way to Cincinnati. We kept the men with us but let the woman scurry off.

We waited. The morning already promised heat—the kind of day that saps the strength of the strongest worker by noon. But the lingering coolness of the night felt like a blessing. And the silence of the station like a meditation. *Lord God*, I thought. *Am I doing your bidding? If I am not, Lord God, send me a sign. Strike me, Lord, if I stray from your path.*

But the Lord did not answer. *He sitteth alone and keepeth silence, because he hath borne it upon him.* The men were quiet, had stopped chatting among themselves. Even the horses' heavy panting had leveled to a soft shuffling. We were alone.

The train whistle cut like a lightening flash through the morning fog. We had hidden with our horses behind the station, holding ourselves at bay until the train came to a full stop. It was not a long train, not more than a dozen cars. Edom could wait no longer. He sprang onto the platform with his horse and a dozen screaming men crowded behind him. I felt the men beside me begin to rustle. "Wait," I yelled, but if they heard, they didn't listen. Wide-eyed passengers crowded the windows, staring at us as if we were a living moving picture. A woman was yelling something. I saw her mouth moving, but I couldn't hear her words. Several of the men had left their horses and were running through the cars. Angry shouts swept like a hot summer wind through the length of the train.

Only one car, the back car next to the caboose, had its shades drawn. When the men got there, the door was locked. Edom started to pound upon it. His screams poured from him like lava pouring from an open crevice.

"Open up, Goddamn it. Open up or we'll hang every one of you. You guards, too. Goddamn it, open up."

"Get the fire ax," I said to the man nearest me, and he ran to the station.

There were two axes, and Edom and Jacob each grabbed one and started to smash the windows on the doors. They were netted glass and did not burst, but caved in gradually like melting mounds of wax. Two scared white faces greeted us.

"Go away, men. This is a federal prisoner. You have no right."

I saw that both guards had guns, but they didn't dare to use them: it would be their death. When the holes in the windows had spread wide enough for a skinny man to slip through, Edom and Jacob stood aside, and three young men leaped through the broken shards as if they were boys diving into the Kentucky River. We would do such feats as boys, fearlessly, as if the river never hid a rock to peril a fall or break a neck. We waited for the three young men, as one waits for divers to surface from the water's depths.

I felt a moment's fear until they reappeared, pulling behind them a man, so tawny colored at first I thought he was one of the guards. But they had vanished out the back door. Then I saw the hair of the man they gripped—matted, tangled in the tight curl of a colored man. All four of them, white and black, crowded back through that broken window, slashing their sleeves and their arms until blood streamed from them all. They came through the window and would have hit the platform like feed sacks falling off a truck, but twenty arms reached up to grab them. I couldn't see the tawny man then. When I saw him next, he was on the ground; his legs had sprattled like a broken horse, but he kept his feet still. I could see he was pulling still, as hard as he could—as if it were all a giant game of tug of war but with only him on his side of the rope.

It was a tug of war he could not win.

"Men," I shouted, and everyone paused and looked at me. "Bring him quietly. We will do this properly. We will have our own trial here." They stared at me as if my words made no sense. I saw Edom and Jacob exchange glances. I was in the stationmaster's small office. "Men," I shouted, "bring him here."

Only ten or so men could crowd into the office, the rest pushing so tight against the window I thought it would cave in, too. I stood behind the stationmaster's desk, the prisoner squeezed in front. We were less than two feet apart.

"Are you Clarence Jones?" I asked him. He was silent a moment, as if he could not understand my question. Then he nodded. *Good. I thought. He does not deny his name. We will not have hung the wrong man.*

"And did you not debauch an innocent child—a child of less than fourteen years old? A white child?"

I waited. He stared again as if he couldn't understand my words, though they were clear. Edom beside him started to say something, but I raised my hand. Finally the man spoke.

"What child? I ain't never been with no child—specially no white child. I ain't never been with a child. Ask anyone. Ask the guards that brung me. They know that ain't true. That's why they taking me to Chicago. They know that story about a child ain't true."

"Lying black whoreson," Edom had broken out. "Hanging's too good for the black bastard. Let's burn him. Tie him to a post and burn him."

"Burn him! Burn him!" The men had taken up the chant. A mob's chant. I waved my arms and shouted back.

"Stop! Stop! We're not burning anyone." I turned back to the man. "Tell us the truth and it will go better for you. Did you rape a child!"

"I ain't rape nobody. Nobody. No child. Nobody. Ask the guards. They white. They tell you."

"Why did they arrest you, then?"

"It's because I ain't got the sense God gave a chicken. Oh, Lord, Lord, save me. Mamma told me not to go near no white woman—even a woman like that Susie. But I had the money—she weren't charging more than two dollar. But it weren't rape. I paid my money. Ask the guard. Oh, Lord, Lord, save me."

It was a pandemonium, a gathering of devils shouting continuously: "Burn him, burn him!" "Ask the guards!" Clarence Jones kept yelling over and over again. But I didn't have to ask the guards. I had asked the Lord for a sign and he had sent it: the man was telling the truth. He had slept with a white whore. He deserved the lash on his back. He deserved to be shamed and shunned.

But he did not deserve hanging.

He had slept with Alice, only this time her name was Susie. I knew what I had to do.

"Men," I yelled again, so loud that for a moment the din was turned, the anarchy stayed. They waited for the signal they thought I would give. "This man is innocent of the crime he's been accused of. We need to let him go."

That moment's silence stretches in my memory as if it were an hour, two hours, instead of three seconds, four seconds at the most. The faces of the men by me stayed still for those moments, as if we were all leaves suspended in the air, caught in a moment's updraft. And then a roar—a slashing roar of a wind like a funnel cloud—broke the silence, sweeping me, them, over the side of a crevice, a pit I have never climbed out of. Some nights, I hear that roar still. I wake and wait. Even Wilma's soft murmurings cannot quiet it.

"No!" Edom was yelling, but so was Jonah. So were all the men. "No!" And they started to grab the black man, but I had a pistol pointed at Edom' head.

"Let him go," I said, and the roar paused—but it was only the silent pause between the flash of the lightning and the crash of the thunder. I waved the pistol in front of them all and they backed off, but we were so tightly packed in the small office no one could move much. We were caught in place. But I put the pistol to the nape of Edom's neck and pushed him forward. He looked like a cur held back only by a strong rope. An inch's loosening of the knot and he would be at my throat. Clarence Jones plastered himself at my back. The three of us inched our way out of the office. *If we can get back to the train,* I thought, *we might make it. Someone might have called for help—the woman we let go. She would have called for help. Wilma would have found out where we were headed. She would have called. Wilma,* I thought madly, *would not have let this happen.*

The passengers were still by the windows, open-mouthed, silent, as if they were like the dummies I'd seen in Lexington stores. As if we were a picture show put on for their entertainment. I wondered if they felt as trapped, as unreal as I did. "Stay by me, Clarence," I said, and he did—so tight behind me we walked like a creature with four legs. Suddenly, Edom stopped.

"Keep moving," I told him. But he turned to face me.

"You ain't gonna shoot me, Deacon. You ain't gonna shoot a white man to save a nigger, especially no black whoreson like this. I don't care if he didn't rape no child. I don't care if he paid his two dollars for a white whore. He gonna hang for that and you ain't gonna stop it."

I'll never know if Edom was right or not. Would I have shot a white man to save a black? Not to save this black—for he would surely have died if I had killed Edom. As would I have. The three of us. I'll never know.

Three shots rang out as I pondered. I felt them ripping through my pistol arm and into my chest. I felt my knee explode with another bullet. I turned and, as I fell, I saw Clarence looking at me, knowing that my fall was his too. I wanted to tell him something, but couldn't make myself speak. I wanted to say something, but arms were grabbing at him and he had no time for me. No time at all. *Clarence,* I would have said if I could have spoken, if he could have heard me. Words I never thought I'd say to a colored man.

I'm sorry, Clarence Jones, I'm sorry. Forgive me, Clarence Jones.

Forgive me.

CHAPTER 12
Nannie Johnson—July 1948

The chickens were next. I sent Eleanor out to pick the eggs. She ought to have done it before light, but I let her dawdle. I don't know why. I just always hate to wake her. She look so peaceful, so safe in her morning sleep. So many things frighten that girl. She not a timid child. Mamma say she just a seeing child—sees things her brothers never notice, not even Franklin. I had roused the boys easy enough. They needed to be out in the field early, helping their Daddy.

"Go get those eggs, sleepy head," I scolded her as if I hadn't been the one letting her sleep. "Your brothers been out in the field a good hour. Who do you think you are? Sleeping Beauty?"

But she wasn't living any fairy story. None of us was. When I heard her let out a scream it took five years off my life. I dashed that two hundred yards to the chicken pen faster than Jesse Owens ran the Olympics. Even still, I barely beat Rudy, who was all the way out in the Hacker field—that's almost to the end of the farm. I don't know how he heard her. It was like the Bible verse where God heard the boy crying out in the wilderness. Rudy's no Lord Jehovah, but when it his child crying I guess the Lord helps him hear.

All the eggs was smashed. The chickens' necks all twisted in place. No blood. We hadn't heard a thing. No horses this time, or shouting. Thieves in the night.

Not thieves. That would make a kind of sense. Vandals. Not taking anything they could use themselves. Just ruining it for us.

After her first scream, Eleanor was quiet. She stood there, panting heavy, but not crying. I tried to hold her, but it was like holding a board. Rudy ran around the pen, pulling up nesting, throwing dead chickens aside as if the men who done this was hiding under some dead broody hen. He looked wilder than I had ever seen him. Wilder than he looked with the dead pigs. It'd been two months since the pigs. We thought we was safe. That's what made him so wild. We thought we was safe.

Herbert and Franklin trailed in five minutes later, breathing heavy. Franklin took a moment to take it all in. Then he turned to me, accusing.

"Ain't no fox that done this! Ain't no fox twisted them chickens' necks, smash them eggs. Ain't no raccoon, either."

I didn't know what to say to him. I let go of Eleanor, still stiff and silent. I reached out to touch him, but he shook my hand off. None of my children ever push me off like that, but I saw in his eyes that he blamed me—blamed me and his daddy. The dead chickens. The dead pigs.

"You lied to us!" He yelled it at us both.

Don't you raise your voice to us, boy, the words popped into my head—the mamma reflex—but I couldn't get them out. I heard all my usual words pass like road signs I've seen so often I know what they say before I read them: *A child raising his voice to his parents! You must have lost your mind, boy.* All my words—hung there. But I couldn't get none of them out. I could see them in Franklin's eyes. He'd seen the same road signs all his life. *You must have lost your mind, boy.*

We all lost our minds. Franklin couldn't stop himself from yelling it again.

"You lied to us!"

He ran out of the pen, back towards the Hacker field where they been topping tobacco for an hour or more. First light. The morning still had a hint of dew about it, still felt so cool I wished I put a sweater on Eleanor before I sent her out.

But I knowed it was just the morning's fooling. It was going to be a scorcher. I've never known nothing but Kentucky summers, but that don't mean I ever got used to them. We'd be needing some nice cool sweet tea before the day was done. I wish Franklin had taken him some before he ran back to the field.

We had lied to the boy. We had lied to all of them. Maybe we had lied to ourselves, too. We was in the wrong place at the wrong time. Franklin knew it. Eleanor knew it. What had made Rudy and I think a colored family could go back to the land in Scott County, Kentucky? If a

Lexington peach tree couldn't hardly make it here, what made us think we could?

I looked around. Miz Lawson was out there with us. I hadn't seen her coming. Her hearing's not all it used to be, but she senses commotion even if she don't hear it. She like Eleanor in that. She had grabbed a potato sack and was throwing the dead chickens into it one by one. I didn't have the stomach to touch any of them. Except for checking under dead broody hens, Rudy hadn't either. Miz Lawson threw each of them chickens in the sack like she was shooting a rifle.

"This won't stand," is what she kept saying. "This won't stand," and she looked so mad at first I thought she mad at us. *She blaming us for these dead chickens?* But then I saw her face when she looked in my direction, and it wasn't me she was seeing.

"This won't stand," she said one last time when Mr. Lawson showed up. He'd been to his church for some early meeting. We didn't even hear him drive up, we was so taken with them chickens. He looked dazed—the way a man does when he first wakes up, as if the world wasn't like he remembered it the night before. Miz Lawson held out a dead chicken, its neck spun like twisted barb wire, its eyes popping almost out their sockets.

"This won't stand, James," is what she said to him as she shot that chicken into the sack. I understood then. She wasn't blaming us for those dead chickens, those smashed eggs. I don't know why. Mr. Lawson sure didn't kill those poor fowl, but she was blaming him.

We went back to our house then. Eleanor let Miz Lawson put her arms around her shoulders. I saw her soften under Miz Lawson's touch like she almost never do with me. I felt a little demon spark of jealousy—*That woman need her own child*—but I pushed it down. Mamma says I'm like one of those broody hens—always thinking something, someone, is out to steal my eggs. Or smash them. Them eggs I had sent Eleanor out to find. I shook my head.

I hope I'm not grudging my own child's comfort, even if she need to reach for it from somebody else. Even if that somebody white.

Miz Lawson was filling glasses with ice. Sweet tea again. The morning coolness already gone. But even ice sweet tea wasn't going to give us much comfort. I see Eleanor put that cold glass to her cheek. She don't drink it. Just rub it up and down that sweet face of hers as soft as any Kentucky peach.

I picked up one of the church fans we got scattered through the house. Sweet Jesus looked back at me, but the sweat still dripped off my face. *Comfort is hard coming*, I thought as I fanned so hard I knew I was defeating the whole idea of cooling off. I sipped the sweet tea Eleanor ain't touched. Eight in the morning, sipping sweet tea, and out of breath. I didn't know where comfort might come from.

Sweet Jesus, I asked the face on the fan, *where we gonna find any peace?*

CHAPTER 13
Wilma Lawson—September 1928

It was September before James was well enough to make it to the church. All that time, only one church lady made it down to visit—Agnes, an old maid who's so timid I don't know that she's said more than five words running to me her whole life. She brought a chicken dish with some dumplings that looked like they'd been carved out of soap they were so stiff. She brought an apple pie, too, but that was from another lady who wasn't able to make it. "It's such a busy time on the farm," Agnes told me, apologizing for the woman.

I had nursed that woman back from near death her last confinement—fed and cleaned her six other children, too. Agnes was so embarrassed I worried she'd faint right there. That would be all I needed. Poor thing. At least she had the courage to make the visit. But telling me about it being a busy time when I've been cooking for sullen farm hands for three months—extra help that we needed since James could hardly make it to the back door the first month let alone all the way to the Hacker field. Well, if that don't take the cake.

No cake. Just a pie, which wasn't much better than the chicken and dumplings. This from a group of church ladies you almost have to hide your sickness from most times else they overload you so with stews and soups and chicken dishes, with cakes and pies and cookies—well, you needed a small army to feed it to. "I guess we're not much in favor," I said to James, who I didn't think cared much. I sure know he didn't care what he put in his mouth. I fed him that congealed chicken and dumplings, and he didn't make the first complaint. I couldn't gag it down myself. I nibbled on the pie for a while before I threw it to Jimmy's pigs.

Jimmy wanted to know what was going on. At first I thought to shush him. "A child doesn't need to know everything," I told him. But I could see right off that wasn't going to work. I had to get down to some serious lying, but I don't think that worked much better. Jimmy would never call his mamma a liar—I don't think he would even think it—but I saw the confusion in his eyes. He was confused because his pure heart knew I was lying, but his brain just couldn't take it in.

But what was the truth that I would tell him? That his daddy who he loved more than the Lord Jesus himself had gone out riding with a bunch of outlaws? Not just riding with them, leading them. They wouldn't have been able to do anything without his daddy showing them the way. And that when his daddy finally saw what he was doing, what he was helping others to do, it was too late. A poor colored man who hadn't done anything different than half the men in this town was hung from a telephone pole, his head almost pulled off his shoulders, his legs scorched from where they tried to burn him before they gave up—too scared and rushed for time to keep the fire going. "You know, your daddy missed the war," I might have said. "That's why he had to wait for the peacetime to get shot by his neighbors. Homegrown Huns." Should I have told him that?

I could hear Jimmy. "What's a Hun?" would be his first question. "Look it up in that big dictionary in the sitting room," I'd say, "the place where your daddy thinks the Bible should be. Or look it up in the Bible. Lots of Huns in the Bible. It's a name we call people who have no sympathy for other people—who burn and ravage and never ever wonder about all the pain they inflict. It's a name for people who hate."

Lots of Huns reading the Bible, too, I could have told him. The Christian Bible.

Better to lie. He'll hear the truth by and by. Not much chance of a truth like that staying silent. Not in Scott County.

"Why don't we look for a different church," I said to James. I still had to help him dress some, especially pulling up his overalls over that bad knee. The bullet went right through his arm and side, but Dr. Klein finally had to dig the one out of his knee.

"You're going to have a limp," is all Dr. Klein said. Never asked how it got there. I guess everyone in the county knew how it got there by that time. I wonder why Dr. Klein doesn't take himself off to Lexington or Cincinnati. It can't be easy for him. But I'm grateful he doesn't. He's a good doctor.

"A new church?" James said, like I had suggested we turn Catholic—he'd worried for years I'd turn back to my childhood church. Or maybe worse. Maybe he feared I'd ask Dr. Klein to take us with him next time he goes to his synagogue in Cincinnati. "This is our church. I helped my daddy build that church. I can't find a new church. I'm deacon in that church."

"In case nobody's pointed it out, James, you and your daddy helped build one of the ugliest churches in five counties. If I hadn't your word that it was always meant to be a church, I would have sworn it had its beginnings as a barn. And it's not our church, James. It's your church. Let's find our church somewhere else. It's not like the county's not full of them."

Calling his church ugly was like pointing out to me that Jimmy wasn't the handsomest of boys. Jimmy's ears did stick out from his head like they were trying to escape, and he could catch whole slices of potatoes in the gaps between his teeth. An ugly church to James was like a homely child to me.

Who cared?

"We're not into making our church a thing of vanity like some Romanish place of idolatry. The Lord doesn't need fancy altars. He abominates them."

He abominates them. *What else does the Lord abominate?* I thought, but perhaps I had already said too much on the subject. Or not enough. What would be enough? I helped him work his stiff arm into his jacket.

You would have thought our straight and narrow path, full of rocks and gullies, was the road to heaven instead of to James' ugly little church. It was our first outing since the shooting: each gully and rock a stab at his sore ribs, a jab at his stiff knee. But he didn't make a sound. If he thought the pain part of the Lord's punishment, it was not worth noting. But James' pain, or mine, wasn't really what I worried about. If I could have left Jimmy out of it entirely, I would have. But a child comes with you, shares everything you have, whether you will it or not.

Sometimes I do miss my Catholic girlhood. Maybe James is right, maybe we did carry on too much about Mary.

But I understand her better now than I did as a girl. Her mother-pain. It's there in her look even in the manger. It's there when she holds her dead boy in her lap. It's a look that says she can do nothing about anything: what will come will come; what has happened has happened.

I think the congregation was surprised to see us, though surely they knew the day would come when we came back. The thought of us seeking a new church would have been as likely to occur to them as it did to James. They would have thought it would be like exchanging a child that didn't suit you anymore. These were people who stayed with what they had—in sickness and in health. For better or worse.

For better or worse. I wonder what my parents would think now.

We were in for the worse.

James limped his way to the front of the church, where there was a space where the minister spoke. James was right. The space surely wasn't any Romanish altar. It didn't even rise above the rest of the church—it was just an area cleared where a man could speak. The minister spoke only about half the time, other men—deacons or elders—often took his place. My heart sank as I saw James whisper something to the minister, who nodded and went to take a seat among the pews.

The church grew very still as they realized James would be the speaker. I saw people exchanging nervous glances. Only Jimmy perked up. He liked to hear his daddy speak. I don't think he understood half of what James preached, but he was proud of how his daddy made people straighten their shoulders, even those who usually dozed their way through the service. Jimmy liked it when people around us nodded their heads and murmured approval.

I feared that we weren't going to get many nods of approval this morning. I prayed. I did not often pray in that church, but I prayed then. *Please, sweet Jesus, please, let us get through this. Let us have some peace. Please, sweet Jesus.*

James waited until the people stopped their shuffling. He didn't need any raised altar; he was taller by six inches than any man in the crowd. Whether they wanted to or not, the congregation had to look up to him.

"Woe to them that devise iniquity, and work evil upon their beds! When the morning is light, they practice it, because it is in the power of their hand.

"Woe to them. Woe to us. You have all heard of my injury—the bullet that went through my shooting arm and out my side, the bullet that entered my knee. *He that saith he abideth in Him ought himself also so to walk, even as He walked.* Even as He walked. All the years the Lord will grant me, you will know me by the shadow of my walk. By my limp. The Lord is merciful. He will not let my sin or yours melt away like a March snowfall.

"So that we *would not forget his deeds but would keep his commands.*

"We have worked evil in our beds—worked evil in our hearts. You came to me. This man," and James pointed to the minister in such a sudden move that the Reverend Edwards raised his hand to his face as if James were going to come down to the pew and strike him—or Jehovah was— "this man came to my house and said, 'Lead our people. They need you to save them.' And in my pride, in my iniquity, I gave heed to his words. I led the people. I led the people into darkness. I leaped into the morning light and I made it dark."

Jimmy had grown stiff by me. I wanted to leave the church and take Jimmy with me, but I knew I wouldn't have been able to drag him away. I hated James that moment: I hated him for what he had done and for what he was about to do. But I could not drag myself away from the words that were going to tear at us all.

"I killed a colored man. He was not innocent; we are none of us innocent. But he was less guilty than many. He was less guilty than I am—than you are. He was a colored man and dark. But he was not so dark that he had blood upon his hands. You"—and James' eyes searched out the men and even the women, one by one, and each set of eyes he connected to flinched, burnt—"have blood upon your hands. And so do I."

I heard a low rumble of anger that I knew would grow. James' voice, loud, soft, was like a pillow pressed upon our mouths. Once he let go, once his words stopped pressing at us, we would die or we would shout. I looked at those around me. My neighbors.

Oh, we would shout. But I wasn't afraid of their anger anymore. I would shout, too.

"You deny it?" James continued. "I hear you say that you weren't even there. And it's true. I don't see one man who rode with me in this church this morning. You are innocent of his blood, you say."

He paused, as if he were considering this point. "Not one man of you was there. Except for me. But I did not place the noose on Clarence Jones' neck. That was his name: Clarence Jones. Have you heard? Has his name been lost already? Clarence Jones. He had slept with a white whore, paid his two dollars and then his life. We thought he had raped a child, but it wasn't the truth. Even then we knew that the story was a lie. But it didn't matter. To sleep with a white woman—even a whore—was deserving of death. So we say. So we tell ourselves.

"But we did not put the torch to Clarence Jones' legs. Clarence Jones' lust, I hear you say, was the fire that consumed him. It is the fire that consumes us all. But we did not stack the faggots about his writhing body. I did not do it. You did not do it. Clarence Jones, we tell ourselves, did this himself.

"The Lord's mercy is infinite. He sends us my limp so that the lie we tell ourselves of our innocence shall not pass. He makes us to walk the crooked line of our lies. His mercy is infinite, but so is His wrath. We will burn in the lies of our innocence. The fire will not just scorch our legs as it did with Clarence Jones. He lies in the arms of the Lord who has forgiven him his iniquities because of the suffering of his body. But my poor limp will not save me from the Lord's justice. My poor limp will not save you. Our guilt is more than the guilt of Clarence Jones' lustful body. We have worked evil in our beds and the morning light brings us no solace. For the fire that burns us will not end, will not consume our guilt away, and the *smoke of our torment goes up forever and ever, and we will have no rest, day or night.*"

Hands grabbed at him. Reverend Edwards leaped from his pew and with two other men dragged him away from the altar. Kate Smollet, the pie woman whose children I had practically nursed, was reaching into the crowd around James, trying to hit James about the face, but the men surrounding him blocked her. Jimmy and I both plunged forward at first into the pew ahead of us—as if we had been in a car that stopped suddenly—but then we both elbowed past our shocked neighbors. Agnes put a hand on my arm as I went by her, calling softly, "Wilma, Wilma," but I brushed it aside.

The fire James had spoke of burst out like smoldering embers in a dry fall. It raced through the congregation, but somehow Jimmy and I made it to James' side. He looked at us in wonder. For better or worse. Jimmy shoved the Reverend Edwards away from James—Jimmy, who'd been taught to almost bow his head to the almighty Reverend Edwards, looked ready to put the might of the Lord behind his hundred pounds and strike the minister dead if he did not let go of his father. I stood beside him ready to do the same. The men backed off.

We walked out. It did not seem to me that James' limp was nearly as noticeable as we climbed the road back to our home. The road itself did not seem as rocky. Or as straight. I thought, *Good. We never have to go this road again.*

I never did. Jimmy never did.

But James still looked puzzled when I suggested again and again that we find a different church. This was his church, his God. He could know no other. Although he never spoke from the altar again, he returned again and again to the ugly church that he and his father had built. Sunday after Sunday, he traveled that road, full of pits and rocks.

Alone.

CHAPTER **14**
Nannie Johnson—August 1948

I told Rudy I didn't have no business going away for a night in town with his mamma. Since when did a farmer's wife get to take a night off in August? If I ain't cooking or canning, I'm out there topping tobacco plants. Everybody works in August. If Harry was tall enough, we'd have him suckering. Rudy says it don't matter; he can take care of things for a day and a night. I don't know how. If he's not off in the corn field, he's making poor Uncle Zeb's old pickup do double duty delivering everything from hay bales to chicken feed. Even made two runs down to Hazard for a couple loads of coal. I told him that truck wasn't meant to be working that hard, but Rudy just says it's going to have to.

"We work harder than that ol' truck, and we ain't break down yet."

"It a race then? Which one of us break down first?"

The Lawsons have been right generous with the split, but tenant farming fourteen acres ain't a whole living. Still, Rudy's put off any more trips for a couple days. And there's one thing about having a small farm, sometimes you do catch up on things. It just a moment, but it does happen—even in August.

"You going to feed the children regular meals? I don't want to come back to find out they been eating oatmeal three times a day. And we got to take them school shopping. They starting a week Monday."

Rudy just smiled and shook his head. You couldn't ruffle the man with a stick but I kept on trying. It was enough for him that his mamma called a special invitation— called Miz Lawson on the phone herself since I don't know when we'll be getting a phone. His mamma hates talking on the phone. Hates talking to white people for that matter. So this was something, her inviting me.

"First the pigs, now the chickens. Mamma knows you need a night away—do you a world of good. And I reckon I can cook my children a couple meals without them dying."

"What about you? Don't you want a night on Deweese Street—the do-what-you-please street? Take your mind off tobacco, which is all you seem to talk about lately. That and corn."

"You need to get away from tobacco and corn, too, not just dead chickens and pigs. I'm doing what I please by staying right here. You go off and have some fun with Mamma."

"Have some fun with Mamma." Not *my* mamma— that would be a night of trying each other's last nerves. She don't let me forget one mean thing I've done in my life and, Lord knows, I've done my share. But Rudy's mamma—she say, "Call me Sally"—could make me laugh so hard I'd forget and almost call her Sally. The best I can do is Mamma Sally.

Sally May Johnson. You wouldn't know she spent the first thirty-five years of her life on a hard-scrabble farm in Estill County—one of the meanest places for colored in the whole state of Kentucky. And Kentucky ain't exactly known for treating its colored sweet.

Mamma Sally don't like that term hard-scrabble.

"*You* got a hard-scrabble place. Simon and me had a real nice spread," she says. "A solid built house with eight rooms up and down. Twice the size you living in. Although there's something about your house that minds me of ours. Both of them care-built houses. Somebody thinking of the little things. Not just throwing on a roof."

She tells me the house was nice and the farm pretty, but she don't tell me the people weren't mean. She don't talk about that at all. She don't explain why she's gone from eight solid rooms to living more than twenty years in a tiny little shotgun in Kinkeadtown—half as big as my mamma's place off Georgetown Street. She don't explain why she thought we be all better off squeezing into her place along with Rudy's daddy than coming out to the wilds of Scott County. When I ask her, she just wave her head. "Oh, that's a story," she say, "that's a story."

After the chicken killing, I wondered if she wasn't right about Scott County. We wasn't going to tell her about the chickens or the pigs either—neither one of the mammas or Rudy's daddy. We feared they'd kidnap the grandbabies if we wouldn't leave. But Eleanor ruined that plan. Oh, she didn't do any storytelling. The child's not one to tell family secrets even to her grandmas. She didn't have to. After she found the chickens, she just wasn't gonna be alone. Not alone meant not even letting you have the length of the whole kitchen between you and her. She just pick out any warm female body and glue herself so tight to it, you almost had to peel her off to go to the bathroom. I had gotten used to it, but the first Sunday dinner after the chicken slaughter, Mamma Sally knew something was up.

"Child, what is wrong with you?" As used to tight spaces as Mamma Sally was, Eleanor had almost tripped her grannie into spilling the whole Sunday feast—we was one tangled set of feet away from a squash of black eyed peas, okra, and fried chicken. "You get any closer, I'm going to have to put on a bigger dress so you can squeeze on in." Eleanor just looked at her but didn't move off much.

The boys weren't much better. Even Harry let you know he wasn't happy if one of us disappeared from sight for more than thirty seconds. And he hadn't seen a thing, but I guessed he sensed something. I say a warm female body, but they clung to Rudy, too. Only he escaped outdoors more than I could though Franklin had begged that trip to Hazard with him.

Each of the mammas turned to me after a little bit of this. Mamma Sally was first.

"What in the name of sweet Jesus has happened to this child?"

I knew there wasn't much use lying myself out of this one. I would have if I could have thought of a way because I knew what was coming—this is what we all got for moving out of the safe and wonderful city of Lexington, where white people was civilized. And polite. They might not let us live in any neighborhood they lived in; we might not be allowed to eat in any restaurant they ate in. And if you wanted to be educated in anything beyond what it takes you to be a glorified maid in a white uniform that you paid for yourself, you be just plain out of luck. If you wanted to see a movie, you needed to climb a rickety stairwell to a balcony so far up and far away from the movie screen, you might think John Wayne a little bitty fellow. And if John Wayne was over at the Kentucky Theater, which didn't have no balcony for you to risk your life climbing, you wasn't gonna to see him at all.

White people might do all that and a lot more in Lexington, but they weren't rude about it. Lexington's white folk are real polite.

Unless, of course, you're where you weren't supposed to be, which is most of the town. Unless, of course, you ask something you weren't supposed to ask and then you a troublemaker.

But, you keep your place and Lexington's a fine town. They surely won't sneak into your backyard and kill your chickens. They surely won't slice up little piglets and hang them from your walls. Polite people don't do them things.

When they heard the story, my mamma carried on worse than Mamma Sally, who carried on bad enough. But Mamma Sally gave it up after a bit. She smart in a way my mamma isn't. Mamma Sally know the way to lose an argument with me is to get my back up. Mamma's never learned that, or she don't care to learn it. Mamma Sally let it alone after a while. She just bided her time. Let me think on it.

That's what this invitation to Lexington was all about: to show me the paradise I had left behind. I knew it, but I didn't care. I needed a good time. I didn't deserve one more than Rudy, though he felt I did. I didn't have enough time to do the things that needed to be done by yesterday. Giving up a whole day and night was just foolishness.

But it's just like Martha and Mary washing Jesus's feet in all that expensive oil. Could sell that oil and feed the poor, one of the apostles said. He was one of them fellows who always looking to see if his neighbors got two coins to clink together and mad because he's only got one. "The poor are always with us," Jesus told the man. But they was only going to have Jesus just a little while longer.

I guess all my chores are still going to be there tomorrow and the next day and the day after that. What seems like a waste might not be a waste. Just like that oil. Of course, I'm not Jesus and Rudy's not washing my feet in any expensive oil. That would be a sight. So maybe it ain't right to take the time off. Like I'm running away for the day. The oil story always confused me some. Maybe the apostle was right. Lots of poor people in Jesus's day. Lots of poor people now. I don't know. Jesus must have known what He was saying. I'm no preacher.

I just know that Rudy was right. I needed a good time. I needed to waste the time even if the time I had wouldn't let me do what I needed doing.

Even a farmer's wife can't always be doing the needed things. Sometimes, just like Jesus, she need to put her feet up. Maybe she won't get nobody to rub expensive oils on her feet, but she need to put them up anyway.

We were headed to the Hurricane. Mamma Sally said it was the fanciest club on all of Deweese Street. Furnished like a first class hotel is the way she put it. And food: pork that just fell off the bone and so sweet you'd think it been a month marinating. It didn't much matter to me, as long as somebody else was doing the cooking. I cringed a bit when I thought of the children eating Rudy's cooking. He might not kill them, but they weren't going to have no Hurricane feast.

That was the name of the club, but it felt a bit like a real hurricane once we hit Deweese Street. I ain't been on the street since before Harry was born, and maybe Friday night wasn't the night to ease back in to it. I'd been five months in the country where Rudy and Miz Lawson might be the only grownups I'd see day in day out—and Rudy too tired most nights to do more than grunt. Miz Lawson talked some, but she a white lady. I know that sounds wrong, but we just don't have that much to say to each other. Mr. Lawson didn't count since he was always going or coming. I don't think we spoke three words other than howdy since we had that conversation about our cousins. I missed talking to grownups. Real-live funny colored grownups. And not about corn or tobacco or cooking or children. I didn't want talk about nothing real. I was tired of real.

I don't know how many in the crowd on Deweese Street could be counted grownups—I know Mamma wouldn't think they did—but growed up or not, Mamma Sally fit right in. Colored folks come in two kinds, the first kind think having a good time is somehow not being mindful of all the bad times you been through. When folks are celebrating something or just sitting back and having fun, they always kind of purse their mouths and you know they thinking it's all just foolishness.

That's Mamma.

The other kind don't forget the bad times. But it seems like the memory of the bad times make them enjoy themselves even more. They draw a line: bad times over there, good times here. If they think about bad times at all, it makes them even happier; they do a little victory dance. *We was near dead, but look at us now*, that dance say.

That was Mamma Sally. Shouting and laughing— sometimes crowding in right on top of you as close as Eleanor ever got to you. Out for a good time. I danced right in.

You almost didn't need to do your own walking. One long block, Mamma Sally and I just got swept along with people pushing behind us just as we was doing the same to the ones in front of us. But laughing. Nobody mad. Nobody scared. Nobody even trying to get anywhere but where they were.

Sometimes the crowd just stopped, and you stopped, too. Like you was in a traffic jam, only this was a sidewalk jam. It took us a good twenty minutes to make it two blocks down Deweese Street. I counted three barber shops, six restaurants, two ice cream shops, and three night clubs. Little bitty night clubs just blasting music. Didn't seem like there was much difference between inside and outside— the crowd on the sidewalk blending into the crowd inside, all of them carrying their drinks with them like they had never heard of any law saying you couldn't drink on the sidewalk. I don't think those rules applied any to Deweese Street. The people kept changing places as the inside crowd probably thought the fun of being right next to the music didn't make up for not being able to breathe. We were sweating enough outside. I didn't want to think how hot it would be away from the night air.

Of course, it didn't help our progress any that Mamma Sally knew every second person and the second person she didn't know, she got to know right then and there. "This is my daughter-in-law, Nannie," she said to half the town. Seemed like they had all heard of me. "The one who moved way out to Scott County? Oh, Lordy, why in heaven's name did you do that, honey?" "Sweet Jesus, did you ever see such a crowd? It's getting worse every week." "Where you headed to? The Hurricane? I hope you get in. Half the town want to hear Duke Madison play that sweet horn of his. Play better than any white boy. I don't want to hear about no Tommy Dorsey." "No, sir, you wrong about that." "Oh, honey, you in for a treat. Ain't nothing like this out in Scott County. You better come on home, honey."

It did feel like home, though a strange kind of home. We never had any white neighbors over on Georgetown Street. Even white people on the street shopping or passing by was uncommon enough for you to look twice. "What's that cracker doing?" "That lady lost?" Of course, when we went downtown we saw plenty of white folks—but we was the ones being stared at then. But I never seen so many whites so mixed in with colored people as on Deweese Street. Every ninth or tenth person in that crowd was white.

"What are all these white people doing here?" I asked Mamma Sally when I could. We had just passed a whole gaggle of them—this bunch looked like college students from over the University of Kentucky. They been laughing and shouting like they owned the sidewalk. One of them—a skinny redheaded beanpole—turned full around and gave me the once over. I wanted to turn around myself and slap him upside his head. He didn't have five years on Herbert. Mamma Sally had pointed out a whorehouse on the corner of Third and Anne Street—girls hanging out the window and calling to men. Guess that young peckerwood thought any colored woman on Deweese Street was fair game.

"Same thing we doing. Looking for a good time. Headed to one of the clubs."

Must have been fifteen clubs crowded into about a mile—some just half a storefront. Some stuck above storefronts. Anywhere they could squeeze in a couple horns or a piano. I saw people dancing on the floor above a barber shop—shouting and waving out the window.

"What's that?" I pointed to a shiny new building—almost finished, though scaffolding still covered part of the roof. It was all sparkly silver metal and glass, so sleek and curved it looked kind of like an airplane on its side.

"That's the new Lyric Theater," said Mamma Sally, as proudly as if she built it herself. "Going to open by Christmas. Band hall, movie theater. Finest all-colored movie theater in the country. Won't have to be near breaking a leg climbing up to those balconies downtown. It will hold three times what the Hurricane holds. They say it going to put us on the map."

I thought we was on the map already. We finally made it to the line to get into the Hurricane, but it was moving slow. "Forty-five minute wait to get in," the man told Mamma Sally, who just shrugged. It didn't matter. Getting inside the Hurricane was only the end of the evening; waiting in line and joking with all the rest of the folks in line was another part.

Only some folks didn't think waiting in line was that much fun. White folks ain't used to being in line with colored. Sure wasn't used to letting colored get ahead of them even if the colored got there first. The college crowd who had passed us was making a ruckus. They weren't all skinny like the one who turned to stare at me. A couple of them looked like they might be football players or something. Drunk players. They pushed through the front of the line like they was pushing through the goal line.

Mamma Sally and I had worked our way almost to the front by then. Both of us got thrown to the ground like hay bales tossed off a farm wagon. I was scared for Mamma Sally. She might act like she twenty sometimes, but she's up there. Too old to be knocked down like a bowling pin at least. But before I could even find her in the crowd of bodies, I felt myself being pulled up. That redheaded stepchild was helping me up, only he had decided the best handles to get me back on my feet were the two cheeks of my rear end. He was smiling at me like he couldn't believe his luck, finding me in all that crowd. Maybe he thought I'd feel as lucky.

Well, at least I wiped that smile off quick. When I pulled my fist back from his face, his nose was making his face about as red as his hair. And he look so surprised. I think I would have smiled at that look, maybe even laughed out loud, only by that time some colored fellows who maybe didn't play college football but knew all there was to know about pushing and shoving, started pushing them white men back like they was a bunch of fourth graders.

Except that they weren't too careful about just pushing the white men. I finally got Mamma Sally on her feet only to be almost knocked over again. The whole line behind us started to sway and curve like we was all in a big rumba line. But we wasn't dancing.

"Whoa," I said to Mamma Sally, holding onto her arm. She hadn't broken anything yet that I could tell, which was the Lord's blessing, but one more tumble might do it. She was holding on for dear life to the man in front of her, but that man looked like he was going down. The night had been full of screams, happy yelling that had changed in the last few minutes. You know when your children are carrying on—making so much noise it's like a whole school ground has moved into your backyard. But you don't pay no attention. Then something in the noise changes, and you stop whatever you doing to listen up 'cause the yelling has gone from happy to hurt. That's the way that crowd's screams changed: from happy to hurt. Then on to scared. Then mad.

The pushing stopped, at least. I thought *OK, it's over*, but that was just the beginning. The line had broke down into little segments—knots of three or four people and then a space. It was like we had forgotten all about getting into the Hurricane. We were waiting for something, but it weren't no horn playing.

The white fellows had pulled back. *Good,* I thought. *They finally realized this ain't Main Street and they ain't the ones calling the shots.* Maybe they just woke up all of a sudden and seen they was on Deweese Street—the center of colored Lexington. They didn't belong on the street in the first place.

I had moved on to mad. I wasn't in Deweese Street anymore. I was back putting dead chickens in gunny sacks. Or watching Miz Lawson doing it. I was scrubbing pig blood off walls. I wanted all the white people gone, even the ones who hadn't made any trouble.

Which was most of them. I know it wasn't fair, but wasn't that the way they treated us in just about every other place in town? I spotted my skinny white suitor in the back of his pack of nine or ten. He was still pressing a handkerchief to his nose. He didn't look like he had much fight left in him. The whole bunch of them should slink on back to the college campus where they belonged.

I forgot what alcohol does to a man: makes colored men stupid and white men crazy. They weren't going back to campus without one more try. Three of the bigger ones made a leap into the two big colored guys blocking Hurricane's door. I think they were the Hurricane's bouncers, and anybody without a whiskey-soaked brain would have known better than to try to get by those fellows.

Even still, I thought they looked like they were going to break through that first push, but the colored guys just swayed a bit and then stood straight.

All of them fellows—white and colored—swung at each other steady like I seen boxers do on the movie screen, when they been caught in a corner and the referee can't get to them. Pounding away. I seen boys fight in Dunbar High School but nothing like that. Dunbar High School teachers never let a fight get out of hand.

And those were boys fighting. This fight was between men, and they looked like they wanted to kill each other. I don't know why they wanted to kill each other. It was just a fight over a line.

I stopped being mad. The crowd was yelling, but I got quiet. I knew that whiskey was making them all crazy—colored and white—but more than that was going on. They was trying to kill each other. They hated each other. The hate ran deep. All of a sudden I thought of the way those dead chickens looked before they got put in the sack—their necks all twisted, their eyes bulging out of their sockets.

At first the fight was punch for punch. All of them getting their share. One of the bouncers—the bigger one—took on two of the fellows who charged the door. It seemed an even fight. The white guys didn't fight for a living and the whiskey was probably wearing on them. But then the fight starting changing. The white guys started to be mashed down. Blood started to stream out of their noses, out of their eyes. Mamma Sally and I weren't three feet away from them, and every time another fist hit their faces, it was like we could hear the crunching.

It was like watching the Brown Bomber on the big screen demolish one of his bums of the month. Only these white boys kept bobbing back to their feet. The bums stayed down. I wished they'd stay down. I heard Mamma Sally shout out, "Stop now. Stop now. You boys stop now!" But they weren't stopping. They were all bleeding—the colored men, too, only somehow it seems uglier when white people bleed. Or maybe I just ain't used to seeing that red against white skin. It made me shudder. I joined in with Mamma Sally. "Stop it, boys, stop it!"

Suddenly a white boy who hadn't even been fighting—he'd been in the back of his friends with the redheaded boy—ran forward towards the bouncer who was fighting the two guys. He was a little fellow, and at first I didn't know what he was pointing.

"He's got a knife!" Mamma Sally yelled, just in time for the bouncer to dance aside and miss that knife like he was a bullfighter dodging a horn. The little fellow swung back towards him again, like you do when you trying to tag somebody. Only he weren't just trying to tag the fellow "it." He was gonna stick that knife in the bouncer or die trying.

"Oh, Lord Jesus," Mamma Sally yelled.

I don't know what the rest of the crowd was yelling. I didn't know I was yelling until I woke up the next morning and found I couldn't hardly speak above a whisper. The rest of the fellows stopped fighting while the little man kept lunging with his knife—first one bouncer and then the other. The three white men who been doing the fighting looked around nervous, like finally they sobered up. They looked around. They seemed surprised to see themselves surrounded by a colored crowd.

One of them, the biggest of the white men, put his hand on the short white-knife man—like he was trying to calm him for a second. *Good,* I thought. *He's gonna talk some sense to his friend. Get him out of here.* But the little man shook him off and reached into his jacket. I had thought it strange him wearing a jacket on a night like this—and pulled out the biggest pistol I ever seen. He pointed it straight at the bigger bouncer.

The crowd stopped shouting. All the noise stopped like somebody switched a radio off. The little fellow stood there and pointed the pistol at the bouncer, who just stood there, too, waiting for it to happen. We was all waiting. Then the little fellow turned and looked at us—all colored except for the friends he come with. Not a white face in the crowd.

"Get back, niggers," he yelled, and swung that pistol in a curve like he was looking for one person to shoot.

He stopped the pistol at me—it was like one of them airplane search lights resting just on me. I knew he wasn't pointing the pistol at me particularly—I was just another colored face in the crowd. But I knew it wouldn't matter if he pulled the trigger. It was like old folks telling us not to take it personal when white folks treat us mean. "They treat all colored like that," they'd say. Well, I was gonna take it personal if I got shot.

It was just a second before he went on, searching. His big friend next to him kept talking to him, murmuring something I couldn't hear, but the little guy wasn't listening.

"Get on back," he shouted again, as if any of us had any room to get anywhere. Sweet Jesus, we tried. There just wasn't nowhere to go. Even his white friends couldn't get away. We was all stuck on Deweese Street in front of the Hurricane. White and colored. Waiting.

When I saw the two colored policemen push their way through the crowd, I thought, *Thank you, Jesus, we're saved. They going to arrest this madman.* I figured the evening was spoiled, but at least nobody was gonna get shot.

It took the policemen a while to make it through the crowd. I thought, *Let them through, let them through.* But people didn't seem to want to move, even when space opened up. I looked at Mamma Sally. She just shrugged.

The first colored cop finally made it to the head of the line. He had sweated through his wool jacket, but his voice was calm.

"Now put that gun away, sir. Put that gun down. You don't need to be waving it at anyone. Somebody's gonna get hurt. Put that gun away."

I don't know what I expected, but the policemen asking the man to put his gun away wasn't it. I didn't think policemen talked that much to men waving guns at people or trying to knife-stab them.

"Why don't they just arrest them?" I asked Mamma Sally.

"Colored cops can't arrest white men. Best they can do is calm them down until the white police arrive. Hope they get here soon."

I looked at her like those church people back in Zion Hill looked at me when we popped on them unaware. They thought we was from another planet. I wondered what planet this was where police couldn't arrest a fellow even when he was waving a gun.

"They can't arrest white men? How about colored? They arrest colored?"

"Already have," Mamma Sally said, and she pointed. The two colored bouncers had handcuffs on them. At least the madman had put away his gun and his knife. The red-headed fellow was already half a block away when I looked for him. The two white guys who had done the fighting was trying to leave, too, along with the pistol man. But the crowd had closed in on them up tight. They weren't able to move. The little white guy was pressed so tight, he couldn't reach into his pocket. I wasn't more than four feet away. His eyes were wild but he wasn't shouting for the niggers to back off anymore.

"What they doing?" I asked Mamma Sally.

"Trying to keep him here for the white police, not that they'll do anything about it. What gets me is those two hired overseers arresting the bouncers. They just doing their job, trying to keep order." Before I knew it, she was yelling at the colored cops.

"Let those men go. You ought to be ashamed of yourselves, arresting them two boys for trying to keep things together. Arrest that man!" And she pointed to the little white guy. "He's the one who's been waving guns in people's faces. He the one trying to stab people. Arrest him if you going to be arresting anybody."

If they could have gotten to Mamma Sally, they would have arrested her—respectable-looking lady or not. But the crowd wasn't budging for them. I thank Jesus I didn't have to ask Rudy to come down to get his mamma out of jail. Have to get me out of jail, too, I imagine, since I wouldn't have let them take Mamma Sally off without a fight.

As it was, the cops was having a hard time holding on to the two men they had arrested. "Let them go, let them go," everybody starting shouting. We pressed in on them so close, they started to get scared. I thought they were going to start waving pistols at us, too, but they didn't have room. Finally, one fellow reached in and snatched the handcuff keys out of one cop's pocket. Both men were out of handcuffs and scooting through the crowd like they was two-year-olds down at Keeneland Race Track. That crowd parted like the Red Sea. I still don't understand how we did that, but we did.

"Won't they arrest them later on?" I asked Mamma Sally.

"Oh, probably. But they free for now." She smiled at me. She looked worn out. I knew I was. I was going to have to rest up back at the farm. "They free for now. I guess that's all any of us can say. We free for now."

We found our way back to Kinkeadtown for the night. I kept thinking that at least I don't have to call Miz Lawson to come get Rudy's mamma and his wife out of jail. The little shotgun house was almost grimmer than any jail. Too late for me to go home to Scott County and we had run out of things to say to each other. I knew Mamma Sally had hoped to talk me into bringing the family back home—back home from the wilds of Scott County. But she couldn't talk about that now.

I had hoped, finally, to get her to tell me the story of Estill County. Those climbing ladder nightmares had to come from somewhere, but Rudy wasn't telling. Or he couldn't tell. Said he didn't remember anything of that time, excepting a little farming.

But it didn't seem the time to be raking up old nightmares when we hadn't caught our breath from the latest craziness. Estill County's story would have to wait. Deweese Street was enough for the night. "Enough was a feast," my mamma always told me when I'd swobble my food. "Chew that food slow," she'd tell me. "Let it go down smooth."

Deweese Street was feast enough to swobble for one night though it ain't gone down smooth. Estill County would have to wait.

Chapter 15
Jimmy Lawson—June 1942, Scott County

Daddy's still mad that I didn't take the farmer-son exemption for the draft. He runs off half a dozen names of farmers who got their sons working on the farms: the Martin boy; Danny, who couldn't plow a straight line if you laid down yard sticks all across the field; the Goode twins, who I bet the Army begged to take the exemption. I was surprised that Tom Bennett took the exemption. His daddy must have got down on his knees.

Daddy didn't get down on his knees, but he sure went on about it. But I just didn't feel right. "Wouldn't look good," I told him. Already people are resentful. The county doesn't think it fair that farmers' boys get out of fighting when everybody else's boys—teachers', mechanics', even the President's boys—had to go to the fighting. Already three boys sent back in coffins, and people said we're not even started. Even the colored were being drafted, though they weren't being sent to the fighting yet—mostly just doing the grunt work, which I expect I'll be doing my share of, too. Funny about the colored. I read in the newspaper that a bunch of them were protesting to President Roosevelt about not being allowed to fight. Think they'd be happy not to have their boys killed, but I guess it hurts their pride. I know how they feel. It'd hurt my pride, too.

But trying to explain that to Daddy doesn't go far. I don't dare mention the word pride: that goeth before a fall and was worth a half-hour sermon all by itself. But just mentioning about how the county felt got him going on, "You got to make up your own mind about right and wrong, sometimes you need to act alone in things. You sure don't let your neighbors pressure you into doing the wrong thing."

He pauses after that, and it's like we're back in his old church and I'm ten years old again. I wait, and he waits. He's back there with me. Then finally I turned to him and said, "Daddy, I thought about it, and I think this is the right thing for me to do."

He can't answer that. Or won't.

I have to have the same conversation with Mamma, though she don't press like Daddy. Not in words at least. I see her eyes following me around, and sometimes that's hard. But what am I going to say? *Mamma, stop looking at me like you already got the telegram?* When I look back, she catches herself and smiles and bustles about some chore like she hadn't been caught out.

Sometimes, I come in from the field at an odd time— maybe mid-morning. I tell her I don't know why but I'm just half-crazy with a sudden hunger. Then I sit back and watch her spin as fast as a June twister rustling up some food for me. When she's finished, I eat that food like I hadn't eaten in days—I don't care if my stomach feels like it's going to burst its seams like an overloaded feed sack. She sits and watches me, so close I can almost see her jaw line chewing along with me. I know she's not thinking anything about telegrams then. Not that little bit of time, at least.

The Army said I didn't have to report until October twenty-fourth so this year's crop will be in. Rainy days we work on the cabin. It's hard to get time to work on it, but we try to get a couple of hours after dark. We had three straight days last week when the ground was too wet to work. Any more rain and we'll be in trouble so we couldn't wish for that. But I did want us to finish the house before the Army took me. I think it'd be a kind of promise I'd be coming back. I told Daddy about a fellow Tom Bennett had working on his place—first-rate carpenter, Tom said. An old colored man named Jesse. Not from Scott County. Estill County, he thought.

Daddy wanted the cabin finished, too. Maybe for the same reason. Don't know. Daddy and I never talked like that. But he looked at me steady when I mentioned the old colored man.

"A colored man won't come to work for me. Wouldn't set a foot on this land."

I looked back at him steady myself. This is how we talked, Daddy and me. Said a whole bunch in those looks. "He might, Daddy. Him being from Estill County. Can't hurt to ask."

Jesse didn't blink an eye when I managed to find him at Tom's place. He was just about done at the Martins, he said. I spoke to him slow and loud, like he was deaf or the old Chinese laundry man in Georgetown who's been here thirty years and still don't speak the language: "I'm Jimmy Lawson," I said, "James Lawson's boy. You know the Lawson place?"

"I've heard something about it," is all he said. "When do you want me?"

Sometimes I stretched that mid-morning food break and sneaked over to the cabin to work with Jesse an hour or two. Sometimes Mamma would bring her sewing or quilting and join me. Jesse would nod and set me to a task like I'd been working for him for twenty years. Sometimes he even got Mamma to put down her sewing and work alongside him. Mamma said it was as peaceful as an Easter morning. We didn't talk much. Most times the only sounds would be hammering or sanding. Sanding made a kind of swish sound. Mamma said it reminded her of ironing—back and forth—back and forth. Jesse was a stickler for smooth. I'd show him something I felt was as smooth as a girl's cheek. He wouldn't say anything—just give it a light touch—and look at me again. I'd go back to the swishing.

He had a son about my age—a few years younger—I found out after working with him a week or two. Mamma had gone back to the house. We had two fellows working the land with us; most summers we had at least half a dozen, but men were hard to find these days. These fellows weren't worth much—one was almost fifty and one looked sixty, though I don't think he was more than forty. A drinker. But sorry or not, they had to be fed. Mamma made a separate plate for Jesse. I had brought it down to him. Her fried chicken had made him talkative, I think. I asked him about his son.

"They got him in the Army down in Alabama," he said.

"Alabama," I said. "Hot in Alabama. How's he like it?"

He paused in his chicken chewing. "He's a colored man in Alabama. How you think he like it?"

I was surprised. It wasn't a subject I had ever heard a colored man mention. Not that I had ever much talked to a colored man. The weather and maybe the cost of whatever we were complaining about that week were maybe the only two subjects I ever remember speaking about. Of course, I didn't much talk to white men, either. Just add corn and tobacco to the mix and maybe the basketball team at the college. Even when I somehow got Daddy to let me do three semesters at Georgetown College before we ran out of money, conversations didn't go too far. Surely never made it to race relations in Alabama. I didn't know much what to say. Jesse bit into Mamma's chicken again. He chewed and talked the next line so I could hardly make it out.

"Of course, hot as Alabama is for a colored man, I reckon I had rather have my boy there than over fighting them Japs. I imagine you gonna find it plenty hot there. My boy don't feel that way. Says he wants to be fighting. Fighting for freedom, he say."

He took a swig of sweet tea to wash down Mamma's chicken. He wiped his mouth and made a sort of grunt sound that meant, "That sure was good." The grunt sound was just being Kentucky polite to me, telling me to tell my mamma how good a cook she was. I had to be getting back to the fields. Daddy had been complaining. He said he needed me nearby if he was going to get any worthwhile work out of those fellows he'd managed to scrape from some barrel. I think maybe he wanted me out there for the company, too. But Jesse had one more thing to say on the subject before he picked up his hammer.

"I told him if he wanted to fight for freedom, he'd be better off staying in Alabama."

The only times Daddy, Jesse, and I worked together was when Jesse stayed a bit after dark. But those after dark working-times were mostly Daddy and me. Jesse would show us what'd he been working on and pack up quick and leave it to us. He didn't tell Daddy what to work on, of course. Daddy usually had his own part of the cabin he was set on. Jesse didn't go near that. He knew what Daddy wanted and did it. Not like those fellows in the field you had to keep looking at to keep them moving.

I don't think Daddy and Jesse said more than a hundred words together the whole summer after their first meeting.

But Jesse and I talked some. It was a week or more before I was able to spend more time in the cabin, but it had started to drizzle some. Daddy had made a trip into Georgetown for some feed. Brought Mamma's eggs in to sell, too.

"How come you agree to work for us? You're from Estill County, but I know you've heard the stories."

It was Jesse's time to look surprised. But he wasn't a man to let on that you had caught him off guard for long. "I hear all sorts of stories. I don't pay most much mind. I do what I want to do."

He drove a nail into a floorboard like that was the last word on the subject. But this was my chance, and I wasn't going to let it go.

"So when you heard that the Grand Dragon of the Ku Klux Klan needed a carpenter, you thought, well, why not give it a try?"

He put his hammer down. This time he wasn't even going to pretend not to be surprised.

"Boy, that's dangerous talk you talking."

I put my own hammer down. I waited.

"Of course, I heard that story. I also heard your daddy got shot trying to stop it. And that he ain't been Grand Dragon since he been shot. I heard all that."

"Clarence Jones. That's the man they hung. You're right. Daddy got shot trying to stop it. But the man wouldn't have been hung if Daddy hadn't led the men to him. Those sorry men never would have found him without Daddy leading them. Daddy told me that, and I believe him. He's pointed out some of the fellows in that mob. Those fellows couldn't make it to Georgetown without getting lost, let alone almost sixty miles to Maysville on horseback."

Jesse took up the hammer again and did three nails before he turned to me again. I was afraid that if I tried hammering, I'd split a board. It'd been fourteen years since I ran at those men attacking Daddy—fourteen years since I pounded on the Reverend Edwards who had just baptized me the year before. I spent my high school years in one fist fight after another—one boy pounding on me because my daddy was a nigger-lover, another jumping on me because he was Catholic and had heard Daddy had been Grand Dragon. I never told Mamma or Daddy about any of it, but they knew. Mamma just cleaned up my cuts and never questioned me.

It had quieted down the last few years. Only one fight my junior year in high school and none my senior year. But Scott County people never forgot anything. At least the white people didn't, and I imagine it was true for the colored, too. Jesse looked hard at me before he spoke.

"So who's your daddy? The man who tried to save Clarence Jones or the man who got him hung? I guess your daddy's both men. I guess you're gonna have to live with that. I guess he's gonna have to, too. But I'm a Christian man, though I don't much like going to church. Especially colored church. They just too damned noisy. Gets on my nerves. But if I remember the Bible—and I mostly don't—I think it say something about knowing a man by his deeds. His last deeds, not the one he done a long time ago. What he doing now. The last big thing your daddy do was try to save a man and not just saying it—lots of folk saying things they wouldn't spend a plug nickel for—but getting shot for trying. I see him limping. He still carrying that shot with him. I guess he's still carrying that other thing with him, too. That's alright. We all carrying something. I don't need to be amening every morning or every church-Sunday to know that I'm carrying something. Maybe I ain't help hung a man, but I've done my share of sinning. I'm working it out. Just like your daddy. Just like you gonna if you live long enough. You think Scott County the only Kentucky county full of stories nobody wants to talk about anymore? You think Alabama's the only place a colored man ain't free? I could tell you stories about Estill County make you thank Jesus you ain't there."

He reached for the hammer. He looked mad. I don't know if it was because of old stories I had made him remember or because of just making him talk so much. He was a quiet man.

"I didn't come to work for your daddy because he'd been Grand Dragon of no god-damned Ku Klux Klan. I came to work because I needed the work and because nobody—white or colored—is gonna tell me who to work for. Your daddy's done bad things. I done bad things, too. Jesus just about the only one who ain't done any bad things. But when they hung Jesus on that cross, just about everybody run away except his mamma. Peter run away. James run away." He took a breath.

"Your daddy didn't run away. That's something. You remember that. Your daddy didn't run away."

CHAPTER **16**

Nannie Johnson—September 1948

The first time I cleaned up Franklin I'm ashamed to
say there a part of me that thought, *Good. He a real boy—
getting into fights.* It a terrible thing to say, but a part of
me worried that he was too much like Rudy. You have to hit
Rudy on the head if you want to fight him and even that
don't always work. I don't mean to say Franklin wasn't
brave. Rudy's brave. And I know that just like Rudy, Franklin
wouldn't think twice about putting his life on the line. Saw
that when the pigs got killed—wouldn't go back into the
house until Rudy made him—until he was sure we was safe.
But just like Rudy, he don't even think about fighting. You
got to draw him a picture.

I know that's a good thing. Most mammas would die
for a child like that. But it's hard to see boys his age and
younger pushing him around. Taking advantage of his sweet
nature. It's taken all my strength not to jump in the middle
of it and start to bang heads. Rudy says, "Nannie, don't be
interfering. It will all sort out."

And he's right, it mostly do. All his boyfriends figure
out after a while that Franklin's got a line they don't want
to cross. He don't have any girlfriends yet, thank the Lord.
But everybody appreciates his sweetness, though the boys
he play with probably don't even know that word; couldn't
form it in their heads. Don't matter. They know they trust
Franklin in a way they don't other boys.

Herbert came home bruised and bloody, too, but that
was just regular business. He's been known to look for the
fights Franklin can't find. But I didn't worry about either
of them. The Lord forgive me, I just thought they outsiders
and got to figure a way to get inside. They hadn't been
around long enough last April. What with the moving and
everything, I don't think they had more than a couple weeks
of school before the summer began. Summer starts early in
Kentucky. This fall was the testing time, where they'd have

to fit in. I wanted to ask them if they fought together—brothers—but I figured they'd tell me if they thought I needed to know. I was proud they weren't running to their mamma with tales.

They were cleaned up when Rudy came in from the field—he stays out there past dark these days. The boys join him after chores. I'm out there myself most days, though Harry don't let me be much help. Miz Lawson keeps him of a morning sometimes. He settles in more peaceful with her than he ever do with me. She give him some fabric scraps, and that boy can spend hours sorting them out. She got the calming touch with children. I never have had that.

Sometimes, that old jealous demon gets inside me and I think all four of them love her more than they do their own grannies—maybe even me—though when I say that to Rudy, he says I'm just being foolish. "Miz Lawson just sweet to them," Rudy say. Both my mamma and Mamma Sally more the "hit you on the back of the head with a wooden spoon if you don't shape up" grannies. That's the way I mamma, too. But Miz Lawson is always trying to think of ways to happy them.

"They ain't used to that," Rudy says, not thinking I might not be too happy about the picture he's painting. "But that don't mean they love her more," he says.

"It don't mean they love her less," I say to him. But Rudy don't understand talk like that.

The second day Franklin and Herbert came home bloody I wasn't so pleased. Franklin had shoved toilet paper up his nose to stop the bleeding, but it soaked right through to his shirt. I still didn't ask any questions, and they weren't volunteering. But I didn't like it. I waited for Rudy to see them, but he was working on a different part of the farm than the boys that night, and by the time he got home he was so tired he couldn't hardly sit up straight at the kitchen table. The boys made themselves scarce—like they knew he'd take one look at their bruised faces and start to ask the questions they didn't want to answer. Maybe I should have made that happen—made him see the boys. But I was trying not to get in the middle of it, like Rudy's told me a hundred times. Hoping things would sort out. Boys can't be running to their mamma every time they get into a scrape. I didn't want no namby-pambies for sons.

Franklin's right eye was swelled shut the third day and his shirt soaked through with nose blood. Herbert's face wasn't so bad, but he was limping. I took one look at them and sent Eleanor out to get their daddy. She came on a different bus than her brothers and been home for a half hour. I figured she knew what was going on by the wide-eyed look she was wearing. The more Eleanor knows, the wider her eyes get. But I know that they had told her to keep shet, and it'd be more energy than I possessed to get her to open up. Besides, I needed Rudy with me on this one. Something was going on. This wasn't no schoolyard scrape.

Rudy came running in from the far Hacker field like Patton had finally called for him. That's a sore point with Rudy. That was one fight he wanted in on. Even after Eisenhower called in the colored troops at that Bulge Battle, Patton took his time. Rudy was in the third batch of colored troops and never did get to the fighting. I bless Patton's cracker-scarred heart every time I think of it, but I nod when Rudy tells that story.

"A doggone shame," I tell him. Like colored don't get enough fight right here in America. Right here in Kentucky.

Rudy stopped short like he hit a wall when he saw the boys. He reached out to touch Franklin's eye, then ran his hand softly over Herbert's face. He looked at me. I told him about the other days; he stood there, just listening. I knew he wouldn't call me out me for not telling him sooner. I knew he wouldn't say I was a hard mamma—a mamma just standing by watching her boys get pummeled to mush and enjoying herself like she'd gotten front row seats to the Brown Bomber. Rudy wouldn't even think thoughts like that. Any hard talk I've ever had coming had to come from me. Or Mamma. Her grandbabies aren't the only ones she's wooden-spooned on the back of the head. Sometimes I wish Rudy would jump in, too. But that's not Rudy's way. He turned to Franklin.

"Boys jump you? White boys?"

They'd been looking down ever since they got off the bus—or trying to. I had pulled their faces this way and that. Made them strip so I could look at their legs, feel their ribs. But now both heads popped up at their daddy's question. Herbert answered first.

"Weren't white boys. Colored boys."

"Colored boys?" Rudy looked surprised. "Why colored boys jump you?"

They got silent again. Rudy was never one for asking too many questions of the children. Not like me. I'm like that radio show Twenty Questions. Rudy says the boys' business is their own. But when he does ask something, they don't know to dodge like they do with me.

Franklin mumbles his answer so low he has to say it twice before we hear him.

"They say we working for the Ku Klux Klan. They say Mr. Lawson's the Grand Dragon and Miz Lawson the Grand Dragon's woman. Say we worse than slave-niggers. One boy said ain't no respectable colored folks worked this land for twenty years."

Slave-niggers. Nobody in our house has ever used that word. It might make even Rudy reach for the wooden spoon. I can't get the rest of what the boy's saying straight at first, I'm so upset.

Herbert jumped in next.

"Told us we needed to go back to Lexington. Only colored man that worked here they run off three four years ago. Said they don't need no Lexington niggers working for the Ku Klux Klan."

It wasn't making no sense to me. I ain't heard of the Ku Klux Klan in years. Far as I knew, it went south to Mississippi. Or Alabama. I know it was in Kentucky years ago, but not lately. At least not in Lexington. I didn't know about Scott County. It didn't have anything to do with us. Or the Lawsons. Mr. Lawson might be a strange man, but he wasn't no Grand Dragon. And Miz Lawson? Sometime she's too sweet. Sometimes it gets on my nerves. I feel like I got to deal with another Rudy, and one's enough. She wouldn't be married to any Grand Dragon. Those colored children had gone crazy with some rumor.

I never would have even mentioned that ugly rumor to the Lawsons. Especially not Miz Lawson. What would I say? "A story's going round that Mr. Lawson's the Grand Pooh Pooh of the Ku Klux Klan. Want to tell me about it?" Miz Lawson would look at me like Eleanor—Eleanor's eyes brim over when you hurt her feelings. I tell the child she need to toughen up, the world won't tiptoe around her. I know Miz Lawson hasn't been tiptoed around. Her boy

Jimmy's gone. Both the Lawsons would have to parade around the chicken grounds in those Klan pajamas before I'd ask them that question.

But I didn't need to. Eleanor had run to Miz Lawson's kitchen after she got her daddy. She hid out there most afternoons, but especially when she was upset about something or other. Something I said probably. But Eleanor must have seemed more upset than usual—said something about Franklin's eye—for Miz Lawson was at the door. She knocked softly like we ain't in each other's kitchens ten times a day. But she always knocked and waited for me to call her in.

"Has something happened to Franklin? Franklin!" She had spotted his eye, and her hand went to her mouth. She turned to look at Herbert. "Herbert!" He hadn't had time to grab his pants, though he grabbed for them now. His left knee was swollen like it'd been hit by a baseball bat. Which it might have been. "Who did this to you? Have some white boys been bothering you?" The boys just stared at her a second. She put down her hand from her mouth and grew quiet. "Have some white men hurt you?"

"No, ma'am." Franklin finally got out. "No white men's been bothering us. Colored boys."

"Colored boys?" She looked puzzled a second, but relieved, too. Herbert's knee took her attention. "We need some ice. My little icebox won't do. Eleanor, go run and get Mr. Lawson. Tell him to drive over to the Martins. They got that big icebox. You have enough bandages? Oh, my Lord, look at that eye. Why did the colored boys do this? I don't understand."

Herbert and Franklin was as likely as I was to tell what those crazy children had said. They just looked down. But Harry picked up strange words every day like a magpie plucks pretty ribbons. He loved to show them off to people, especially to Miz Lawson, who cooed at him like a pigeon dove every new word he trotted out for her.

"Klan," he said now to her, and, when she didn't respond to him at first—she had Franklin's face in her hands and was looking at his eye close up—he said it again. Loud now and clear. "Klan." And Miz Lawson finally turned from Franklin's eye and stared at Harry. She didn't repeat his word like she usually did. Didn't dance around him like he was the cleverest child this side of the Mason-Dixon line. Her very own colored Einstein. Miz Lawson never worried about the children getting big heads from too much praise like my mamma did. Like Mamma Sally did. Anything any of them did was just the smartest, finest, prettiest she had ever heard from any child.

But not this time. Though Harry said it twice more, though his face started to crinkle in disappointment, a crinkle that everybody knew was going to end up in a wail, she didn't say anything. Her hands stilled in her lap and her face got white. So white I thought she might faint, and I reached out for her. But she sat there steady and I took my hand back. She didn't faint. She just got whiter and whiter. Made me feel blacker sitting next to her. Made Rudy and Franklin and Herbert—even little Harry with his crinkling face—seem blacker. I don't know that I ever seen a face as white as Miz Lawson's, whiter than new snow, whiter than the Reverend William Price's hair. Whiter than a Ku Klux Klan's sheet covering.

"Klan!" Harry let out one final shout. And Miz Lawson looked at me, and I knew it was true. Mr. Lawson was the Grand Dragon. And Miz Lawson—so sweet and nice my children all thought she was that angel in the Reverend Price's church window come down to earth—sweet Miz Lawson was the Grand Dragon's wife.

That night Rudy had the climbing ladder dream. First time in months. I woke him up, and he moved in close like he always wants to, but I wasn't up to it. It's only because his body's worn to the bone after close to fourteen hours in the field that he got to sleep at all—though I know he rather be awake than have that dream. I lay there staring at the log loft where the boys was sleeping. I hoped they was sleeping. Probably were. Boys can sleep after anything. And they didn't see that look on Miz Lawson's face. They didn't believe what I believed. What even Rudy believed now. No, Rudy might want to get close for comforting, but I wasn't up to it.

I lay there wondering what we was going to do now. We couldn't stay on the farm—I knew that. Couldn't live next to the Grand Dragon—the Grand Dragon's wife. But we had to finish the season. Rudy had worked too hard not to. We all had. But how was we going to live thirty yards away from Kluxers when everything in me screamed to get away? As fast and as far as I could. And to take my family with me.

I thought about Mamma warning me. I thought about Mamma Sally, too. Something she wasn't telling me about Estill County, something that made her almost shake when she came out to Scott County. Something that made Rudy climb those rotten ladders in his dreams. Rudy couldn't remember. Or didn't want to. But Mamma Sally was going to tell me. I was determined. We weren't going to be ambushed by any more secrets. She was going to have to tell me.

I hadn't said anything to Miz Lawson yet. But she knew I knew. Her hands was shaking when she left. Mr. Lawson had brought the ice from the Martins, and he wanted to make sure Franklin was OK before he left, but I wanted them out of there and Miz Lawson knew it. She grabbed Mr. Lawson's arm and almost pulled him out the doorway. He looked surprised. Then he saw her face. He didn't look surprised anymore. He looked like he knew what was going on. He nodded like a person does who's been expecting something all along. He didn't even say goodnight when he went out the door.

We didn't either.

CHAPTER 17

(Mamma) Sally Johnson—September 1948, Lexington

You been wanting me to tell this story a long time, Nannie. Well, it's a long story. A long, hard story. Hard for me to tell. Maybe hard for you to hear.

I hear that those Jewish people who came out of them Concentration Camps won't set ten words running about what went on in there. They go mum like they the guilty ones instead of them Nazis. My neighbor Viola can't understand why that is.

"You'd think they'd want the whole world to know what happened to them," she says.

The woman doesn't have the sense the Lord gave the average hound dog. At least when that dog smell something bad it knows not to go back sniffing.

I know why those Jewish people don't want to talk about that stuff. It's not just that some of the memories act like they're not even memories—not something stuck in the past. It's somebody beating on your head right now instead of twenty years ago. And your heart don't know time's gone on, either, pounding like you still running. Like you ain't safe yet.

It's not just that. It's that you do feel guilty. Only you don't know what for most of the time. I know there's things I shouldn't have done. I got things weighing on my conscience I think about almost every day. It's what keeps me judging people too hard—even white people.

I see you carrying an anger on your shoulders, Nannie, that's gonna wear you down. You got reason to be mad. Lord knows, I know you got reason. But it's gonna wear you down.

But I ain't talking about those times you know you've been wrong. You bring those things to the Lord, and He helps you let go of them. Or if you can't let go of them, He teaches you how to carry them. But how you gonna let go of something when you don't know what it is you letting go of? How you gonna let go of feeling that you should have done something different? Not let them people treat you like they did when you know you couldn't have done anything about it.

Don't go telling me that don't make sense, that there wasn't nothing me or those Jewish people could do. I know that. I've thought long and hard about it and everything I think I might have done, I know I couldn't have. It would have got me or somebody close to me killed. And the way I hear it told, the whole German army had a gun to those Jews' heads, so I ain't blaming them, either. I'm just telling you the way it feels. The way it hurts.

But you tell me that some stories got to be told— that it's wrong keeping secrets just 'cause the secret's painful. And I know you right. I know you right.

We had the prettiest spread you ever seen in Estill County. Right outside Ravenna. We called it the village those days and it was a fine place. Daddy had come to work for the railroad back in 1910. I was almost grown by then. Felt like we was heading back to Mississippi when Daddy said we were leaving Louisville. For the sticks? But I was just thirteen. Almost grown but not quite, so I had to follow.

Only thing is, I loved it almost from the start. I thought we'd be the only colored folks 'round, but there was a whole group of us. The railroad needed workers and they didn't seem to care 'bout hiring colored. Later on that changed, but not then. Daddy said you showed up, and they put you to work right next to a white man. The white man might grumble, but was nothing he could do about it. Same pay, too. That didn't happen much them days. These days, either.

It was good wages, too. Weren't more than a couple of years before Daddy saved enough to buy him a nice little farm. He worked on that farm every hour he weren't working for the railroad. Simon, Rudy's daddy, did the same thing. Colored men working themselves near to death, but they didn't care. It was their chance, and they didn't get many of them. The land was cheap—and it was good. You let the Kentucky River flood your bottom fields some years, and the next year you got as much corn from that land as any land this side of Iowa. And the corn didn't go begging. At least not during the war—the first one. The Army bought up every cob you could give them.

I wasn't much more'n a child when I married Simon. Went from working my daddy's field to working ours 'cause Simon had done the same thing Daddy did with all that good wages. Daddy helped us build our own house. I was carrying Rudy. I'd sit and lazy, watching Daddy and Simon and Simon's friend Jesse worked on that house right up to three days before my time. I'd say, "Child, look at your daddy building you a home. You the luckiest colored baby in the whole state of Kentucky." Oh, it was a fine house. Simon and Daddy were good solid builders, but it was Simon's friend who added the touches no other house had—none I ever seen, anyway. Prettiest built-in cabinets. A staircase that curved its way up to the second floor like it was a piano note come off the page. Jesse even carved a wooden cradle for Rudy so fine I hated when Rudy outgrew it. I think about that cradle. Always meant to save it for my grandbabies when it came out that Rudy was the only baby I was gonna get. But it got left behind. A lot of things got left behind.

The house you in now reminds me of our place, except ours was bigger. It got all those little touches that don't leap out at you at first. You can tell they built it for that boy of theirs, the one killed in the war. Somebody took care to make a home. Not like the sorry shack we living in now. It's built just to get as much rent money as it can before it give up the ghost and fall over.

Our house weren't more than a quarter mile from Daddy's place. Could see when his kitchen light was on from our back porch. I'd sit there and see Mamma in my mind's eye, bustling about making sure Daddy didn't die of hunger. Oh, the way she spoiled that man. But at least he had the good grace to know he was spoiled—not like some men who think it all their due. I serve up Simon a king's feast, and he act like I'm just doing what I'm supposed to. But then I ain't Mamma. Rudy more like Mamma. The Lord's grace leap about like that.

We were up on a knoll—didn't mind the Kentucky flooding the lower fields, just didn't want it going through our kitchen. Looking down that knoll, gazing at that Kentucky River when it was behaving—well, it weren't like we were back in Mississippi. I don't know that I told my daddy how I felt—that was the kind of child I was; he had to figure out for himself that if I weren't griping I was happy—but I sure didn't miss Louisville.

But something or somebody is always wanting to spoil a good place. Look what happened down on Deweese Street. Folks having a good time, laughing and carrying on but nobody getting hurt, and somebody—somebody white usually—comes in and makes a misery just for meanness' sake. I ain't saying Ravenna was any Paradise—I guess Adam and Eve were the last people that see Paradise, and they couldn't hang on to it long enough to give Abel a baby taste of it. At least Rudy got a taste. Much as I fuss about you and Rudy moving out to Scott County, I know that the Kentucky countryside is the nearest thing to Eden we got this side of Heaven.

Daddy had a half dozen peach trees the other side of his house. They were up on a ledge that protected them from the wind some—kept them from freezing most years— and high enough so that they didn't flood. They were halfway between Daddy's home and ours. It was a sight.

Your Eleanor would have loved them trees. A walk as pink as a sunset in April. I wish I could have shown them to her. I don't know that your boys would have thought much about them blossoms, though Rudy couldn't get enough of them, but they would have loved the peaches. Everybody did. Didn't have a real market for them, so we had to do the best we could with them. What we didn't trade for other fruit—apples, pears, watermelons—and what we couldn't eat of a summer, we canned and ate all winter. Mamma complained sometimes that the house smelled like a peach pit the whole year round. But she weren't really complaining. She knew we had it good. We all did.

But it's like good ain't the natural way for colored. Daddy had the first real trouble. His land was just about the best 'round and some white men just didn't think it was right that a colored man should have that land. Just because Daddy had worked harder than any man I ever knew—white or colored—just because he seen his chance and took it, that didn't mean he had a right to it.

I think it started with the tobacco war. You know about that? It weren't so much around here—mostly out West—but the trouble spilled over. Trouble always spills

over. The farmers were fighting the big tobacco companies—the big one, American Tobacco Company—trying
to get a fair price. Daddy was all for that. So was Simon.
We only had two acres in tobacco, but it was good money.
Real good money. And then it wasn't—wasn't worth
bothering with at the price American Tobacco Company was
offering. So we were all for the farmers.

Except then the farmers started night-raiding
farmers who didn't join their Co-op. Colored know that you
get a bunch of men yahooing it around the countryside and
even if the first thing they got in mind is fighting the tobacco
company, the second thing they come up with is making
trouble for the colored. They knew Daddy was one of them—
had signed the paper saying he wouldn't sell except at the
price they all agreed to. And that was a hard thing for Daddy
to do. He had about ten acres in tobacco—more than half
his money came from it. Touch and go whether he could
hold out, but he did. Said if they didn't stand together, might
as well hand over their land to the tobacco companies and
let them run it the way they wanted. Might as well go settle
back in Mississippi and pick cotton for the man.

And after a while things got better for the farmers. I
don't know if the tobacco companies gave in or what, but
the price of tobacco went up to where even a small grower
could make a fair living. Weren't no need for the Night
Riders no more. Except for that second thought they got: if
night riding worked for American Tobacco Company, it might
work for that other thing that was nagging at them—getting
the colored off land they thought was too good for colored.

I was still nursing Rudy the first bad night—I
remember because I was out on the back porch, shucking
corn with one hand and patting Rudy with the other—when
I spotted Daddy's two milk cows just mashing down a whole
row of my tomato plants. I stuck that baby in the corn basket
and ran out to try and save my tomatoes, but it was too
late. A whole section of the fence we kept those milk cows
in had been just torn up. It wasn't just one section being
pushed over by an ornery cow who sees something better
to nibble on the other side. I'm saying there wasn't a plank
left standing.

That was just the first of their meanness. Folks say
the men doing it—riding around, tearing up and burning

things—weren't the tobacco Night Riders. That these were different fellows. I don't know about that. I know they wore masks same as the other ones. Maybe they called themselves something else. A skunk can call itself a cat, but it still stink. I know these fellows weren't trying to punish tobacco farmers who were selling to American. They were trying to run off colored farmers—especially the ones with good land. If you owned something not worth owning, they left you alone mostly. At least at first. Except if you had a good job with the railroad. They didn't like that, either. Then even if your land weren't good, they didn't want you as neighbors. I guess if you were colored and were making a decent living—or even if you weren't—you were in trouble.

All through Rudy's growing up, things got meaner and meaner. The peach trees still bloomed in April, the Kentucky River in the springtime still made you feel the Lord's bounty was just rushing through the land—but the meanness made life hard, made you feel like you couldn't make it to the next day sometimes, let alone to the next peach blossoming. We had a good colored community in Ravenna and Irvine and in all that land around it. But more and more folks just decided it weren't worth it. More and more just sold out if they could or just left everything if they couldn't and moved on to Lexington. Lexington ain't no Harlem. I know that, even if sometimes I tell you different. But it sure beat having to deal with Night Riders.

It wasn't just Night Riders plaguing farmers. Colored railroad workers had it bad. Six or seven white fellows might wait for a man after work. Jump on him. Break his kneecap so he can't walk, let alone work. You recollect that fellow who begs sometimes over at Do-Good Tavern? He was one of them. That's why when I heard about Herbert's knee all swell up like that I about faint right over. It's like I was a girl again. I know you say it was colored boys did that to Herbert, but it the same thing. Meanness is meanness. Once a fellow was jumped like that, he didn't have no choice but to hobble himself down to Lexington, try to pick up a job that didn't need him standing. If he found one—which weren't likely—it sure wouldn't pay what the railroad did.

Colored fellows started to make sure they always had a group around them. Leastways, even if they were outnumbered, they'd give a good fight back. But farmers ain't like that. They don't have no group around them, except maybe at harvest time. A farmer is alone. He don't have neighbors practically sitting in your lap like we do in Kinkeadtown or you did out on Georgetown Street. That's why he's in the country in the first place. Just his wife and children to keep him company. Just the Lord to protect him.

I ain't criticizing the Lord, but sometimes I think He's a heavy sleeper. I've always been a light sleeper, myself, and some August nights I don't think I sleep at all—Mamma used to say you got to pay for everything in this world, so I reckon Kentucky August is our payment for April. The air so wet and hot, it makes me feel like I'm choking. I put me a cot on the back porch and fought for breath when I weren't fighting mosquitos.

Nights like that seem to go on forever, so I weren't really surprised when I saw the first light. I figured I had fought the night through straight to dawn, though it sure didn't feel like I had gotten any rest. I was still half-sleeping. I sat up and wiped my eyes and thought it was a strange sunrise—still dark as blackstrap molasses on the porch, but bright as a flashlight over near Daddy's place. I stared at that brightness a good minute before I finally figured out what I was looking at.

Daddy's barn was burning.

I called out to Simon, and he came running. His friend Jesse had been helping with the harvest, and he came up from our barn where he'd been sleeping. Other neighbors came running, too, none of us were that far apart. White neighbors came to help, too—I ain't saying no. We all formed a line down to the Kentucky, but it weren't no use. That barn was gone—two cows, a horse, and most of Daddy's crop with it.

Daddy didn't have no choice but to sell off then—at half the price he should have got. Had to. Owed too much and with no crop to sell—or not much of one—he wasn't going to get out of debt this lifetime. Simon asked him to move in with us—I begged him to, but he was stubborn. Mamma, too. Didn't believe in crowding their children. Went back to Louisville. All them years of double work, and they ended up back in their old neighborhood. Like running a race for thirty years and finding yourself back at the starting line. Only you ain't young no more.

Wouldn't you know just about the first thing the new white owner did was chop down them peach trees. They were getting old, but they still bloomed. Still gave lots of fruit in a good year. But the man said there weren't no market for them, that they were more trouble than they were worth. Thank the Lord Mamma never saw that. She asked about those peaches, and I'd lie, telling her, "The blooms are as pretty as ever. Of course, I don't know about the peaches."

I could lie like that because Mamma and Daddy never would visit us for all our asking, though we lived on there a good five years more. It was for the best. Would have broke her heart to see those peach trees gone. Broke her heart again. Took a year or two, but I imagine the place finally didn't smell like a peach pit anymore. Or maybe it did still. Some smells linger. Like a skunk's. I'll never know for certain. Once Momma and Daddy left, I never went in their house again. Would have broke *my* heart.

Simon was determined that what happened to Daddy wasn't going to happen to him. To us. He stayed up nights roaming his land with a rifle handy. Working all day and roaming all night. I didn't think it could last too long even with his friend Jesse and other colored men taking turns. But I was as determined as Simon—maybe more so.

I said, "Give me that rifle. I can't sleep no ways, and you need your rest."

But he never would. "Them Night Riders find you out there and they might not stop with burning barns. Maybe Rudy your only baby,"—I don't know why, Simon and I kept working at it—"but Rudy need his Mamma just as much as if he be ten children. Maybe more."

I didn't want to hear that. "He need his daddy, too.

"Yes," Simon said. "He needs his daddy. He needs his daddy to be a man."

I only have two pictures of Rudy as a boy. One as a baby. We didn't take pictures much in those days—not like nowadays. I know I'm his mamma, but he was the sweetest-looking boy. You know how that is, Nannie. You a mamma, too. Your Franklin favors Rudy. Sometimes I'd look at Rudy and want to gobble him up like he was one of Mamma's peach cobblers. Other times, he just about made me pull the last hair out of my head. Not from meanness. Rudy boy is like Rudy man. He just ain't drunk from the meanness cup.

You a good woman, Nannie, but you and I both have drunk our share from that cup. You know it's true. Of course, somebody's got to be the mean one. Especially dealing with a child like Rudy. Or a husband like him. And how we know nice if we ain't seen mean?

I'd send Rudy off to school with three corn pones wrapped around some bacon, an apple and a good chunk of Mamma's peach cobbler, and he'd come home hungry as a weanling calf. I'd find out that maybe he ate the apple. Gave all the rest away to some "poor" child. I say, "You gonna be poor if you keep giving my food away," and he'd hang his head like I caught him stealing.

It drove me plumb crazy. My momma said he was the walking Christ child. I said, "He ain't gonna be walking long if he keeps that up 'cause I'll cut a branch and switch his legs so hard he'll think twice about feeding the poor on my cooking." Oh, Mamma would just look at me and shake her head. "The living Christ child," she'd say again, 'cause I think she knew it drove me crazy.

How you gonna switch the Christ child's legs?

I think I threatened Rudy ten times for every switch he ever got. I don't know that his daddy ever touched him. Rudy ever switch the children? No, I reckon it's all on you like it was all on me. Some mammas get to threaten their children with their daddy coming home. Yours and mine would just laugh at that. Not that Simon don't have a mean streak in him—same as me. But he never could bring himself to lay a hand on Rudy. "What? I'm supposed to beat the child 'cause he gave his lunch away? Lord have mercy, woman, you done lost your mind."

I worried sometimes, and I know Simon did, too, that we weren't making Rudy tough enough. A boy's got to be tough in this world. A girl, too. I laugh at that now—like we got to be practicing toughness on our children—like the world won't be tough enough on them in time. Especially colored children.

My neighbor Viola is always yelling or beating on her children—her grandbabies now. I say, "Viola why you treat that sweet child like that?"

"The world don't know it a sweet child," she say. "If I don't harden this *sweet* child, the world gonna take its sweetness and crush it, just like a juice squeezer crushes an orange—leave just some dry rinds behind."

I don't know. Maybe she right. Lots of colored folk think like that.

Seem to me, though, they just doing the world's dirty work first.

Rudy didn't have to wait too long before the world started its dirty work on him, started pounding on that sweet face. He hid the first time it happened. He about twelve years old—maybe shy of it a couple months since he's a Christmas baby and they just started school. We start school early out in the country, so it was still August. That'd be about 1926. He was out helping his daddy after school who didn't notice half the time if the boy got on pants let alone that he's sporting a big bruise mark above his left eye. I say, "What happened to you, boy?" His daddy finally look at him, then.

"Ain't nothing," Rudy says. "Just a fight with a-nother boy."

Well, I was just too surprised to ask any more questions, which was my fault. I look at Simon, who's as surprised as I am but covers it like a man does. "Well, boys fight," is all he said.

Maybe so, but Rudy fighting was a first for us.

I went looking for him next day. I had a worry in the back of my head that I didn't even know was there. Just uneasy. It was that idea of Rudy fighting. I couldn't shake it loose. Rudy was off doing some chore in the field next to where Daddy's peach orchard used to be. I made him pen the pigs there. Their stink was more than I could bear close to the house. Rudy was never a one for neglecting any chore, but he didn't run to do them first thing. He'd want to play first, work later just like any boy.

Whatever Mamma said, he weren't the Christ child every day, which I can't say I minded that much. I weren't no Mother Mary; I didn't need to be raising no Jesus. Sure enough, when I found him he was nursing an egg over the right eye this time and a whole bunch of scratches. Both eyes were circled black and blue like he was some raccoon. "What happened," I asked again, and when he said, "Just some fight." I asked, "Who's this boy you're fighting? What's his name? I'm going to see his mamma because this ain't right."

One thing Rudy never really learned how to do and that was lie. I wish you could teach your children how to lie. I know that sounds terrible, but a good lie can save you a whole bunch of misery. That Eleanor of yours can't lie to save her soul. One thing sure, she won't grow up to be no card player. Even when she make her lips say one thing, her face is yelling out the truth like she's flashing the latest movie down at the Strand. Rudy was the same way. I watched him struggle to come up with a boy's name, but he couldn't do it. He couldn't have done it if I had promised him ten of Mamma's peach cobblers, which he loved more than anything in this world. He couldn't have told me the boy he fought if I had cut down half a dozen peach branches and switched him all the way to Powell County. Wasn't a boy who bruised him like he'd gone ten rounds with the Brown Bomber. Weren't two boys, either. Or three boys. They were men who done that to my boy.

White men.

The story didn't come out easy. Rudy didn't lie, but he didn't tell tales, either. This time I did call for his daddy. Not to beat him—I guess he'd been beat enough—but to make him tell. He kept telling us that he could handle it. Just some trouble we didn't need to worry about. Rudy had seen how much I had worried about my daddy—how much I grieved over that orchard. He had seen how it just about killed Mamma to leave. He didn't want to be worrying us anymore. He didn't want to give us the idea we had to leave, too. I yelled at that boy—you know I'm a yeller. You a yeller, too, Nannie. The more upset I get, the more I yell. But even when I was screaming, screaming so hard that next morning my throat felt like I had swallowed a rose branch, thorns and all—I was thinking was this the boy I worried weren't tough enough? He had a soft heart. That didn't make him soft. He still got a soft heart, Rudy. But it's a soft heart that never gives an inch when it comes to loving. It's a soft heart you could pummel and pound all you wanted and it was going to go on beating. That soft heart was as tough as they come.

But tough heart or not, his daddy and I just wore him down. Some secrets too heavy to keep—you keep telling me that, and it's true. Too heavy especially for a little boy, and he weren't twelve yet. He was a little boy, though it'd be worth my life to call him that to his face. He breathed heavy sometimes when he told us his tale, but he didn't cry. *He ain't crying so I won't, either,* I said to myself. Fact is, I didn't feel like crying. Fact is, I felt like grabbing the rifle and finding me some real coon. Some white man coon.

Rudy didn't know the names of the men, but we figured out who they were quick enough. Bunch of day-workers down at the railroad yard who only worked about half the time. Rest of the time, they spent their children's food money in them bars down there on Geneva Street. That was a rough street them days. The colored had a bar on the edge of it, other side of the river. Needed a river to separate them. Those men hated everybody who had full-time work. I ain't excusing them, but I know the feeling. You ain't got two dimes to keep each other company and you see folks spending money like they think money flows like the Kentucky and is never gonna run dry. The Bible tells me not to covet, but it's hard sometimes. I tell myself, *Sally, don't be hating rich people. They can't help it if all that money makes them stupid.*

But it weren't just rich people those men hated. They hated colored. Hated colored like it was a sickness that went into their gizzards. They breathed that hate. They burped it up and tasted that hate. That hate for colored people filled up their mean lives. It got them up in the morning, it kept them running the countryside long after the tobacco companies gave in.

It ain't like I don't know about that kind of hate. Sometimes I hate white people. I got reason, Lord knows. We all got reason. But when I see the ugly hate done by them crackers—sometimes, they so full of hate, they don't look human. Well, I say, Lord. Save me from that.

Those crazy crackers hated rich people and colored. And colored rich—or what looked like rich to them—just made them crazy. The drinking helped with the crazy, but that weren't it. If a job was to be had, it was the white man who was supposed to have it. That was Bible-written as far as they were concerned. Bible-written. I wanted to ask them where it was Bible-written to hate your neighbor 'cause he's colored. Right here, they would have told me: Isaiah something or other. Hebrews something. A Bible-hating man can always cite you text and verse for why he's supposed to be hating. He's got the Lord on his side.

These Bible-hating drinking fools weren't crazy enough to go after the colored railroad workers, leastways not after they started making sure they always traveled in a group. But colored boys—little boys coming home from school, too big for their mammas to be walking with them but little enough for them to chase and beat—they were fair game. I couldn't in Jesus' name figure how grownup people could be picking on little boys, but hate don't see children. Them Nazis didn't see Jewish children when they killed them. They just saw Jewish. And Lord have mercy on me, I didn't see white children later on when I helped Jesse. Hate's like some cold you pass on to your neighbor just by sneezing. Pass it on to a whole crowd if the wind's right. You look at your neighbor, all red-eyed and wheezing, and you think, "Thank Jesus, I ain't him."

But you could be me, Nannie. You don't take care, you will be. Only it ain't no cold you passing on.

Rudy weren't the only one they set on. That trash had pounced on half a dozen children, maybe more. Rudy changed his walking path; they wait for him his new way. If we'd been going to church like I maybe should have been, we would have found out about it way sooner than we did because people had been talking, trying to figure what to do. But I ain't much of a churchgoer. Not like your mamma, Nannie. Not like mine was, either, but with her in Louisville I had stopped going.

I wasn't one for looking for the Lord in a little church so crowded you knew who was sitting next to you just by their smell. I didn't need a black man up front taking more than his share of air telling me how many ways I was going to Hell, and that he knew the way to the Lord and was going to show me. I found the Lord all by myself in Daddy's peach orchard. And when the man cut the peach orchard down, I found the Lord somewhere else. Sometimes it was hard. The Lord ain't just a heavy sleeper, He covers himself better than any child playing hide and seek. He knows all the best hiding places. But I've always found Him sooner or later. And it ain't ever been in church.

I was ready to go shoot up Geneva Street, but it was Simon who was going to be sensible about it all. "We are going to the law," Simon said. The law? I wanted to laugh out loud, but Simon looked at me hard. We had taught Rudy to respect the law. It wouldn't do to let him know what we truly thought of it. That's what I mean about lying. It comes in handy every once in a while. Simon was going to gather a dozen or so men. Maybe a whole bunch of colored had left for Louisville or Lexington lately, but a dozen votes representing two dozen others weren't something that sheriff would overlook if he wanted re-election. And it can't be good for a town, letting a bunch of no-count white drunks beat up on little colored children.

The sheriff seemed to listen to Simon at first. He was a cracker like all them who ran the town, but he was a cracker who needed votes. He said he'd make sure to talk to them boys—make sure they left the children alone. "Talk to them," I yelled, when Simon told me about the meeting. "How about corralling the lot of them down to the Kentucky River and making sure they stay under till they drowned dead? How about hanging them from their ugly feet and then turning them around and giving their necks the next round? How about just shooting the whole lot of the stinking cowards, picking on little children because they too afraid of grown-up men?"

Rudy's eyes just got bigger and bigger when I carried on like that. Another reason I didn't go to church too much. I was never one for turning the other cheek. Especially if the cheek you hit was my child's cheek. But Simon just kept saying that the sheriff said he was going to take care of it and we had to give him a chance. It was either that or go to war against the whole county and how could we continue living in Estill County if we did that?

I knew he was right. But it was hard going down. My throat was already rubbed raw with all my yelling. But it weren't a thorny rose bush I'd been swallowing. It was Daddy's barn burning; it was Daddy and Mamma leaving their land and going back to live in a Louisville slum for their old age. It was that man buying their place for pennies on the dollar and then not even knowing what he bought, chopping down that peach orchard like it hadn't been one of the Lord's sanctuaries. It weren't no rose bush I was swallowing. I was swallowing every last insult them white trash had been hurling at us for two hundred years.

But I did it. I looked at Rudy's big eyes getting bigger and I did it.

Things did get better. For a little bit. I made Rudy almost strip most days, looking him over from feet to head, searching for any scratch. One time he had a skinned knee and I almost made him swear on the Bible that he just had tripped. I never stopped worrying, but I began to think that maybe I should—maybe the worst was past and I should just calm down. That's what Rudy kept telling me. Even Simon said it once—when I was going on about that scraped knee—but I don't think he believed that bad times had passed any more than I did.

Hate like them crackers had for colored didn't pass like no summer cold. Didn't sneeze itself out. Hate like that was a wasting disease. It got into your bones and just ate its way out till there weren't nothing left to eat. Till it was all gone.

Rudy's school ended at 2:00 in those days. Gave the children time to do their chores and help out in the fields. I'd start waiting for him about quarter past. When Rudy didn't come home by 2:30 I went out looking for Simon. It was coming on mid-April, our busiest time. We had given up on the tobacco acres and gone all corn. Corn has to be in the ground by May, but Simon just had his friend, Jesse. He didn't want to keep Rudy home. It would have been better for all of us if we had kept Rudy home. But we didn't want to. Thought he'd have a better life than a farmer's life. Guess Rudy thought different about that.

Simon didn't want to come in at first, said I was worrying for nothing. I told him it only took Rudy twenty minutes to walk home.

"He's just dawdling," Simon said. "Good Lord, woman, you going to drive the boy crazy hovering over him like that. He coming up twelve in December. I was almost out in the world by myself at twelve years old. I sure didn't want my mamma dogging my every step. Rudy be waiting for you when you get back to the house."

Simon talked like that to convince himself as much as me. He came back with me, and Rudy weren't there. He knew as well as I did that Rudy didn't dawdle his way home. He knew it'd worry us too much, and Rudy wasn't gonna do that. Simon stopped talking about me worrying too much. He took his rifle down from the wall. I went and found the bullets. I said I was going with him, but he shook his head. Somebody had to be home if Rudy showed up. I saw that was true. Waiting is a lot harder than doing. I ain't never been much good at it.

CHAPTER 18
(Mamma) Sally Johnson—September 1948, Lexington

The rest I just hear from Simon. And his friend Jesse later. They didn't want to tell me, but I made them. Just like you making me tell this story. Some they got from Rudy—other parts they get from Rudy's friend, Toby, who walked with Rudy. We made them all promise they wouldn't walk alone. Toby said they spotted a group of white men drinking by the river, over near Miller Creek Road. Must have been more than a dozen of them and the boys hear them before they see them. They were carrying on like they were celebrating something. What they celebrating ain't clear to this day except maybe that the sheriff was away— gone down to Franklin for some business. Or that what he say later—said he weren't around to stop the trouble. I think that mighty convenient him being away but I don't know. I just know the mice play when the cat's away. Except them men weren't no mice.

More like rats.

Toby said as soon as they spot those men, they turn around and run the other way, but it too late. The men spot them and give chase. At first Toby says the men shouting and laughing like it all a game of chase. They call out to the boys to stop, they weren't going to hurt them. But Toby said they knew better. They keep running, and the more they run—the more the men have to chase them—the madder them men get. They run the whole length of the river, and those men keep on them like the boys was foxes and the men hound dogs.

Toby said they don't know where they are after a while, but there ain't no colored around. They pass white folks sitting on their porches or working in their yards and they yell for help, but the people stare at them like they watching a parade. Sometimes it worse. Sometimes people join in the crowd chasing them. Soon there's a big mob chasing two little colored boys. "What they done?" People yell from their porches. "They stealing?" What they done? But nobody knows the answer to that or nobody's telling. Like you need a reason to chase some colored boys. They just some varmints the hounds are after. You don't need no reason to chase varmints. It just fun.

But it ain't no fun for Rudy and Toby, who think they gonna die. Toby said he thought maybe they should jump in the river, but don't neither one of them swim. Better to drown in the river, Toby said, than be torn up by those men. "Let's jump," Toby kept saying, but Rudy kept shaking his head no. "Keep running. Those fellows will give up sooner or later."

But it weren't all the same men who had started the chase. The new ones had fresh legs and weren't gonna give up no matter what. Some of them by that time probably thought Rudy and Toby had been thieving. Ever see that? How a question becomes an answer before you know it. They were yelling, "Stop them thieves!" and even more men joined in. A few women, too. Nobody bother to ask what they stole. They just kept chasing. The boys kept running.

Only they couldn't run forever. Their legs weren't fresh. Toby said he kept looking for some tree they could climb, but they didn't have time. Besides, he didn't want to be up a tree. He feared that mob would shake that tree till they fell out of it like they were possums. Rudy was the one who spotted the barn loft with the ladder leaning from it.

It was better than a tree, Toby thought. Maybe they could scramble up there and push the ladder down. They'd be trapped, but maybe folks'd calm down after a bit.

They didn't have much choice nohow. The men chasing them weren't twenty feet behind them and catching up fast. They got to the ladder, and Toby said it was so long and spindly he had a moment when he didn't think he could climb it. But Rudy said go and he started—one rung after another, pulling himself up. He felt Rudy three rungs behind him, the ladder swaying, worrying all the time the whole thing was going to fall apart. Not strong enough for one boy, let alone two. It was a rickety, rotten thing, Toby said. More than one rung was missing, but they were scrambling so fast they hardly knew it. They probably didn't even have to tip the ladder over when they got to the top. No grown man with any sense would risk it.

Toby said when he got to the top, he just dived over. He landed in a little bit of hay, but it weren't enough to soften his landing. He thought Rudy was right behind him. He turned to push the ladder over, but Rudy wasn't there. He heard a high screaming that scared him more than any of the mob yelling. He lay on his belly and crawled to the edge of the loft. It took all my pleading to get him to tell me what he saw then. Took all Simon's and Jesse's hard looks, but he told us finally.

He said the mob had made it to the ladder just as Rudy got to the top but before he could jump off. They grabbed that ladder away from the loft but didn't let it fall over. Not at first. Rudy didn't weigh more than a hundred pounds, and they were strong men. They held that ladder straight up with Rudy at the top. First they yelled at him to come on down, but when he wouldn't do that, they just held that ladder straight. That ladder was probably twenty feet, narrow, homemade, and not too proud. But those men held on and Rudy swayed at the top like he'd been caught at the top of a tall sapling in a May twister. "He hollered for help. He hollered for you, Miz Sally," Toby told me, and it was like he shoved that sapling right through me. Yelling for his mamma made those men laugh and shout all the more. They rocked that ladder back and forth, Rudy crying and screaming, them yelling.

But even strong men can't hold onto a twenty foot ladder forever. Toby said the men claimed they didn't mean to let go. I don't know if that's true or not. It don't much matter. It's like saying you didn't mean to kill nobody when you aim a pistol at them, just scare them. Then somehow the pistol goes off. Somehow the pistol always goes off. That ladder got away from them men or they let go, and Rudy came tumbling down all that twenty feet. Falling like I hear boys jump off them palisades they got over on the Kentucky River. Toby said Rudy had stopped hollering when he began falling. Stopped calling for his mamma. Everybody stopped hollering, Toby said. Everything stopped as they all watched Rudy floating down like he was an angel swooping in from heaven.

Only he didn't have no wings to land himself soft. He didn't even have the Kentucky River to take his splash.

I try to remember to thank the Lord for not letting Rudy be killed—or paralyzed like one of Viola's grandnephews was when he broke his neck in a fight. I don't know why Rudy didn't break his neck, or his back. He broke an arm when he landed and conked his head so bad he didn't wake up for three days. Three days we thought he was dead. But on the third morning he woke up, looked around, and said he was hungry. We were afraid if he didn't die, he'd be an imbecile, but he was the same Rudy. Knew us all. Only he didn't remember nothing about what happened. Nothing. The doctor say sometime it go like that. The memory just gone.

"It's a blessing," my mamma said. "A blessing."

And I know it is. Only thing, every time he had that ladder dream as a boy—every time he have it as a man—I thinking that memory ain't gone. Just hid. Like all those stories. Waiting. Waiting to come back when it ready. Good and ready.

Simon was always just a half mile behind that mob chasing Rudy, but he catch up with them finally. Rudy hadn't fallen more than five minutes when Simon got there. They all just standing around, like they just woke up, when Simon find them. It's amazing they didn't lynch him—a black man with a gun in the middle of that crowd—but I think they too stunned by what had happened. It's amazing he didn't start shooting when he saw Rudy lying there, but he didn't, thank Jesus. They really would have lynched him then. But he had Rudy to care for and I guess that took his mind off shooting. And Toby had to be taken care of, too. Took him ten minutes coaxing that boy down the ladder. He was afraid to touch that ladder, but Simon couldn't climb there and get him. Sure wouldn't hold a man and a boy. He came down finally, trembling. Calling for his mamma, Simon says.

Nobody laughing though. Might have been a shooting after all if they had.

Jesse was with him when they brought him home. Jesse had gone a different direction, looking for the boys, but he joined up with Simon at the doctor's office. Doctor patched up his arm, but said there was nothing else to do but wait. I told you I ain't good at waiting, but didn't have no choice. Simon joined me when he could, but he worse at waiting than I am. Jesse sat with me. Jesse didn't have no children of his own then and I think he thought of Rudy as half his.

Jesse sat with me and we brooded. We sat there and we brooded such a hate as to make war on the whole world. The whole white world. I never understood hate before, never understood how people could do such terrible things to each other. But I understand it those three days. Jesse understood it.

Simon was down to the sheriff. Simon wanted people arrested. Like that was gonna happen. Our piddling few votes weren't gonna make that sheriff arrest white men over a colored boy getting hurt. Not even killed, just hurt. Just shook up a little. Just a little fun. Arrest white men over that and lose every white vote in the county? It weren't gonna happen. White people didn't care about colored children. The only children they cared about was their own.

White children. "Suffer the little children," the Bible says. These Bible-hating folks thought the only children that should suffer were little colored children. I meant to show them they were wrong about that. Lord have mercy, I was going to show them they were wrong about that.

CHAPTER 19

(Mamma) Sally Johnson—September 1948, Lexington

I said before I understood why the Jewish people in them camps didn't want to talk about them. Of course, I don't understand it all. Nobody who weren't there can understand it. And even being there, living through it, don't mean you understand most of it. But I'm guessing Jewish people did things to survive in there they don't want to think about. I'm guessing they wondering how they did such things.

I know things about me I don't want to tell. But they part of the story, too. Part of the secret. You tell me secrets are secrets we got to dig up, and you right. But I wish I could bury this secret in the blackest hole there be. They say they got some mine pits in Harlan County that you throw a stone into and you never hear it hit. I wish I could throw this story into that hole and never hear it echo back. The past echoes by you sometimes so loud you think everybody else must be hearing it, too. The past like a radio that don't have no off button. It don't stay dead. Sometime it feel like the past ain't even past.

Easter's my favorite holiday. I love to see the little girls in their white dresses and the little boys all spruced up. Simon says I should be ashamed to flaunt myself to church on Easter Sunday in my new hat when Christmas maybe the only other day I make it. "How you show your face, woman?" he ask. I say, "I show my face like all the other sinners. Easter is about hope—about rising up when you down." I said. "If Judas could have made it to Easter Sunday, he might have been OK."

I've already been through my three days of sorrow—three days of waiting to see if Rudy was going to wake up from the dead. I know how them apostles must have felt those three days waiting. I know how His mamma must have felt.

Rudy woke up, but I didn't thank Jesus. Everybody around me was thanking Jesus, but I went off to do the worst thing I've ever done. That's what I remember. That's what I know about me. I woke up, too. I woke to know that I'm capable of the worst crime. I ain't no Nazi. I ain't no Judas. I didn't go down that road as far as they did. I ain't no Ku Klux Klan. But I know how they got down that road. I told you I didn't know how those crackers hate like they did. They didn't have no reason, and I still don't understand that. I had reason. I had lots of reasons. But the hate that take over me, that take over Jesse, is a hate I never want to feel again. It's the worst thing they did to us: make us hate like they did.

I need my Easter morning. I need my fancy hat. Simon just teasing me. He knows I need it. I ain't a church-going woman. I find Jesus on my own grounds. But it was a long time, a long time, before I found Jesus again. Simon found Jesus before I did. Rudy never lost him. I don't know if Jesse ever found him. I never seen him again. Sometimes, I look for him on a Easter Sunday. I wish I could see him strutting the sidewalk in a brand new suit. I ain't seen him yet, but I keep looking. Jesus can find him if Jesse gives Him a chance. He found me.

I don't know whose idea it was. It don't really matter, does it? They always blaming Eve for bringing Adam the apple, but he ate it, didn't he? He could have said, "No, Eve, you bring that apple back." But instead he said, "That look like a good apple. Give me a bite, sugar."

He'd been wanting that apple a long time. Wanting to taste that sweet apple. Dreaming of that apple.

I been wanting to taste that sweet apple ever since they knocked over Daddy's cow fence. Ever since they burned his barn and chopped his orchard down. I'd been wanting to bite into that apple from the first time I seen the bruises on Rudy's face, the swelling of his eyes. I was done wanting that apple. I was done waiting.

Jesus said it'd be better to tie a millstone round your neck and throw yourself into the sea than to harm a little child. Them crackers that hurt my child weren't tying millstones round their necks. They slunk back down like they usually did after they done something really terrible, so terrible they feel the need to hide out. Simon said that when he drove back from the sheriff's he didn't see practically nobody on the street—surely no men hanging out drinking. Like that meant things was changed. I didn't say anything. Jesse didn't say anything either. Simon went and got the pastor to come sit with us, to come wait by Rudy's bedside. But I told him no. I didn't want no pastor preaching forgiveness to me. I wasn't ready to forgive.

I was looking for a millstone.

When Rudy woke up, I don't remember rejoicing that much. Simon did. Lord, Simon let out a shout of joy that brought all the neighbors in from the porches where they had gathered. "Praise Jesus! Praise Jesus!"

Colored people sure know how to praise Jesus. Where was Jesus, I wanted to know, when them crackers was chasing my boy and Toby over half the county? We was supposed to praise Jesus for bringing my boy back from near death? Why didn't Jesus keep him safe in the first place?

I knew half the colored community were crowded in our house, though I didn't really see them. I heard them like you hear a road noise off in the distance. They'd come by me where I sat by Rudy, patting at my arms, trying to hug me. It's hard to hug a person who don't hug back, but they did their best. I know that at least three women had crowded into my small kitchen because they kept asking me where things were. They managed enough food to feed most of Ravenna. They tried to feed me and Jesse, but we weren't hungry. I don't know if Simon ate any.

They had enough food to feed even the white part of Ravenna, but of course white folks weren't coming by. White folks had tortured my boy and his friend Toby. Had left him for dead, but *they* weren't coming by. If I wanted to see any white folks, I was going to have to go looking for them.

We kept close watch on Rudy that first night he woke up, but he kept breathing easy. He even ate some, though he didn't speak much. Just looked wide-eyed at us. We didn't know then that he didn't remember none of what happened. We didn't want to question him any. The women, and even some of the men, kept petting him. He just smiled, letting the women feed him.

I don't know why I didn't pet him any. I just sat there and tried to calm myself, but it weren't working. The longer I sat there, the less calm I got.

I know some say I didn't even wait long enough for my boy to half recover, but I waited most of that night. And Simon didn't leave him. Simon had collapsed in a chair by the bed. Couldn't even get him to leave Rudy long enough to make it to our own bed. I waited until all the neighbors went on home, the women taking one final pet on Rudy. I could see them glancing at me sideways, wondering what was going on. I sat there silent. Rudy would open his eyes and smile at me every once in a while.

I didn't smile back.

It was coming on dawn when I joined Jesse on the porch. He was waiting for me, though we hadn't said nothing. We didn't need to say anything. We looked at each other's faces and we knew we felt the same thing. We weren't going to sit around and praise Jesus like some nice colored folks who take the leavings and call it a feast. I love chitlins and pigs' feet, too. But the only reason we got to eat them is because the white folks didn't think them worth eating. Colored been doing that too long. Thanking Jesus for just surviving. Listen to the choir. Hallelujah. Not no more. I wasn't no Mary raising no Jesus.

I've seen them gangster movies they have down at the Strand—all them fellows racing their cars through the streets, shooting their Tommy Guns out the windows. Raking down whole lines of other gangsters, shooting down anybody who gets in their way. Lord knows what might have happened if Jesse and me could have jumped in a car like that—loaded up some Tommy guns.

But Jesus slowed us down. Put us in an old farm wagon and on Estill County roads.

Nobody had no cars in them days. Maybe six cars in the whole town of Irvine. Two maybe in Ravenna. I didn't know any colored folks that owned them. Simon had an old Champion farm wagon we used to haul just about everything in. That wagon had high sides all around it and in the back, so high you couldn't see the road when you were in the back and it was empty. Most times we pulled it full of something—corn or hay—tobacco. We hauled pigs in it once. They quieted down once we got them inside, like they didn't know where they were headed—or they were resigned to it.

We had two old mares, one big brown thing and one little gray. Most folks had mules to do their plowing and hauling, but we got these mares cheap. A lot cheaper than a good matched pair of mules. They did the job mostly. The little gray mare wore out quicker than the brown one and would just stop when she did. The big brown one almost never thought it a bad idea to stop. No amount of coaxing or even hitting would get them horses moving then. You'd just have to let them take their rest. Simon was better at letting them rest than I was. He never even touched them, just pulled out his food or his sweet tea and sat down with them. The few times we had Rudy running them—he was a bit young to do the plowing—it took a morning to do half a field. I told Simon he might as well hitch me for all the progress we was making. But Simon and Rudy are a pair. "All in good time," is all he said. "All in good time."

Jesses hitched the mares to the Champion, and we started out. We didn't know where we was going. We didn't even know what we was looking for. Well, that weren't true. We knew what we was looking for; we just didn't say it out loud. Jesse had his own pistol; I grabbed Simon's rifle. I look back now and I think we was crazy. Crazy. Two colored folks—a big woman and a little man, as mismatched as our two mares—armed and ready. For what? I didn't feel crazy at the time. And Jesse didn't look crazy. I remember seeing the road ahead of me like it was a big, broad highway, like it had signs pointing the way every ten yards just in case you forgot where you was going.

We knew just where we was going.

Simon said he hadn't seen any of the crackers who had chased Rudy and Toby down. The sheriff had probably told them to lay low. Jesse and I didn't talk it out, but if we had we would have said we was looking to find a stray from that crowd—maybe two—who had wandered away from the rest of his herd. We knew we couldn't handle the whole herd—we were crazy maybe, but we weren't stupid—but if we got that stray off to the side. By himself. Like a dog rounds up a sheep who wanders off. Only difference is that dog is aiming to bring that sheep back safe.

We wasn't.

I wonder now, did I ever think I'm going out to kill a man? Maybe two? Those ain't thoughts that form whole in your head. At least they didn't in mine. Maybe if you a Nazi those be regular thoughts. I don't know. I didn't think. You notice what people say when they done something foolish, something bad, "I didn't think." But you don't think. I've been angry lots of times in my life—Mamma says I came out of the womb mad—yelling my head off. But there's mad that goes way beyond yelling and that's where I was. That's where Jesse was. If we had come across some lone cracker, he would have been a dead cracker. We didn't need to discuss it any; we didn't need to put it in words.

We didn't think.

But we didn't come across anyone the first hour. The horses plodded slow—there weren't no hurry. This weren't a field we needed to get plowed by noon. We didn't have any one place in mind. We were near the creek—we could hear it tumbling, but we couldn't see it. We weren't far from the river. The air smelled like it might rain later on. The river fog still clung to the tree branches like some giant caterpillar nest. I pulled my jacket 'round my shoulders and kept Simon's rifle inside my coat, pressed next to my right breast. Its barrel poked by my shoulder like a broom handle.

We kept looking, but it was hard seeing with the mist—like looking through a glass darkly. You'd see what you thought was a person, but you'd get close and it was a fence post. One time a scarecrow raised up. I don't know that it fooled any crows but it sure gave me a start. Sometimes it felt like it was just us and the horses in the whole county.

When we first spotted them—three of them—they were straight ahead on the road about a quarter of a mile. I glanced at Jesse, but he'd spotted them, too. I couldn't tell that distance if they was men or women. They could have even been colored. All we knew is that they weren't animals. And they weren't fence posts. They were some kind of people. I pulled Simon's rifle down so it didn't show. If they saw us, they didn't seem to mind one way or another. The horses kept plodding closer and closer.

We were almost on top of them before they turned and looked at us. Not scared or anything, just curious as to who was behind them. Two boys and a girl, headed to Ravenna to school. The little girl smiled at me, a Kentucky "hi." She was about seven with that tow-headed straw hair that look like it don't have no color at all. Like all the color went into her blue eyes. Her brothers were older—ten, maybe, and twelve. Their tow heads had started to brown some, as if the brown earth they'd been trodding barefoot since they were born had started to filter upwards. They weren't so friendly. A colored man and woman didn't rate a howdy. They nodded, though.

If they'd been just a few years older, I think I would have taken Simon's rifle and blown a hole right through those children. You think you know me, and you say I ain't no killer. I ain't no Nazi looking for some Jewish person to kill. I ain't no KKK looking for any stray colored. But I'm telling you that if they'd been older—grown, or mostly grown—I would have shot them right there. That's why I was out there with Jesse—leaving my man and my boy come back from the dead alone in the house. I was out there to kill, and I didn't much care if I got killed in turn or not. Can you understand that?

If you can, you understand more than I can.

But Jesus saved me from that much. He sent that mist down and hid all the grownup crackers, sent me some cracker children, instead. He hoped my heart would soften. Hoped I see people, not just crackers. But it didn't. Not yet, it didn't. I only saw crackers. And I thought them crackers didn't spare my children—them crackers chased my boy and Toby all through this land. Trapped them like you trapped a possum in a tree. Shook my boy out of that tree like he weren't worth no more than that possum. They never thought how it'd feel to the mammas and papas of those boys.

Well, they were going to find out how it felt.

I pulled that rifle out of my jacket and pointed it at the oldest boy. "Get in the wagon," I told him, and his jaw just dropped. "You, too," I said to his brother.

Jesse had looked at me quick when I first pulled my rifle, but he followed my lead. He stuck his gun in the younger boy's face, who looked like he might try to run for it. "You heard the woman," he said, "get in the wagon."

The little girl let out a high scream—a kind of scream a rabbit make when you cutting its throat. I leaned over and slapped her full across her face. "Hush!" I said, and she hushed. Jesse bent over to pick her up and put her in the wagon with her brothers. I kept my gun pointed at the boys.

What were we going to do with them? I don't know. Jesse didn't know. We just kept making those horses plod that road for an hour more. Maybe two. The children kept silent in the wagon for the most part, though I heard the little girl whimpering a bit and her brothers trying to shush her. The sun finally burnt off the mist. We just kept rolling on. We were considerably outside Ravenna. We left the river and traveled up. The road got narrower and steeper. When the little gray mare decided she had had enough for a while and started to graze at some alfalfa poking through a wooden fence, Jesse let her. The brown mare joined in. We sat there and watch them chew.

Stopping must have frightened the children even more 'cause the little girl started to cry again. One of her brothers joined in. His crying was kind of that jerky sobbing that tears right out of you—the kind that the more you try to keep it in, the more it rips itself out. The horses were panting as they chewed. They weren't used to such workouts. And it was hot for September. The sun high in the sky. We hadn't brought no water. I hadn't even thought of it until we stopped. But my mouth felt dry then, parched. Like it do the morning after you'd been sick, fevered. "Dryer than a creek bed in August," Daddy would put it. *The children must be thirsty, too*, I thought.

We sat there, Jesse and me, listening to the horses panting, the children crying. I don't know what Jesse was thinking. I could still feel the sting on my palm from where I had slapped the little girl. It seemed to leave a bruise. I don't think I had ever slapped anyone before. Not like that. Surely not a child. Those few side swipes I'd branch on Rudy's legs never amounted to much.

Suddenly I started thinking.

Jesus, Jesus, I thought.

What have we done?

"We have to get these children back home," I said, and Jesse nodded. Like he had woke up the same time I did.

The children were huddled in a corner of the wagon all together. When we poked our heads over the slats, both boys let out a yap. The little girl hid behind them. But Jesse kept talking quiet to them—ten minutes he talked, and somehow he got them to forget he had aimed a gun at their heads not two hours before. Jesse had a calm voice, all one level like some kind of hum. They finally began to listen to him. He patted the older boy's shoulder. The boy trembled like a colt does when you first touch it, but settled down then. None of the children would even look at me. When Jesse reached over to pick up the little girl, she let out a small squeal but didn't say anything else. The boys watched him steady as he pulled the little girl over the truck slats, then climbed over themselves. The way they hopped the walls, I know they could have done that sooner only that they didn't want to leave their sister. Brave boys. Brave little girl, too. Their mamma would have been proud of them.

They had brought their lunch with them—just corn pones with some bacon grease smeared on them. Some of them poor children Rudy was always sharing my chicken with. A big jar of sweet tea, too. None of them had thought to eat or drink any. I guess if you ain't pigs, you think where you might be heading and it takes away your appetite. The younger boy even offered Jesse a swig of his sweet tea. Imagine that? Jesse thanked him and told him no. The children still weren't looking my direction.

We set them on the road—pointed the direction they should head to. We offered to turn the wagon around and head their direction, but none of them was willing to get back into the wagon. Just as well. They turned and looked at us standing there once or twice before they went out of sight—making sure we weren't following them, I guess. The little girl even waved a tiny wave as she disappeared.

Kentucky polite until the end.

We hadn't been thinking before, but we had to do some quick thinking now. Jesse released the brown mare from the team. She wasn't as worn out as the gray. He fashioned a bridle out of a piece of rope, and jumped on. He was going to cut across the mountain road and beat the children back home. He had to get back to Simon. Get back before the valley went crazy. Warn everybody. Everybody colored.

He gave me his money. It weren't much, but I didn't have a penny on me. He took another piece of rope and made a short bridle for the gray, but I could tell looking at her she wasn't going anywhere for a while. Not even if I beat her. And I was done beating.

"There's a train running from Irvine," Jesse told me. He looked at the gray mare. "Walk if you have to, but keep out of sight. Don't try to go home. The children will get there before you can. That little girl..." he didn't go on. "Get to the train depot and get a train to Lexington. Don't try to go back home." He looked at me hard. We ain't never had that thing between us—never out loud. He was a good friend to Simon. More a brother. But he looked at me hard.

"Don't try to go back home," he said one more time.

I spent ten minutes pulling on the gray before I gave up. Maybe if I had had a real bridle, but that thing Jesse looped together didn't make much impression on her. The children had left their empty sweet tea jar behind. I filled it with creek water and poured it over my head. I filled it again and drank for five minutes, but I still felt dry. I hoped there weren't no cows upstream to make me sick, but I was past caring. The gray had wandered over to take a drink herself. "I hope you don't get sick, either," I said to her and reached out to give her a pat but she winced her head away. "That's OK," I said. I left her there and headed the direction towards what I hoped was Ravenna's train station.

I had got so turned around I didn't even know if I was still in Estill County. We'd been headed north mostly. Some west. The river had followed the road near enough, and it was my bearings now. I ain't no pioneer. I could have passed over into Madison County or even into Powell County for all I knew. What I did know was that I had to keep out of sight as much as I could. A big colored woman toting a rifle wasn't going to be welcome in any Kentucky county that I knew of. I had to keep out of sight and make it to the Ravenna train depot, buy what ticket I could with the three dollars Jesse gave me and not get lynched trying. I didn't know how I was going to do all that. Since I had begun thinking again, I'd begun to get scared. Real scared. Thinking will do that to you.

I kept close to the river except when the land made me climb away from it. Woods and hills so thick and so empty it felt like I *was* a pioneer. One time I saw a cabin with a little twirl of smoke coming out its chimney. It scared me plenty. I could see they had a garden out the back way, though, and I was hungry enough by then to risk it. I got down on my stomach and crawled my way into that garden. It had sweet ripe tomatoes and some corn so tender it didn't need cooking. Good thing. I crawled back out and continued trekking. I didn't know where I was headed. I didn't stop and ask Jesus to guide me. I got some pride. I didn't think I had the right. If Jesus was gonna help me, He was gonna have to do it without my asking.

I didn't see any more cabins the rest of the day. It got chilly at night. September can even bring a frost at night in the hills. I had lost the river. It was all cliff and rock now. I covered myself with some leaves and slept the sleep of the righteous. When you as tired as I was, even the wicked can sleep the sleep of the righteous. *What am I going to do, Lord?* I remember thinking just before my eyes closed. I know I said I wasn't praying, but some things just slip out.

I was dreaming I was in the back of the big Champion where the children had been. They was still there—huddled in one corner as far away from me as they could get. The little girl weren't whimpering, though. Just staring at me wide-eyed. I close my eyes and I can still see her to this day. Staring at me. Kind of like your Eleanor when something's frightened her. None of us, children or me, could see a thing but those tall wooden slats. I was thinking, *This road is rougher than I thought because we shaking something terrible.* I be trying to keep from hitting the walls, but I couldn't help bouncing from side to side. The children didn't bounce. They stayed in their corner, away from me. But I was thinking, *I'm gonna be tossed right over the slats.* I couldn't understand it. Those two old mares must have been galloping. Those mares never galloped. "Whoa!" I shouted out. "Whoa!"

"Whoa yourself." I opened my eyes to see a tall, thin white woman shaking my shoulder. "I've been five minutes trying to rouse you. I've never seen a body who could sleep so, especially not on this wet ground."

I stared at her—not really knowing what I was seeing, like you do when you come out of a sleep so deep it's like you're swimming on the bottom of the Kentucky. Then I looked round for my rifle.

"Your rifle's over there by that tree if that's what you're looking for. But I don't think you'll be needing it. Times so hard just about every squirrel treading a tree branch has already ended up in somebody's stew pot. And if you're thinking of shooting me with it, well, there's time enough for that. Time enough for that."

Time enough for that. The way she said it just relaxed me, made the tension go out of my shoulders better than my neighbor Viola, who knows how to do the best shoulder rub in the whole city. If that stranger settling back and waiting for me to rouse myself hadn't been a woman, if she hadn't been at least twenty years older, if she hadn't been white, she would have minded me of Simon. Time enough for that.

She waited while I brushed myself off as best as I could. I waited for her to ask me what I was doing there—who I was running from. What I had done. I felt the tension seeping back into my arms. I thought about what I could tell her, but I couldn't think of a thing. Not anything she'd believe.

"My name's Abby Marson," she said and put out her hand to shake—like I've seen politicians do in election time. Though most of them take care not to shake colored hands in front of no white voters. Out on the farm alone, they might risk it. I looked at her hand now like I didn't know what to do with it. But she kept it there so I finally took it.

"Sally Johnson," I mumbled back.

"Well, Sally Johnson, I bet you could use some coffee and some eggs. Maybe some biscuits if you can wait a bit." A small speckled mare had appeared at her back and was pushing her. "Oh, look at you," the woman said. "Jealous already." She smiled to show a row of teeth so perfect they almost didn't look real. "This is Frosty. She needs to be the center of attention all the time. Why don't you climb on up her? My cabin's just a half mile hike over those hills, but you look like you've been hiking enough."

I don't think Abby was a talker most times, but she was the kind of person that knew when she needed to. She filled both parts of the conversation and let me wonder at it all silently. Frosty didn't seem to mind me being on her back, though I weighed considerable more than Abby. She led the way in front, but she didn't pull at the reins. Frosty knew the way. I hung on to the saddle's pommel as we climbed the hill to Abby's cabin. It was so steep a hill, I thought I might slide off. Abby walked it like she was a young girl, though the closer I looked at her, the older she got. I finally said something about the climb.

"Oh, you get used to it. I've been riding these hills for more than twenty years—delivering babies, fixing broke bones and whatever else needs fixing. Thought I'd be preaching the Lord's word, too, but I found it doesn't much need preaching. At least not from me. These mountain people don't much care for a woman preaching. Anyway, the Lord's word is there for those who need to hear it. Don't need me telling it." She paused a second. Even Abby had to catch her breath once in a while. "Do need me with the babies, though." And she smiled again. I can see that wide grin even now in my mind's eye. I imagine that smile was all the preaching she needed to do.

The cabin was two rooms built like an L. It wasn't Jesse-built, but it looked tight enough. A garden stretched out in back where the trees had been cut to let the sun shine through. A half dozen chickens were scratching a patch by the garden. A small outbuilding—for Frosty, I supposed—stood next to the garden. *How she keeps those chickens from being snatched by some wild critter?* I wondered. Even back in Ravenna, foxes, even skunks, had done havoc on my chicken raising.

I got my answer when two dogs near the size of Frosty came bounding down the hill, headed straight to us like we were on the menu instead of chicken. "Sampson, Delilah! We have company! Don't be jumping on anybody." She said it firm but friendly. The dogs calmed at her voice but still quivered in that way dogs do when they're just so pleased to see you. Simon says he'd have to move out if I moved a dog in, and I know it's true. The house we live in now couldn't squeeze in a poodle let alone one of them farm dogs. But I do miss them. A dog don't have no pride when it loves you. He just shake all over he so happy.

I slid off that horse feeling as stiff as if I was the old woman, not Abby. The cabin inside was big and airy—I hate a closed-in room. Abby looked me over critically then opened a chest that was one of three pieces of furniture in the first room. She pulled out what looked like a tent at first.

"It's what I wear when I'm feeling my age or the weather just won't let me get outside—though I'm out in most anything. Babies don't come by the Farmer's Almanac. I don't get to wear it much, but when I do it's real comfortable. I think it will fit you fine while we wash those clothes." She smiled again, so I shed my clothes like I was five instead of thirty-five. She started banging things around in the small kitchen space—a wood stove and a pie safe. A small sink with a handle was in the corner. I smelled coffee and knew I was hungry. The tomatoes I had snatched seemed a long time ago. I thought of all that food going to waste in my house. Well, I hoped it wasn't going to waste.

I ate and ate. The coffee just cleared the way for more food. Abby kept smiling, like my appetite was the best thing she ever seen. She didn't ask any questions even as we took turns scrubbing my dress. It seemed like it done picked up every stain Kentucky had to offer. When we done our best, we hung it on the clothesline she had strung pointing west from her back porch to a beech that had somehow survived the garden clearing. September was back pretending it was August. My stockings and jacket joined my dress and hung there like they had a story to tell. Abby wasn't asking, but it was time I did some telling.

Abby didn't interrupt much as I did my talking. "Powell County," she said, when I asked where I was. "A good ten mile from the county border. I can't believe you made it so far without running into anybody."

I didn't tell her about slapping the child. I just couldn't. But I told her everything else.

"The children alright?" She asked once.

"Yes," I said, "as far as I could tell. Just scared and tired. But those boys will find their way home. We didn't take them that far away."

"Sure they will," she agreed. "They're Kentucky country boys. They'll be alright. And they'll take care of their sister just fine," she said, like it had all been an adventure. "That little girl will forget about it all by tomorrow. Young girls are tough out here. They got to be."

I didn't think that little girl was gonna be forgetting any time soon, let alone tomorrow, but I took the comfort where I could get it. It hadn't sunk in completely what I had done, but it was beginning to.

"I heard about your boy—about both boys." I looked at her, surprised. "Oh, you'd be surprised at how quickly news travels around here. Sometimes I think those big-city newspapers should call us to check on things. Of course, I acquire more news than most people—traveling around as I do. Estill County is on my regular route—the northern part of it at least. People tell me all sorts of things. I heard about your boy and thought it a terrible thing. Chasing those children just for meanness. Torturing them. I heard one story that they were dead. You need to wait a while before you believe the news. Not all of it is right. Or it takes time to get right. I'm so happy he's doing fine and the other boy, too. Thank you, Lord."

"Thank you, Lord." I hadn't done much thanking of the Lord. I'd been so angry, so full of madness, I hadn't been thanking anybody. Abby didn't say it like she meant for me to be joining in. She just thanked the Lord like she was thanking Him herself, not telling me to thank Him. Maybe that was it. Maybe that was all I needed. Suddenly I just started to cry. I began to sob like the child had sobbed jailed in our Champion—big jerking sobs that tore at my anger and shredded it like an iron hoe tears at a tree root. And I began to thank the Lord. *Thank you, Jesus.* I didn't say it out loud. I didn't amen myself like I was a whole colored church. I said it deep, quiet. I said it inside those sobs tearing at me like Rudy had torn at me being born. *Thank you, Jesus. Thank you for saving my child.*

Abby just sat there. She didn't pat me or try to calm me. She sat there quiet as if she were waiting out a thunderstorm. When I calmed some, she looked at the clothes hanging on the line. "Those clothes will be dry in no time," she nodded approvingly as if she had arranged the sun all by herself. She frowned. "Going to be trouble. Jesse—that his name?—is right. You can't go home right now. We're going to have to get you to Lexington. I'll have to think on that."

When I thank Jesus now—and I do, every Easter I do. People think you got to be thanking Him over and over like He's some forgetful old person, or like you got to convince Him you're really thankful. You don't think He knows when you're really thankful? That He's like some forgetful stupid old person? No, when I thank Jesus now, I'm not just thanking Him for saving Rudy, or for keeping me from killing some silly cracker. I thank Him for Abby, too. Abby didn't just save me from a lynching. She keep me from hating all white people. You know that's a danger colored people face. Maybe not colored like Rudy. Or even Simon. But colored people like me. Or you, Nannie. You in danger, too. They give us so much reason to hate them—all of them. But if we hate them, we become just like them crackers, like the Ku Kluxers. It so easy to hate them all.

Then I think of Abby. I know other white people be Christian people. But they still white—they still get on my last nerve even when they trying to be nice. But not Abby. Abby stay in my mind like she the special ambassador of white people. She never looked at me and thought, "Here's a poor colored woman in trouble." I just somebody needing help. She knew I was colored. She weren't blind. And she knew being colored put me in real danger. She weren't dumb, either. She just never thought of me as colored. I ain't never met a white person like that. Hardly even met any colored like that.

She went off with Frosty and was gone a good hour. I began to worry a bit, though she told me she'd be gone a while. When she come back, she was sitting next to a man driving a Model T Ford. I don't know that I had seen more than a few of them up to that point. The city was full of them, but they didn't make it up to Ravenna much. Horses did the work—or mules. Kind of like we weren't quite in the new century yet. The car couldn't make it all the way to the house—the road stopped about a quarter mile away and there weren't no driveway. Why would there be? I froze when I saw the white man. He was about my age, maybe younger a year or two. He didn't look happy. Abby was talking to him. When she turned and saw me, she smiled and waved me on. I came on.

That man didn't say a word to me the whole drive, and it was a long one. We didn't go directly at Lexington but circled round the back way—making stabs up one highway and then over to another. Roads in them days were hard going anyway. That man didn't talk much even to Abby— never even got his name—but Abby kept up the chatter. Made sure we didn't have time to think about each other. She didn't say it direct, but I gathered he owed a whole bunch to Abby—saved his wife twice over and the babies she was carrying. Wasn't anything he wouldn't do for Abby, and that included helping a colored woman escape from the county. But he weren't happy. No, ma'am, he weren't happy.

We got onto Paris Pike, finally, and edged our way into Lexington proper. I had been in Lexington only to pass through from Louisville to Irvine. I was too worried about Rudy and Simon to give it much notice. I didn't think this would be our home now forever. I thought we'd be going back to Ravenna. Mamma and Daddy were smarter. They knew when they left that was it. Abby directed the man to a big house off Sixth Street—about five times bigger than the shotgun we living in now. She told us both to wait while she went and knocked on the door.

We waited while she was inside, never even glancing at each other. Abby had sat between us. We left the empty space. If I had spotted him on the road when I was scouting the country with Jesse, I would have shot him without a thought. If he'd been part of a posse looking for me and I'd been unlucky enough to fall into his hands after I let the children go, I imagine I'd be swinging from some rope. Now we just sat there waiting for our friend, Abby, to make arrangements for me. She was a blue-eyed angel I never thought to see, the "better angel of our nature," Mamma always used to tell me when somebody did something that surprised you with its goodness. People almost never surprise you with their meanness. Abby surprised me. Maybe she surprised that white man sitting two feet away. She kept us from killing each other.

The lady who showed me into a small back room of that big house looked about as pleased with the situation as the white driver, but Abby had her ways. I was to wait in the house until Abby got word to my family. "I'll get word," she promised, and I believed her. "They'll be safe," she promised, too, but that was harder to believe.

"Just have faith," Abby told me. She smiled and squeezed my hand. Was it only a day that I knew her? It don't matter. I still remember that smile.

I waited two days in that lady's house. I never saw the lady again. I ate my meals in the kitchen with the maid and cook. They never asked me a question about anything. Colored people are like that. They know when your business is too personal to pry into—even when their prying is meant well. "I'm praying for you," the old cook whispered to me once, and I nodded. That was nice. I needed praying for.

Maybe I hadn't whooped in joy when Rudy woke up from his deep sleep, but I sure did when Simon showed up at that lady's back door. Rudy stood next to him. He looked tired, but he smiled as big as Abby when he saw me. Simon had two big packages he was toting, Ruby a smaller one. I was to find out later that that was all they got to salvage from our big home, but I didn't care about that then. Except for a few more photographs they couldn't grab and some of

Mamma's plates that got left, I still don't care about it. They was both safe, and I was through being mad. I thanked Jesus. I thank Him, still.

It'd been hard, hard going. When word got back what Jesse and I had done—kidnapping those white children— the whole town just went crazy, Simon said. Colored people everywhere had to run for their lives. Men were pulled out of barber shops and beaten up. They jumped on men in the middle of the day on their jobs at the railroad.

"Anybody lynched?" I asked, fearing God's judgment on my head.

"Nobody lynched, thank Jesus. But you remember Wesley? Wesley Hatch? They found him wandering the railroad track almost stripped naked. He weren't the only one. Only Jesse and me sitting on the porch with guns kept four men from rampaging through our house, taking what they wanted. They were rounding colored up like they were cattle—putting them on any train leaving town. Not giving them any time to collect anything. The sheriff not doing anything to stop them. Newspaper either. It come out the next day—look, here. I got a copy."

Simon pulled out the thin Irvine newspaper from his back pocket. He pointed to the line:

All negroes have been ordered out of this place because of sentiment against them.

I looked at the paper a while. It was hard seeing it in print like that.

"Who ordered them?" I was getting back to being mad. Simon shrugged. "The powers that be, I reckon."

"How'd you get out?"

"It calmed down the second day some, but I knew that calm wouldn't last. The whole town had a look on its face like it just couldn't wait to dress itself in white hoods. Jesse and I helped shepherd a group of colored down to the railroad station. Everybody crying and carrying on, but we knew we didn't have no choice. Able to buy our way out of town at least like it was our choice. I reckon those men we scared off that first night made a beeline for our house once we went, but couldn't think of that anymore. Had to make it safe to Lexington."

Make it safe to Lexington. That's what we did. We been here ever since. Abby made sure we got something for the house and land, but it weren't much. But I grateful. The Lord taketh, but He let us have enough. And that a feast. Abby did what she could. We got enough.

We never went back—not even to visit. They say it's changed now—not like it was. I don't know. One thing for certain. Almost no colored in the whole county anymore. Not in any of them counties, but especially not Estill. About as many colored there as in the other Ravenna, the one they named it for in Italy. Of course, I don't know that. Ravenna, Italy, might have plenty of colored.

Ravenna, Kentucky, sure don't.

CHAPTER **20**
Nannie Johnson—September 1948

Mamma's told me stories of old times all my life. Mostly how them old times was just better. Or maybe it was just that the people were. The children surely was better behaved. Even Daddy liked to mosey through good time memories, though mostly he was drinking when he told his stories and mostly they involved him getting the better of somebody. You think he and Mamma should have been on Easy Street the number of times he came out the winner in his telling, but that's not the way it was.

But the people in Mamma Sally's story didn't seem better—not most of them, anyway. And the times she talked of sure almost make our times look good. If Mamma Sally came out a winner, she won like in one of those races out in Keeneland. They've started taking photographs at the finish line, I hear. Even then, even studying those photos, they not always sure who passed the finish line first.

Of course, I think she won. I hope she think she won. But win or lose, she ran a hard race and that all anybody can ask.

It changed me, listening to that story. I had the children half-packed and ready to go before I heard that story. If we even passed through Scott County ever again, it be on the way to somewhere else. Anyplace else would do.

But that story changed me. I got to thinking. At least they been running in Kentucky. Colored have been running away from so many Kentucky counties for a whole bunch of years. It ain't like Mamma and Daddy didn't get encouragement to leave Wolf County. I asked them once, but they ain't talking. I don't imagine it anything like Mamma Sally's story, but something ain't being told.

I think it might be time not to run away anymore. I don't know. That's the way I feel. I don't know if it's right or not. I have to think on it.

I half wish I hadn't made her tell me that secret.

But it wasn't just the running away—the leaving of that roomy house and that pretty land for the cramped little shotgun over in Kinkeadtown where you can't hardly see the land, it so jammed pack. It was she and Jesse kidnapping those children. If you had put a gun to my head, I never in a million years would believe Mamma Sally could kidnap children. I don't care if they white, black, or green. And that she slap that little girl? Lord help me. That's not the Mamma Sally I know who look at me hard when she think I too hard on her grandbabies. She had to do the telling. Those words had to come out of Mamma Sally's mouth herself for me to believe them.

The story calmed me down enough so that I could go see Miz Lawson. For a few days, I was all but hiding indoors when I seen her outside. I just wasn't up to the conversation I knew was coming. I think she was hiding from me, too. Leastways, she was never outdoors when I was hanging clothes or tending to the two poor chickens we had left. But finally I walked the fifty yard between our homes and knocked on the screen. August had been mild for Kentucky, but September was making up for it.

Her white face stared at me a second before she opened the door.

I think I might have carried on against her something fierce for keeping her secrets before I heard Mamma Sally's story. But I'd grown a new appreciation for secrets. I understood better why people kept secrets: the bigger the story—the more hurtful—the deeper the secret. I guessed Miz Lawson had good reasons to keep her counsel. Telling your new colored tenants your husband was once Grand Dragon of the Ku Klux Klan wouldn't fall easy into any conversation.

We both stood there looking at each other. Sitting would have made it like a social visit, and it wasn't.

"We can't live here on Ku Klux Klan land. We going to have to move. I'm here to figure out when."

She just nodded. She did point to a chair then. I thought she'd argue it weren't Ku Klux land, but she didn't.

"Please. Leave the door open. The only air this kitchen gets. Let me get you some sweet tea. When do you think the weather will break? I swear it's hotter than August."

"It is, isn't it?" I agreed. I know that sounds silly—us chatting about the weather when I just finished telling her that I couldn't be living fifty yards away from a woman who was married to the Grand Dragon, but it seemed rude not to agree. Not Kentucky-like. And it was hot. It's always hot in September, and we always surprised—like we think summer should pay as close attention to the calendar as we do. Same in winter. We always thinking snow should happen up North, though every winter we see it—sometimes piles of it.

But that the Kentucky way: we think what we think. Sometimes it don't matter what we see. And sometimes we can't help seeing even when we don't want to.

I took a long swig of sweet tea before I continued. "The trouble is we can't afford not to finish the season. We need the money from the crop to find us a new place. Rudy and I got to find jobs. So we going to have to keep on living here for a while, but I don't know how."

She nodded again. I had a whole speech in my mind— railing against her and Mr. Lawson for letting us settle when they knew the story, the whole county knew the story. All those people, white and colored, startling like they seen a ghost when they heard where we was living.

Of course, they seen ghosts—ghosts of that poor man they hung. Ghosts of all the colored that been terrorized on this land. Maybe all over Scott County. Oh, the details all came tumbling out once I ask. The church women said they thought we knew about the Ku Klux. "How I know about it?" I ask, and they look like I ask how I know about it being hot in summer.

"Everybody knew," that look say.

But the Lawsons knew we didn't know. They let us settle on this land when no colored would even work on it. I put the sweet tea down. I felt my temper rising again.

"How could you let us sign that contract knowing what you knew? How could you let my children play in the house of the Grand Dragon? My little girl. Eleanor. She sit right here and cut out quilt scraps while your man—the Grand Dragon—watched her. Was that his fancy robe, she be cutting? That why he upset? I don't understand it. How could you do that?"

Her head jerked when I mentioned the children. I saw her swallowing hard a couple of times before she answered. I saw tears, but I didn't care. The time for tears was long over.

"He's not the Grand Dragon anymore. He hasn't been for twenty years. He's changed. Repented."

"Please, don't talk to me nothing about Grand Dragons changing. I don't care if they change into grand hogs, which wouldn't be that much of a change. I don't want to be around them, and I don't want my children around them. And I don't want my children around anyone married to a Grand Dragon. Especially anyone who stayed married to him all these years."

The tears did drop then, but my heart was hard. I was through being polite. I shoved the sweet tea across the table and headed for the open door.

"And what about them pigs being killed? And the chickens? That his people coming back?" I was yelling now. She knew I yelled at the children or at Rudy, but I don't ever expect she think I'd yell at her. Nobody probably yelled at her since she was a girl. She got whiter and whiter.

"You so caring when the pigs get killed. Spent half the morning helping us clean up that blood. I knew you wasn't that nice. I knew there be something behind all that niceness. But I never thought to think you knew anything about it. Now I find out you known all along about who done it. But you still didn't tell us. You let my children be put in danger. I can't forgive that."

She stood up now like she'd been insulted. Her mouth tightened. "Your children were never in danger. I never would have let anything happen to your children."

I stared at her. I stopped yelling. "You don't know that," I said quietly. "I don't even know that. The children might be in danger now. You can't protect children even when they babies, let alone when they grown."

I remembered too late who I was talking to. She knew all too well about not being able to protect children. We was living in Jimmy's cabin. At least we would be for another month. But the thought of my children being in danger was making me crazy. I began to understand Mamma Sally, knew how she must have been feeling when Rudy was near death. Everything in the world just falls away. Nothing else matters. It's like you not in the same world anymore with everybody else. You just got to keep them safe. You just got to keep them safe.

I started yelling again.

"Now, don't you be talking to my children any unless you see a coyote headed their direction. Not even then if you can avoid it. And only talk to me when pointing can't do the job. If Mr. Lawson has anything he got to say, he be saying it to Rudy. But I hope he don't need to say nothing. Don't neither of us ever want to hear his voice again. Or yours. We'll be moving as soon as the tobacco's cut and hauled into Lexington. When the last cob of corn is cut, we be out of here."

I paused at the door. Miz Lawson had her head down. I could have pitied her, but I didn't. She had married the man. Had stayed with him. She had put my children into danger. Put my husband back on the battlefield like she was Patton—and he just another colored body. Maybe she think men who could butcher piglets and wring chickens' necks wouldn't stoop so low as to hurt a little colored child. But I knew better. Mamma Sally knew better. If Wilma Lawson didn't know better, she didn't know the world she lived in.

"You advertised for a good family. You got one."

She looked up at me then. I met her eyes head on.

"We didn't," I said.

I told Rudy the next morning we was moving as soon as the harvest was in. He just nodded. The way I tell it, it like Rudy's not the man in the family. Like I'm the one making all the decisions. But that's not how it is. Rudy was the one who decided we was coming out here in the first place. He was the one who decided we were gonna be farmers. He's the one who decides most things in our life. I don't mind. That's the way it's supposed to be. A strong woman don't mean a weak man.

But some things are beyond his soft heart. I know he'd end up forgiving the Lawsons, and I won't allow that. I won't allow it. I guess I'm not Christian down to the roots like he is. I guess I'm too hard for that. Mamma Sally said I wasn't hard—just a sensible colored woman who knows the world is hard, especially for colored children. What did she say about Rudy?

Sweet's good for dessert, but it's not the whole meal.

"We going back to Lexington," I told him. He kept nodding like there weren't another word to be said. Good thing I got Mamma. Gotta have somebody arguing back at me.

Rudy talked to the Reverend Crenshaw about the fights. The Reverend spoke to the teachers in the school and the fights stopped—just like that. The children began to talk about other children at school. I don't know if they was friends, but they seem on their way to becoming them. Not friends to bring home—no colored children on this land except ours—but that was something. The boys seemed happier. Herbert even said one boy had called him brave for living so near to the Grand Dragon. Herbert seem near to bragging about it. He stopped that story when I looked hard at him.

Eleanor weren't happy, though. She couldn't understand why I won't let her go near the Lawson house let alone go inside it. She always a quiet child—loving doing quiet girl things. I got to bite my lip so as not to snap at her to get a move on, to make some noise, for goodness sakes. Make some mess.

Mamma thinks I'm the most unreasonable mamma on the face of the earth.

"Most mammas would give their eye teeth for a daughter like Eleanor," she tells me.

I know it, and I'm ashamed of myself, but we just ain't alike. I'm a whole lot more like Mamma Sally than my own mamma. Maybe that's the way of the world. That don't mean we don't love each other. That's just the way it is.

I love Eleanor, but she a whole lot more like Miz Lawson. Miz Lawson never had a daughter. She might have think she had one now—a little colored daughter—but she don't.

I'm sorry for Eleanor. Sorry she got such a mean mamma. But I'm not letting her near Miz Lawson. She ain't her mamma.

That's just the way it is.

CHAPTER **21**
Rudy Johnson—Late September 1948

Just six months since we drove up that sorry road, the kids trying not to bounce out the back of the truck. Seem like years. Now we in the home stretch, and I can't help feeling bad about that. Of course, Nannie right. She always right about things like this. Fellows at work used to rag me, say I was woman driven. They don't know Nannie. Anything I want, she more than happy to do her best to make sure it happen. Anything *she* want, she put aside till she see whether it be possible. She always like that, putting everybody else first. Daddy say Mamma the same way. And just as bossy. I done marry Mamma, Daddy say the first time he meet Nannie.

"Well, you could have done worse," he say. That high praise from Daddy. "You listen to that woman, now," he tell me. "Because you never did have no sense."

So when Nannie say she won't be living on no Klan land, won't be working for no Grand Dragon and I ain't gonna either, I gotta listen. Only it make me sorry some.

The thing is it don't feel like Klan land. The boys don't know the Elkhorn they jump in to cool off is running through Klan land. That tree house I help them make solid so they won't fall and break their necks don't know it looking over land that been spoiled. I climb up there with them. I try not to let them see how scared I get climbing up anything. Don't want them thinking their daddy's some chicken, though I sure hate ladders. Nannie say not to worry about it. We all scared of something. When I get to the top, that view sure is worth it. The land roll and curve like it dancing. The breeze blow the tobacco leaves, and it look like a whole field of church fans waving. I feel like waving back.

I know I don't own any of this land—ain't never gonna own it. But it feel like mine. I worked it hard enough. It sure don't look spoiled. One bad crop don't spoil a field. Plow it under and plant again.

And Mr. Lawson sure don't look like no Grand Dragon I ever heard of. He changed, Miz Lawson say. But when I mention that to Nannie, she just let me have it. She don't want to hear about no change.

"We gonna change," she says. "Change ourselves right out of here back to civilization." She mean Lexington.

And how do I know Mr. Lawson's changed? "What change look like?" she ask. "You see his heart? He have a different heart than he did when he led those outlaws and chased that man all the way to Maysville where they hung him? How do you change a heart like that?"

"He tried to stop them," I tell her. "Got shot trying."

"Too little, too late," she answer. And she look at me hard. None of us—the children or me—say anything when she look at you hard like that. No answering Nannie when she make up her mind about something.

"Too little, too late," she say again. "No changing a heart like that."

I don't know about his heart. I just know I work with the man every day, from first light to past dark. He getting up there in years, but I hardly keep up with him. Right now we chopping and stacking. Should be done by now, but rain in August put us back some. Mr. Lawson got more than ten acres tobacco of his own we got to do. Don't know how.

Chopping and stacking. There a rhythm to it that makes you think almost like you dancing, 'cept you don't stop. The music don't end for a whole day. You pause to take some water or maybe eat something. Nannie bring me something when she get a chance, though most days she over with the corn field trying to finish up there. Mr. Lawson bring his own food. Chopping and stacking. It a wearisome job.

The boys come out to do their share soon as they get home from school. They good boys—Mr. Lawson think so, too. I see him looking at them once every little while like a farmer look at something he thinks worth looking at. The boys never complain—not even Herbert more than a grumble or two. But they just boys—not even such big boys yet. Two hours and they wore out. I send them home. Or off to that tree house.

"If they got energy for climbing trees, they got energy to keep working," Nannie frets, worried we ain't ever gonna get done.

"They boys, not men," I tell her. She get quiet then. When Nannie get quiet, it mean you won that argument.

When they go off, it just Mr. Lawson and me again, chopping and stacking, up one row and down the other. I stop to moan and straighten my back every so often. If he do the same, I never catch it. You get the feel of a man working by him like that. I know Nannie say it too little too late and nobody can change his heart.

I think, *If nobody can change his heart we in a whole heap of trouble.* But I don't say that out loud.

You don't say things out loud to Nannie when she give you that hard look.

We was trying to figure out when we'd finally get the tobacco to market. It be touch and go making the auction the last week in October. It might not be cured in time. I wish the boys was older or we could hire some help. But help is scarce as hens' teeth in harvest time, even if we could pay for it. Which we can't.

We still got all the tobacco to hang. They got some auctions in November we might have to try for.

"You going to be around in November?" It was the first time Mr. Lawson even mention our leaving to me. Sometimes the conversation itched at us—hung there in the air—but we never put it into real words. I never knew a man to talk much. Daddy sure don't. I try to talk more to the children, but it hard. Women just seem to be a whole lot better with words.

I know Mamma talked a whole lot to Nannie about what went on in Estill County when I was a boy. Took a whole day telling her tale—me in the fields, the children at school. Told her things she ain't never said to me.

I never asked her. Never wanted to hear it. Maybe that why she ain't never told me her story.

"It's your story, too," Nannie said, and I see her circling around it. I just shake my head. She stop.

Now I see Mr. Lawson circling his story. I don't want to hear his story, either. His story is making us leave this land in the first place. I like to tell him that, but it wouldn't be polite. Wouldn't be Kentucky.

"I reckon I'll be here as long as I need to be. Nannie might leave with the children."

He nod. "Sorry to see you go. Should have told you the truth in the first place."

He went back to chopping and stacking then. I took a second and joined him. He was right. Didn't need a whole lot of words to tell the story. Sorry to see us go. Should have told us the truth in the first place.

What else was there to say?

When I saw Nannie waving to me late afternoon, I thought, *What now? Them two chickens we got left been eaten by a fox?* We should'a ate them long ago, but we couldn't bring ourselves to it. Or the children wouldn't let us. They got to be what every farmer warns his children against making farm critters: pets. But they was survivors, so we took the few eggs they laid and let them be. I'd hate to think a fox had ate what we turned down. I even felt a little sore about the chickens. "Soft heart, soft head," Mama says.

But it wasn't chickens she was waving about. "Come see," she kept yelling. Mr. Lawson stopped his chopping. Her "come see" seemed a general one, though she didn't look at him. She never looked at him. We went to see.

A whole quarter section of the fence between the Martin land and my corn field been mowed down. Two of Martin's cow was chomping contentedly in a field just ruined. We almost finish the harvest of the sweet corn, but we planted late. Nannie would hike out there of a morning and try to glean what was left. We still had a whole two acres of feed corn to harvest. We been waiting until we got a handle on the tobacco. Didn't look like we were going to have to wait on that.

"Some of your friends' doing?" Nannie still wasn't looking at Mr. Lawson, but her words aimed at him.

He turned to look at her. "Haven't been my friends for a while, but I have a good idea who they are. It's going to stop now." He looked at the corn—more trampled than eaten. He turned his words to me now. "You and I are going to have to figure out how much these cows ruined. Come to a price and we'll settle up on that." He looked at the cows. "I'm going to have to settle up with Dick Martin, too. I don't think those cows will survive of a morning. Help me drive them back over the fence line. Or maybe your boys could do that. I got to make a visit to some people."

JOSEPH G. ANTHONY

He paused. "Your woman's right. I guess they used to
be friends of mine. Or something like that. I'd say we were
more fellow coyotes in a pack. Used to have lots of coyotes in
these parts when I was a boy. Don't see them much anymore.
I think the last time I saw a pack was back before the war,
and it wasn't much of a pack then—just two or three of them,
half-starved looking. Packs used to be bigger. Meaner. But I
guess just because you don't see them, don't mean they aren't
still there. Hiding. Ready to take their chance."

It was a long speech for him. Most I heard him talk
all summer.

"Can your boys take care of those cows? Maybe you
could wander over to Dick Martin and let him know what's
up. Tell Miz Lawson I might be late. I'll be obliged."

I let him go half a field before I shouted out to him.
"Hold on. I'm coming, too."

Nannie turned from watching him go to looking at
me like I done lost my mind.

"What are you talking about? You not going
anywhere. That man has to take care of business he should
have took care of a long time ago. It's not your business.
You staying right here."

She was shouting now. Nannie's a shouter when she
upset. Mamma's the same way. The cows stopped their
chomping a moment to look at her. Mr. Lawson paused when
I shouted but then went on walking. I'd have to hurry up
some to catch him.

"I don't know whose business it is if it ain't mine," I
said to Nannie. "Whose chickens got their necks wrung?
Whose chicken coop got dead pigs hung up in it like some
butcher set up shop in the middle of the country? Whose
children still wake up seeing that? Of course it my business,
Nannie. It all our business. You get the boys to help you
with these cows—get Franklin to run over to the Martins.
And tell Miz Lawson where we at. I don't got time now. He
almost out of sight."

Nannie stopped shouting. She got quiet. When
Nannie get quiet, it mean I won the argument.

"You take care," is all she said. "That's *my* business.
You take care."

*   *   *

When I caught up with Mr. Lawson he tried to argue it wasn't my business, too. But he gave it up when he saw I weren't budging.

"Might make things more chancy..." He paused, considering.

"Because I'm colored? Well, that's what's it's all about anyway, ain't it? Besides, you going alone make it seem like it just something between you white people. Maybe it mostly is, I don't know. You fighting about something that go way back. I just know I'm coming with you. I'll take my chances. Besides, my fight goes way back, too."

He didn't say anything more. He weren't a man to use two words when one would do.

Nothing more to say.

We stopped at the barn. That's where he kept his guns. Miz Lawson didn't want them in the house. He kept them up in the barn loft, wrapped in burlap locked in a case. He told me where they was at when I first moved in. The ammo was in another locked case. Varmint control, he explained. I figure that by the time he climbed up to the loft, opened both cases, and came back down again, any varmint would be long gone.

Unless it was a mighty slow varmint.

Or unless you had a good idea where the varmint hung out.

He picked a single shot sixteen-gauge shotgun. He opened the ammo case and took six shells. He handed me the other gun, a 257 Roberts.

"My daddy had one," he told me. "'Bob,' we used to call it. Kids start out with that gun. Lightweight. Not much of a kick to it. Only trouble is, you almost got to hit a deer in the head to kill it. Sometimes you hit an artery and they bleed to death, but that might mean trailing it five miles over rough country."

It's like he decide today was the day to do his talking.

"Jimmy's gun. He liked to hunt. I was never one for it. Before the war, we hunted some to put meat on the table. But everyone was trying to put something on their table during those times. I think maybe he killed one deer with that rifle. No, two. The first one he had to track two days before he got it. Just a boy—maybe thirteen. Wanted to give up on it, but his mother wouldn't hear about it. 'You shot that creature,' she told him, 'now you go make sure it's dead.'"

He rummaged around and found a cleaning rod. We spent some time cleaning. I could hardly make it up the bore of the Bob the first couple times. Mr. Lawson looked at me struggling.

"Jimmy kept that rifle real clean. Guess I let it rust some."

It took me several swipes, but the rod finally came out clean. The shotgun weren't as neglected.

We looked over the ammo. My rounds looked tarnished.

"Should be OK. Kept it dry up here, at least. Wilma won't have guns in the house. Worst thing happen is that they won't shoot."

Worst thing happen is that they will *shoot*, I'm thinking.

"I don't think we'll be needing these, but..." He didn't finish.

Like I said, he a man of few words.

We was almost to his car—a clean getaway—when Miz Lawson came out to the front porch. We was quiet. I don't think she heard anything. But women got a sense about things. They don't have to hear or see anything to know something's up. She looked at us. She looked at the guns.

"James," she said, and waited.

He didn't answer right away. He placed the shotgun in the backseat—took mine from me and put it next to his. He paused a second more before he turned to her.

"Back fence cut and knocked down. Dick Martin's cows ate themselves to death on the feed corn. What they didn't eat, they trampled. Whole field mostly lost. Going to take care of it."

She didn't say anything at first. Just stared at him. Nannie be yelling questions. Mamma, too. But Miz Lawson just stared.

"James," she said again. That was all, but the word tore at me. Tore at him, too.

"Wilma, you told me when the chickens got killed that things couldn't stay. Couldn't stay. You said I had to do something. You were right. I'm doing something."

They looked at each other. He didn't try to duck her gaze. They just looked at each other. I don't know what they thinking. They been married a long time. Close to forty years I reckon. A long time. A boy grown, gone, and killed. Maybe they thinking that. Maybe they not thinking nothing, just looking.

She don't say nothing more. He don't neither. He finally gets in the car and cranks its up. I get in beside him. I don't turn my head to look and he don't neither, but we both know she back there on the porch watching us drive into that cow patch they call a road. She back there watching us go. And when she can't see us no more, she listening to us grinding our gears down that road.

And when she can't hear us, she still standing there. She still standing there.

We didn't say nothing for a good while. Not that that grinding old Ford and pit-road let you have much conversation. But when we made it to the church crossways, Mr. Lawson looked over at me.

"Headed to a fellow used to work for me. Twenty years ago. Edom. Edom Wachs. You might have passed his land walking to the church over at New Zion."

We been driving to church when we could make it. But I remembered that first hike.

"One fellow didn't seem too friendly. Made us walk all 'round his property."

Mr. Lawson nodded. "That'd be Edom."

We turned down off the main road into a driveway rut that almost made our road seem like a highway. Both sides of that driveway was piled high with metal—parts of cars, bed springs, tractor pieces. Everything rusted brown like it been there for years. I don't know how it missed all them metal drives during the war when anything hard got melted down. But maybe they didn't want this—maybe some metal's just too worn out.

Or maybe it too far off the road. It felt like we was driving through some abandoned city rather than way out in Scott County.

It weren't entirely abandoned. I saw two children— six or seven years old, I figured—scrambling over some barrels. About eight or nine barrels was piled high, open-ended. No telling what they had in them. The children was jumping off one onto another. Sometimes one got on top and tussled with the other. King of the mountain. Or the barrels. I couldn't tell if they was boys or girls—or one of each— they was so dirty. Just covered in brown rust. Nannie would have hosed them off before she let them in the bathtub.

"I sure hope them children got their tetanus shots," I said.

Mr. Lawson glanced over. "Not likely. Not likely to have had any shots. Edom wouldn't want to spoil them."

"His children?"

"Grandkids. They're all living here, I think. I don't know. Haven't been on this place for twenty years."

The children stopped their tussling when they saw us and hightailed through the dump. We had to travel on that driveway, so they beat us to the house. Three women— one old, two not young but younger—stood on the porch waiting for us as we drove up. About five or six children spread themselves about. Mr. Lawson turned off the motor but didn't get out. He nodded to the older woman, who didn't nod back.

"I'm looking for Edom, Sandra. Do you know where I might find him?"

She stared at him a second before she answered. Her eyes widened when she saw me sitting in the passenger seat. "What you want him for, James?"

"Got some business I need to talk to him about."

She nodded towards me. "Business include that nigger beside you?"

Nobody said nothing for a moment. The word just hung there. Funny about that word. It just a word—I don't know why we give it so much attention, but we do. Like she fire a shot when she said that word. All the children scramble up to the porch to gather round their mammas. Their grandma. It a sad looking porch—just clinging to the house. Glad them children don't look like they weigh a hundred pounds wet or the women neither, otherwise that porch might just give up the ghost and slide on out to the road.

"My business is with Edom, Sandra. Do you know where he is?"

She didn't even nod yes or no. Just stood there, arms folded 'round her thin chest, staring at us. Hating us. I've known people in my life who ain't much cared for me. One fellow in the Army wanted to fight me every time he saw me. He another colored man. Weren't nothing black or white about it. Finally one day we drinking and not fighting and I ask him about it, why he always ready to come at me.

"I don't know," he answered. "Something about you I just don't like. But you a fine fellow," he say to me. "A fine fellow. I just don't like you."

He just didn't like me. Me. Like you can't put enough sugar on rhubarb for me to put it in my mouth. Like that fellow. He try me and he didn't like me. I can accept that.

But I never understood people hating you who ain't even tried you. I don't understand people who don't even look at you. They just know they hate you.

One of the barrel children—I could tell now she a little girl—had inched herself next to her grandma. She was a pretty thing under all that dirt. Pushed herself so tight against her grandma, her grandma was near to being pushed off the porch. Finally, she had to give in. She unfolded her arms and let the little girl press her face right next to her bosom, kind of squashing it with her chin. It was a funny sight. 'Minded me of Eleanor and how Mamma says she feels sometimes they only need one dress between them. The little girl stared wide-eyed at me. I smiled at her.

"Nigger!" she yelled so loud all three women on the porch jumped. She looked surprised herself. The other children giggled.

"Hush," her grandma said to her.

I pulled my head back so she couldn't see my face. *You the one should hush*, I thought. *Where you think your grandbaby got that word?* But I didn't say anything. That word. Hurt a lot more than I ever got hurt fighting that fellow who didn't like me. Left a taste in my mouth a whole lot more sour than rhubarb. That word was rhubarb without any sugar.

We drove three more places, down roads almost as rough as the first one. Trash heaps on two of them, but nothing like that Wachs' place. No men at home. A couple boys near grown. But mostly women and children. Nobody pleased to see us. Me, especially. Some of the boys looked like they might like to say something, but their mammas brought them back sharp. They couldn't see the guns, but they knew this business weren't something boys should fool themselves with.

Everybody—women and boys—seemed to take it as a kind of special insult Mr. Lawson brung me with him.

Well, they could take it like they wanted. I knew all about special insults.

We weren't getting anywhere—driving away from our fourth empty driveway when we spotted a little boy, not more than nine, coming in from the field. Little as he was, he was herding two big milk cows who kept wandering away from him. He get one going one direction, and the other one head the opposite. Mr. Lawson stopped the car and leaned out the window, smiling.

"Howdy Davy. Those milk cows giving you trouble? Ol' things more trouble than they're worth. I came out to talk with your daddy. Do you know where he is?"

Davy looked surprised to see anyone, let alone Mr. Lawson and a strange colored man. But Kentucky find it hard not to be polite to a friendly howdy. Don't seem natural not to howdy back.

"Daddy ain't here. He at a big meeting at the church with Mr. Wachs and all the other men."

"That's right. The church. I plumb forgot. Thank you, Davy."

And he waved. Davy waved back, but looking like he just remembered the meeting was a secret. Both cows wandered clear off by the time he turned to look for them.

The church was walking distance from the house. Could have saved a lot of time if we knew where we was headed. But ain't that always the case? There was four cars and a pickup in front of the little yellow-bricked side building. The dog run that connect it to the church had the light on. A light on in the building, too. It was getting dark. I always hated losing the light in the fall. Not enough daylight as it is to get things done. No light in the church. It's painted some kind of brown, but in twilight it almost look black. Nannie thinks it the ugliest church she ever see.

"It just a plain building," I tell her. "Plain people like plain churches."

But she right. It sure ain't pretty.

I don't know if Davy got word to his mamma and she got word to the church, or one of the other places we tried did it—one of them might have had a telephone—but anyway the motor ain't been turned off more than ten seconds before three men came outside. They didn't look surprised to see us. All three was carrying some kind of rifle, straight up like they was on parade. *Just three*, I thought, but then two other men joined them. One of them had a pistol on the outside of his pants—no holster, just something that looked like a .45 stuck through his belt. The other man wasn't carrying that I could tell. We sat there a second. I wondered if I should reach over and get our guns. Mr. Lawson put his hand on my knee.

"Wait," is all he said.

We waited. The unarmed man started to walk towards us. When he almost got to the Ford, Mr. Lawson opened the door and got out. He didn't reach for his gun.

"Reverend Edwards? You running this meeting? You the Kludd of this Klan?"

I was glad the man didn't have a gun with him, the way he pulled his head back sharp at Mr. Lawson's words. He took a second. "I'm no Kludd and this isn't any Klan, James. It's just a meeting of concerned Christians. You used to be one yourself."

"Concerned Christians?" He looked back at the men. "You running a Bible study meeting?"

The minister looked over towards me.

"You used to have more sense, James. Are you looking for trouble? Bringing a colored man along with you."

Now it was Mr. Lawson pulling his head back.

"Don't remember having more sense," he say. "Seems I remember not having any sense at all. And I haven't looked for trouble for a long time, Reverend. Don't need to. Trouble seems to find me easy enough on its own."

He nodded his head toward me. "I reckon I can bring who I want with me anywhere I want to go. Besides, the colored man here has a stake in all this. His name's Rudy Johnson. *Mister* Johnson thought he'd come along with me. Thinks it's his trouble, too, seeing as it's his pigs and chickens being killed. His fence being torn down. His field corn ruined."

The man with the pistol in his belt came closer but stayed twenty yards away. He yelled, though he didn't need to. Mr. Lawson's and the minister's words traveled the distance just fine.

"His corn? Don't you still own that land? You give over the title to that black man already?"

Mr. Lawson turned to him.

"Howdy Edom. Been looking for you. No, I haven't given over the title. Not yet."

The "not yet" made the man grab for his pistol, but the reverend waved him down. "Edom, you said you'd let me handle this. No need for guns, now." He turned back to us.

"I don't know anything about dead pigs or chickens, James. If you have any concerns, you should take them to the sheriff. Not go running about the countryside with a colored man, toting rifles. That's the way to get yourself killed. We've had enough of that. We don't need those times again."

"Those times." The words hung in the air. The kind of times that got us run out of Estill County. Mamma's always wanting me to remember something I just can't reach for, but I remember enough. I remember being beat up and chased. I remember Papaw's farm and the barn burning. I don't need to remember any more of *those* times.

Besides, seems to me those times ain't gone. Not all gone. The man with the pistol in his belt sure don't think they're gone. The men with those rifles sticking straight up like MacArthur gonna inspect them any moment don't think they gone.

But one thing different. I ain't running. My family ain't running. Maybe I ain't remembering what Mamma wants me to remember, but I remember running. And I ain't doing it again.

Mr. Lawson had listened closely to the minister. "Those were bad times for sure, Reverend. But I wonder if you remember them as good as I do? I don't remember you worrying much about me getting killed twenty years ago. I don't remember you even worrying about, Edom, either." He paused and looked towards the men in back.

"Who else is back there? Tommy Butler? Aren't you too old for this? I know Edom and me are. And you brought your boys with you. They're too young and we're too old."

He turned back to the minister.

"I remember what you told me twenty years ago. Said you needed me. The colored were running wild. White men, too. Said the Lord and the congregation were in need of a strong leader. The white men would turn into a mob. A bunch of hooligans. Quoted the Bible to me. Always seemed able to find the right Bible verse, Reverend. Something from Isaiah."

The minister put his hand on Mr. Lawson's arm.

"Here's more Isaiah, James. '*Jehovah, thou wilt ordain peace for us; for thou has also wrought all our works for us.*' Let the Lord obtain peace for us, James. It can't be got from the barrel of a gun."

Mr. Lawson shook his head. "It's really something how you can do that—just pull a line out of the Bible when you need it. I guess after thirty years, a man gets good at what he does. But you were good twenty years ago. Only you weren't preaching peace. In fact after listening to you— and to Isaiah—I led a group of Christians out to find and kill a black man."

The minister shook his head no. "I never told you to kill anyone. That blood's not on me."

Mr. Lawson thought about that a moment. "Well, I guess it's on me then. And Edom. Tommy was with us. Hope it doesn't pass on to those boys. Guilt of the fathers onto the sons. Wouldn't want to think Jimmy was guilty because of me. The man we hung was an innocent colored man. Well, not innocent. Aren't none of us innocent. The Bible tells us that. Isaiah tells us that. Aren't none of us innocent. But he wasn't guilty of what we said he was guilty of. He was an ordinary sinner. Just like the rest of us."

He paused again. "That's not true, either. Far as I know he hadn't killed anybody. More than we can say."

Mr. Lawson went on. "After we found that out, the man being innocent of the crime, I thought maybe you'd find another Bible verse to come to terms with what we done. I've been waiting twenty years, and you haven't come up with one yet. I don't know that you've even tried to find one. You're so quick with the Bible verse, I know you could find one if you wanted. Blessed are the guilty, the ones with blood on their hands. Blessed are James and Edom and Tommy because without them..."

He looked at the minister, then over at the man he called Edom. "What'd he be without us, Edom? Just another sinner?"

"Speak for yourself, James Lawson. One thing I ain't. I ain't a traitor. I ain't a nigger-lover."

Mr. Lawson kept looking over the minister's shoulder at Edom. "You aren't a traitor, Edom, if you mean by that you haven't changed. Thirty-five years I've known you,

you've been afraid of the colored man. Blamed him for everything."

"You turned on your own kind, James Lawson."

Mr. Lawson nodded. "I did. You were my kind and I turned on you." He looked to the minister again.

"You know, Wilma keeps telling me to find another church. Says the Bible—at least the Jesus Bible—is full of forgiveness and mercy. Mercy is what it's all about, she keeps telling me. Women won't let go of something once they got on to it. Worse than you preachers. But I told her no. This is my church. I don't want to run off to any church where everybody's so ready to forgive you, you can hardly remember what your sin was. I don't want to forget what my sin was. No, I'll find out the answer right here—right where I sinned—why the Bible seemed to steer us so wrong twenty years ago. Why you steered us so wrong twenty years ago."

The minister looked like he wanted to say some‐thing, but Mr. Lawson put up his hand, and he stopped. It like Mr. Lawson's twenty year quiet burst like a mud dam in a spring flood.

"Only the Bible doesn't steer us wrong. We just hear wrong. I heard wrong. Maybe I heard you wrong. So I've been waiting twenty years to hear right again. Knowing that you'd find the right place in the Bible eventually—maybe not Isaiah this time. Maybe something from the New Testament. Maybe something Jesus said, like Wilma is always talking about. But now I find you'll still back there preaching to the same folk you were preaching to twenty years ago. In the same way. To the same good Christians still out there looking for the wild black man like nothing's changed all these years."

He waited—as if he expected the minister to answer him—as if he was still hoping he would. But the minister stayed silent. Didn't even quote Isaiah no more.

"But lots of things have changed," Mr. Lawson went on. "Colored changed. Won't put up with things like they used to." Edom made some noise, but Mr. Lawson ignored him. "Another thing changed: Jimmy's gone. Sometimes I think his going is the Lord's punishment, but Wilma says that's just this church talking.

"Jimmy stopped coming to church here right after all that happened. Jumped on you and Tommy there, trying to get you off me. Didn't weigh a hundred pounds, but it didn't matter. I tried to get him to forget that. I told him his granddaddy helped build this church—gave the land for it. One fight shouldn't make you leave something that's a part of you. Told him that when he married—he never did get a chance to marry—but I told him when he did, he couldn't leave a wife every time they got into an argument. Go through more wives than an old-time Mormon.

"But he wouldn't come. Stayed home with his mamma. She and he did quiet things together when I came to church. Made him feel peaceful, he said. I told him the church wasn't meant to make him feel good. Well, he said— made his mamma laugh when he said it—it was doing what it was supposed to, then. This church wasn't what he wanted. Didn't have much Jesus in it. That was his mamma talking. But he was listening to her. He'd just stay home with his mamma."

The minister was indignant. "Jesus Christ is the founder of our church. We are a Christian congregation."

"I told him that, Reverend. Over and over. But he didn't agree. Didn't think our church had enough Jesus in it."

He looked back at the men standing apart. "You men didn't reckon on a sermon, did you? I'm sorry about that. It comes from being silent too much of the time. I guess that's what happens to a farmer. When you get a chance to talk— to preach—you can hardly let up. So I'll bring this short." He waited while the men came closer to hear him. "Somebody's been doing a lot of damage to my farm—to my tenant's farm, Mr. Johnson, here. Killed his pigs and his chickens. Scared his children. Tore up his fence. It's going to stop. I know who you are, and I will stop it. You know who I am, too. You know I will do whatever I need to."

He turned to that Edom fella.

"Edom. You were always a man who needed straight talk. I remember when you worked for me. If I didn't tell you to do something real exact, it didn't get done. So I want to be real clear with you. You and I go way back. You put a bullet in me. Two bullets. I still limp a bit with the knee injury. That's over and done with. I'm glad to limp. I'm glad to remember. I hold no grievance against you about the bullets. That's all the past. Only understand me now, Edom. I will put a bullet in you if you do anything else, to any pig or chicken or fence line. If you hurt anyone near to me—and that includes Mr. Johnson here. My tenant. My friend, too...If you step on my land and I haven't invited you, or Mr. Johnson hasn't...Hear me. I am a Christian man, Edom, but not Jesus, and not Isaiah. Not anything or anybody will keep me from what I have to do. I swear I will kill you."

He turned back to the car then, like it was all over and not just beginning. Suddenly Edom pulled the gun from his belt. I leaped over the seat and grabbed the Bob, but it was too late. Edom was shooting, and the men behind him started shooting, too. I aimed the Bob at Edom, but the first bullet didn't fire. I could hear that click in the middle of all that blasting. I saw Edom staring at me—looking past Mr. Lawson falling to the ground—looking for the black man who had brought this all on. I aimed again at him—aimed for his head, his face. I clicked again and this time his eyes widened a second, and I wondered if it misfired again, but the blood start to ooze out from his forehead—then the hole start to grow and widen till that hole swallow his whole white face.

I ain't never been in a battle. Patton kept us away from all that—ain't never killed nobody. And oh, Jesus. Jesus. Don't let me never do it again. I know Edom a bad man—a man so full of hate, he like a boil full of puss. Just like them Nazis. But he still a man, and it make me sick to shoot him. The bullet I aim at his head turn round and hit me in the stomach.

But I don't got time to worry over it. I grabbed the shotgun and shoved the shot up the barrel. The three men in back had stopped shooting. Mr. Lawson and the minister lay on the ground. I got out of the car and went to Mr. Lawson. He was still breathing.

"Somebody call the hospital," I yelled to the men in back who stood watching me but wasn't moving. "Help me get these men in the car." My shotgun was pointed at them. The men held their own guns in front of them. "Your minister's hurt. In his back and leg. One of you shot him." We still pointed our guns at each other. They wasn't budging. "They need help. Somebody go call. Somebody help me lift them."

I could hear Nannie now in my mind's ear, so clear like she standing right next to me. She always knew what I was about to do. "Are you crazy?" She was asking me now.

"These the same crackers who killed our pigs and strangled our chickens, the same crackers who terrorized our children. You just shot their leader. Three of them pointing a gun at your head. Only thing keeping them from shooting is the gun you're pointing back. Don't put your gun down. Rudy!"

Somebody gotta, I tell her in my mind, though I don't know as I would'a had the nerve to say it to her face. *Somebody gotta put the gun down first.*

Or we'll all be dead. We all end up like Edom with big holes where our brains been.

I put my gun on the ground beside James.

It took a second—though it seemed like an hour— but finally the older boy ran back into the church building. The man, Tommy, lowered his gun after another few seconds. The minister was groaning. I knelt by Mr. Lawson. His breathing was quick. I touched his arm.

"Hold on there, Mr. Lawson. Hang on there. We gonna get help. You gonna be OK."

He opened his eyes a little, just a slit. He said something low. I put my ear to his mouth.

"James. Friends..."

I took his hand.

"That's right. You got that right, James. We friends. You hold on now."

James got quiet. Tommy came close and was kneeling by the minister. I looked over. The minister wasn't fixing to die. One bullet might'a hit the back of his left knee, another bullet gone higher up. He'd be limping, but it didn't look like he'd be dying.

I didn't dare move Mr. Lawson. He was bleeding bad. I tried to press the worst spot, but it just kept seeping.

Mr. Lawson—James—made another sound. I leaned in close.

"Tell Wilma," he paused. "Tell Wilma...sorry, everything. Clarence."

"I'll tell her. I'll tell her. I'll tell Clarence, too, who- ever that is. But you gonna tell her yourself. Clarence, too. You tell her yourself."

But he was done with telling. Never was one for talking much. Except for this last bit. Like he saved all them words up for the end. Good words.

But he was done now.

I looked up. The younger boy, he weren't more than sixteen—just a couple years older than Herbert and Franklin—was still aiming his gun at me. Like he was scared to lower his gun. I knew how he felt. My friend James would'a knew how he felt. I put my hand on James' forehead. I ain't no preacher, I can't give no blessing. But I can pray like everyone else.

"Remember his good words, Jesus," I said out loud, making sure my Jesus carried all across that field like I've heard preachers shout it back to the last pew. I saw the boy lowering his rifle a little.

I bowed my head. I thought of Edom, the man I killed. The man who killed James.

"Forget all the ones he said in anger." I racked my brains for a Bible verse, but I couldn't think of a one. "This is James, Jesus. He was my friend in the end, whatever he might'a been before. Be his friend, too, Jesus and remember all the good he done. Don't be remembering all that other stuff. Amen."

Well, I thought, *I wish I could'a sent him off with better words than that.* But I guess all those Jesuses done the trick. When I raised my head, I saw the boy had lowered his. Had lowered his gun, too, right along with his head.

CHAPTER 22
Wilma Lawson—October 1948

Jimmy, that last summer before he went off to the war, always used to accuse me of acting like I'd already received the telegram from the War Department. I told him it wasn't so, that I knew in my heart he'd be returning home safely.

"I just dread the coming quiet with you gone," I said.

"Oh, Momma," he laughed, "I'm going to come home and give you so many grandbabies to take care of, you'll long for all this quiet."

He'd look out over our yard like he wanted to take some of that quiet with him. Then he'd come back and start to bang his fork on the table demanding food, like he hadn't eaten in days. I don't know where that boy put all that food. He always was skinny. I told him one more bang on the table and I'd be doing some banging on his head. He'd laugh as if I had told the funniest joke, but he stopped treating the kitchen table like a drum. Thank goodness, he wasn't a picky eater. Ate what I managed to rouse up no matter what it was.

But he and I both knew I was lying. And when the telegram finally did come, I wasn't surprised. I just wondered why it had took so long.

James kept looking at me strange after the telegram. I didn't cry. Didn't shout my grief like I've seen women do. Men, too. I sat there as frozen as the January ground surrounding us. One day. Two days.

On the third day, I walked out into the fields. The land was so bleak. The furrows where James had plowed in spring were unmoving, stuck. As if they would never yield again. At least Jimmy was in a green land when he died, I thought, and something ripped inside me. I felt something tearing. I heard a crazy woman shouting and crying. And James was there, trying to hold me, but I would not be held. I pushed his arms away, and I hit him. I hit him on his arms, his shoulders, his face, and he just stood there—letting me hit him. He just stood there.

I didn't get a telegram for James. Just a visit from the sheriff. I didn't walk into the fields, fields still full of green, still full of life as if to mock me—mock my whole family. Gone now, gone. I didn't shout and carry on like a crazy woman. Though I *was* a crazy woman. I could feel the craziness well up in me like vomit. Like gore. But there was nobody left to yell at. Nobody left to hit and hit again.

James was gone.

I can't remember the last time the sheriff came to the door. Maybe to tell us about Alice. How long ago was that? Of course, this wasn't the same sheriff. This boy looked about Jimmy's age. I wondered if he had known Jimmy.

I watched him walking up the pathway, knowing he dreaded every step that brought him closer to me. I felt sorry for him. If I could have spared him the story he had to tell, I would have.

But that wasn't my job. My job was to stand there and listen. I could spare nobody. Nobody had spared me.

The young sheriff had been a friend of my boy, Jimmy, though I didn't recognize him. Now he told me of the shootings, the killing of James—Jimmy's daddy—of Edom, the wounding of the Reverend Edwards. And I listened like if I listened hard enough, deep enough, I could change something in what he was telling me.

He told the story matter of fact. As if he were a farmer, talking about the weather. Storm damage. As if he was just reporting. With a farmer's stoicism. It was what it was.

James would say that when I fussed about something. Some silly thing past changing—it was what it was.

It's all past changing now.

I saw Nannie running up from Jimmy's house. She had seen the sheriff's car.

"How is Rudy?" I asked the sheriff, and he looked confused for a second.

"The colored man? We got him in the jail right now. Shot Edom Wachs right between the eyes."

Nannie was coming quick. Edom dead was not my concern. But fear had crept past my numbness.

"What was Edom doing at the time?"

"That's what we're trying to figure out."

I stared at him silently. He did that little dance grown men do—boys, too—when they don't want to say something. "Reverend Edwards—he's going to be alright—Reverend Edwards said Edom had shot....well, was fixing to shoot the colored man."

"After Edom shot James?" I said it calm myself. Just more storm damage.

The boy looked very uncomfortable, but I wasn't feeling sorry for him anymore.

"Yes, ma'am. After he shot James...Mr. Lawson."

Nannie had made it to the porch. The sheriff barely looked at her. "Then it seems an open and shut case of self-defense. The Reverend Edwards wouldn't lie. Not for a colored man, at least. Why is Rudy still in jail?"

"He killed a man, ma'am. A white man. We still got laws in this county. We got to figure things out."

He killed a white man. I was suddenly afraid. Confused. James dead. Jimmy. That other man—so long ago. A black man, dead. Nannie was looking at me, pleading. I made myself come back.

"But it's the same law for white men and colored now. Isn't that right, sheriff?"

Nannie wasn't saying anything. That surprised me some. She stood next to me on the porch. She looked at me and waited. Then she turned to the sheriff.

The sheriff hadn't made it all the way up the porch steps—had stopped on the middle one. He was a tall young man. The three of us were almost of an eye-level. Nannie stood a bit taller.

"That's right, ma'am," and he could have been talking to Nannie. "Same law for the colored and for the white. We just got to do a little more figuring. Should be out by morning."

I felt Nannie breathing heavy beside me, but she was letting me do the talking. "Is he safe, son?"

He turned to me. The word "son" had made me Jimmy's mamma again.

"He's safe, ma'am." And this time he did turn to Nannie.

"Those times are done. He's safe, ma'am. I guarantee it."

Safe. Guaranteed. I felt something pull then. I felt myself slumping. The sheriff made a grab for me but Nannie

JOSEPH G. ANTHONY

waved him off. She had me. She held me, and I let her. "James, James," I whispered as Nannie held me. "What have you done, James?"

Looking back, it's surprised me some that the Reverend Edwards had backed Rudy's words as to what happened, though one of the others—a boy just turned sixteen—also told it the same way, so I guess he didn't have much choice. I don't know that he would have lied—just not been clear. Like the other two men—the ones who accidentally shot the reverend—who claimed they hadn't been close enough to see what happened. Close enough to shoot the minister, but not close enough to see Edom shoot anybody. Still, I wasn't surprised enough to let him do James' funeral even if he had asked to. Which he didn't.

James had never stopped being a member of that ugly church, but I had. And a funeral's for the living, not the dead. But I didn't have a church and it seemed wrong to bury James without one. Jimmy and I had made our own little church—quiet mornings when James had taken himself down to the Calvary he didn't seem able to stop going to. A Calvary he carried with him all the time. I didn't want that Calvary, but I needed something.

"Have the funeral at our church." Rudy had come home from jail and started back in the fields, jumped right in. Said the tobacco didn't care what happened. Still needed cutting. They hadn't even kept him the whole night in the jail. Stephen, the sheriff, had driven him home himself.

"Your church?" I saw Nannie's eyes open wide at the very idea. She opened her mouth, too, but must have thought better of it. Rudy and I both waited for a moment. Nannie deciding not to speak was a new phenomenon for both of us. We hadn't spoken much the last day. But she had allowed Eleanor to come over. "To help out," Eleanor said she'd been told.

"You help out just by being here," I told her.

I shook my head at Rudy.

"Have you asked the minister? What is his name?"

"Reverend Crenshaw. Yes, I asked him."

"And he's alright with a colored church burying the former Grand Dragon of the Ku Klux Klan?"

I don't know that I had ever said those words aloud before. They shocked me. They shocked all of us. Rudy took a second.

"He's alright with burying my friend, James, who died trying to protect us."

I suspect not everyone in the congregation felt the same way, but if they did feel differently they were too polite to let me know it. So there I was, the only white face but one in a sea of colored ones.

The only white face but Agnes. She'd been the only one from James' church to brave a visit after his shooting. His first shooting. Brought us that dreadful chicken and dumplings. I never liked the woman, never gave her two thoughts, and here she was again. I didn't even know she was still living, though I suppose I would have heard if she wasn't.

She looked so scared I made her sit by me. Like family. My only white family. Everyone else gone, or cousins too far removed to have to claim me. But I had my colored family. They closed in around me as if it would be impolite to give me any breathing space.

I think it would have been.

The choir was singing a beautiful hymn. I don't know that I had ever heard it before. Must have been a colored hymn.

"There is a balm in Gilead. To make the wounded whole. To heal the sin-sick soul."

Oh, James. I had been so composed—I was trying to be a dignified widow—but the words cut at me like a knife. "To heal the sin-sick soul."

Oh, James. That is what I hope for you. Your sin-sick soul healed. A balm in Gilead.

I bent over and my tears flowed. Agnes looked frightened, as if I were having an attack, but the other women made noises like they had been waiting for my tears—almost as if they thought my tears a long time coming. Sally—Rudy's mamma—just reached over and covered my shoulders. She didn't try to pull me up. She let me bend over and groan. "That OK, honey," she kept saying over and over.

"That OK, Abby," I thought she said, then caught herself. "That OK, Wilma, honey. That OK. You keep on crying."

"There is a balm in Gilead," I heard the choir sing over and over again, and Sally sang it with them. "If you cannot sing like angels, if you cannot preach like Paul..." she chanted, and I pulled myself back up. Agnes looked relieved. I took her hand, which frightened her again. I leaned over to her.

"Sing it with me," I said, and she nodded. We sang it together with the choir, with all the women surrounding me, with all the congregation. *James, James*, I thought and squeezed poor, frightened, brave Agnes's hand till I think I might have bruised it. But she never let on. She was too busy singing.

"There is a balm in Gilead to heal the sin-sick soul."

Time came and went, and then I asked Rudy and Nannie to switch houses with me. I think they were surprised, but this house is too big for one lone old woman, and they're mighty cramped over there. Besides, it's Jimmy's cabin. I know he never lived there. That doesn't matter. Or maybe it does. If he had lived there, he'd be gone now—too small to raise a family in. But now it's like he just hasn't come home yet—like I can wait for him there in the cabin he and his daddy built. They built it well, better than this house. I'm getting the better bargain, but there's more room in the big house. Rudy and Nannie can spread out. The boys will like it.

Nobody talks about moving back to Lexington anymore. I wonder if Nannie thinks of it, but she hasn't said anything. Nannie not saying anything means she must agree with staying. Good thing. I couldn't run this farm without them. I tell them it's going to be theirs when I'm gone and to treat it like it's theirs now. They wave their hands at me like I'm saying something outrageous, like they've never heard of an old woman dying. Later Nannie asks me if I'm serious—if I don't have any family I need to leave the land to.

"Any white family, you mean?" And I think Nannie actually got a little misty. Nannie's not one for tearing up. Even at the funeral, I think she had the only dry eyes in the church. Rudy bawled like a baby.

No, not like a baby. Like a grown man with a full heart.

"Did you see any white family at James' funeral? He had a sister, Alice, but she's many years gone. And Jimmy. No, you're the only family I have."

She nodded. Didn't say anything. She looked mad for a while like she does when she's upset. Eleanor couldn't do a thing right the rest of the afternoon. I couldn't, either. One thing about being part of Nannie's family, she doesn't feel the need to be polite anymore. Rudy and the boys took one look at her and made themselves scarce.

She talks of trying to go to nursing school even after Good Samaritan turned her down. I told her I knew the nun who ran St. Joe's. Sister Claire. Nannie looked surprised at that. My maiden name was Stein, I told her. Good German Catholic stock before I married James. I used to try and keep up many years ago. Even after I married James. But it was too hard.

"Sister Claire is a fair woman," I told Nannie. "Maybe we could do something."

Nannie looked dubious. She had reason to be. Times are changing, but they're not changing that fast. People still give us the oddest looks when we shop in Georgetown together. We're the stuff of local legend. But people are polite. Kentuckians are always polite if you're not family. I run into Stephen, the sheriff, once in a while. He's almost too polite to me. I think I may have gotten too used to Nannie's manners.

The sheriff told me Edom's family wanted to bring charges against Rudy, but there wasn't any chance of that.

"His widow is the one pushing it," Stephen said. "She's real angry."

Well, I could understand that, I told the boy. I remember Sandra vaguely. I hadn't seen her in twenty years. But being married to Edom would make a saint angry. And Sandra wasn't any saint.

"Maybe I should sue them. Edom killed James."

The sheriff looked at me, scared I was serious, as if they had anything. Anything I wanted. They had taken what I wanted. And there was no giving it back.

Rudy has wanted to go over to Edom's house, to try to explain in person what happened. Keeps talking about the grandchildren—one little girl especially—and how maybe he could help make things easier for them now that Edom is gone. The sheriff, Nannie, and I have all jumped on the man—telling him he couldn't have a worse idea than showing up at Edom's place. Times haven't changed that much. He might get himself killed. His showing up just wouldn't help. Couldn't help.

"But I did kill the man," he keeps saying, "I owe his family something. I owe the man"

Owe Edom? You owed him the death you gave him, I want to say, but of course you can't say that to Rudy. *As for his family, if a killing can be a blessing, you gave them one.*

But of course you can't say that either. Nannie and I look at each other. She's biting her lips so hard I worry they're going to bleed. Later on she lets it all out to me:

"The way Rudy talks it's like he thinks it'd be better if he'd been shot instead of Edom. I don't think Edom be worrying too much about owing us anything if things was switched around."

"Rudy's a good man," I tell her, but she gives me that look—I've seen her give it to her mamma—like I've gotten on her last nerve. I don't need to be telling her he's a good man, that look says. You try living with a good man and see how much you like it, that look says too.

But there are some things you don't say aloud. Even to family.

I did live with a good man, I would have said. Only he didn't know it. And I didn't believe. Not always, anyway.

I finally had to promise to sneak help to Edom's family through the church. Only I couldn't let them know the help was coming from me—that'd be almost as bad as knowing it came from Rudy. The Reverend Edwards was happy to oblige—especially as I made him keep it all secret. I hear even some of his congregants are grumbling, not happy about his role in all that happened. A little generosity might help to smooth things over. In return I made Rudy promise—Nannie made him promise, too—that he wouldn't contact Edom's family at all. He gave his word when he saw there wasn't any way around it. We all relaxed a bit then.

Rudy's word is money in the bank.

The few times we've gone into Lexington it's been almost as bad as Georgetown, people so surprised to see an old white women with a passel of colored, the children all treating me like I'm their old nanny. I'd love them to call me that, Nanny, but I don't want to push it. Too close to Nannie for one thing. Still, I have to come up with something friendlier than Miz Lawson. Maybe Oma. That's what I called my German grandmother.

I mentioned it to Nannie, and she gave me a look. "So you want to be my colored children's German granny?"

I laughed when she put it like that. I let it be. But I guess that is what I want. Why not?

I see people in Lexington trying to figure it all out when we go into town. Of course, Lexington people would never come out and ask you. Telling them I'm the adoptive German grandma of the four colored children they see me with would probably confuse them even more. I imagine they just conclude that I'm shopping with my help. My very young help.

They wouldn't be wrong.

CHAPTER 23
Nannie Johnson—April 1949

I hate it when Easter comes early. Last year I put the prettiest white and pink dress on Eleanor. Mamma and I worked a month on that dress. Eleanor kept stroking the material. She couldn't believe we was making it for her. "Who we making it for then," I yelled at her. "Herbert?"

Herbert and Franklin both hit the floor laughing. Mamma just shook her head at me.

Mamma had gotten some silk—pink silk—not enough for a whole dress but nobody's seen nothing like it since the war. Just as soon ask for diamonds as silk during the rationing. We wove it into the fabric like it was a quilt. Looked as fancy as those quilts Wilma gave us, only without them deep purple and green blocks. I asked Wilma once where she got those purples and greens. I never could imagine her wearing dresses those colors. She just smiled and said I wouldn't want to know.

If Wilma says I wouldn't want to know, I probably don't.

Anyway, Eleanor's dress didn't have purple and greens, but she was just the picture of springtime wearing it. That first springtime, when the leaves and buds so tiny and fragile, you just know a freezing is gonna blow them away, snap the buds right off. She near broke my heart to look on her.

Only trouble, she about the only springtime around. A March Easter. Two inches of dirty snow on the ground and freezing. Eleanor still wanted to go bare-armed and bare-legged like it was eighty degrees outside, but I made her cover that pretty white and pink dress with a sweater, a scarf, wool leggings, and a coat that almost touched the ground. She wasn't gonna be frostbit if I could help it.

But this year Easter comes when it's supposed to— April 17th. Mamma and I tore last year's dress apart, added some blue silk to blend in with the pink, and have just about reduced Eleanor to a state bordering on idiocy. It tears at me that she still got that feeling of getting more than she deserves. She deserves a lot more than I can give her.

I snap at her, "Stop acting like you the last girl standing at a dance. Be a little sassy. The boys be lining up."

She so happy with the dress she don't even hear me. Which is just as well. Mamma hear me, though. Give me that look. Even Wilma give me a little shake of her head. Just what I need: two mammas thinking I'm the world's meanest mamma ever.

I never in my life much cared about what's on my back—Mamma used to try to dress me up pretty but gave it up after a few tries. Just wasn't interested. Eleanor is the feast she's been waiting for. I see Wilma wanting to jump in, too, but she holds back. She gets Eleanor a whole lot more than Mamma does.

"Why do the children call her Oma?" Mamma asked me. "I thought her name was Wilma. Besides, it's not respectful for them to be calling her by her first name."

"Oh, it's a German word," I told her. "Means something like friend, a term of respect for older people."

Mamma nodded her head. "Long as it's respectful," she said.

Don't want to tell Mamma it's the German word for grandma. Don't know how that would go down.

We got the boys new suits, too. Herbert and Franklin, I mean. Just keeping Harry in any clothes—he's in that time when if he's not cold, he don't see the use of them—is challenge enough. I think the boys like their suits but feel like it might violate boy manners to let us know that. I tried to talk Rudy into a suit, but he just smiled and asked me, "What a farmer need a suit for?"

"Easter Sunday," I told him. "So Mamma Sally can loop her arm into her baby boy's and not be worried her new hat won't get the outing it deserves."

He just laughed, "Daddy and me give up years ago trying to keep up with Mamma's Easter hats. Besides she don't need nobody trailing 'long beside her. She her own parade."

Mamma Sally and Simon are coming out for Easter dinner along with Mamma and Uncle Zeb, if Mamma can persuade him. Uncle Zeb is nervous about Scott County.

Mamma says the man thinks everything outside of Fayette County is the next thing to Alabama. "I wonder where he got that idea," I say. Mamma just make that grumbling sound she does when she don't want to answer.

Easter Saturday Mamma Sally wants me to join her in Lexington. Says the Lyric—that's that new theatre we saw lying on its side like an airplane last August—has been open now since Christmas. Easter Saturday is going to be a big night. Cab Calloway himself.

I told her our last visit to Deweese Street had ended up in a near riot, but she said it would be different this time.

"Go on," Rudy say, "you deserve a good time."

"You do, too," I tell him. He went through a real rough time after the killing, but he doing better now. Hasn't had the ladder dream that I can tell. Had a few other dreams— Mr. Lawson, Edom—but even those seem to be passing. "A good time will do you good," I told him.

"I'm gonna have a good time," he says. "I'm gonna sleep in late, then I'm gonna help them church ladies hide the Easter eggs for the hunt on Sunday." Late is seven if I know Rudy.

"Whooee," I tell him. "You a wild man."

He just laugh and say, "All sorts of good times. You go have your own with Mamma."

"How am I going to get back late Saturday night and still have Easter dinner ready for the crew of us? I count at least ten, and Mamma will probably drag a couple stragglers with her even if she can't get Uncle Zeb. She always does."

But Rudy just waves that all away. "Oma will get things started."

Rudy's been calling Wilma Oma, too—like to drive me crazy the first few times. ("You got a German grandma, too? What else you got in your family history you want to tell me about?")

"You can't fill up on 'startings.'" I snapped. The man didn't know tittle about putting on a big meal.

"And your mamma and my mamma will bring half the dinner anyway," he went. Calm. You couldn't shake the man with an earthquake. Then he waits for my next excuse.

But I don't have no more I can think of. I guess I'm gonna see Cab Calloway.

*   *   *

I start nursing school in August—St. Joe's over on Second Street. Told me my old white uniforms from Good Samaritan would do fine, but Rudy says I should buy new ones. "Why would I want to do that?" I ask him. "The old suits will do just fine." But he and Mamma both say I need to throw those old rags away.

"Hush," Mamma tells me. "You acting just like Eleanor with her new dress."

That hushes me.

I passed all the nursing tests. Sister Claire said it wouldn't be fair to keep me out. *Wouldn't be fair? What's fair have to do with colored?* I wanted to ask her, but I'm learning to keep my mouth shut. Sister Claire's from up North. She been here a while but still ain't got used to how we do things down here. My good fortune. She been around long enough, though, to know there's gonna be problems. Won't be able to live in the dorm they have for nurses. Not right away, anyway, she says. Just as well. Cheaper to squeeze in with Mamma Sally and Simon when I'm not running back to the farm. Mamma is coming out to help with the children. She and Wilma will keep things going as best as they can. It's going to be hard. But good hard.

We done bad hard. Good hard's better.

I just hope one of the children don't slip and let Mamma know what Oma really means. We don't need that kind of hard. A Sunday week ago I heard Mamma call Wilma Oma. Wilma gave her a little strange look but didn't say anything. Thank the Lord.

I tell Mamma Sally it seems a bit heathen to be out partying the night before we all show up for Easter services, but she just says it's all part of it: dance on Saturday, pray on Sunday. I show up at her house, and she gets one look at what I'm wearing and takes me back to her closet. She makes me put on something orange and brown—all flowing and clinging at the same time. Three pins and it fits me like it was special tailored.

"I'm the mother of four," I tell her. "I don't need to be dressing like some nightclub singer."

"You going to be a college student," she says back to me. "A nursing student. You don't need to be dressing like you my age."

Since when have you dressed your age? I want to say but don't. I'm getting used to keeping my mouth shut. I know I've said I never care what I'm wearing, but looking in Mamma Sally's full-sized mirror—the woman really has no shame—I think I know a little of how Eleanor feel in her new dress. I can't help wishing Rudy could see me. I smile and say that to Mamma Sally.

"Oh," she says, "Rudy don't need to see you dressed all in sparkles to know you're pretty. You can wear a potato sack and sparkle for Rudy."

She don't say that's what I usually wear. She's learned to keep her mouth shut, too.

I thought Deweese Street been crowded last August, but it was like the whole of Lexington was showing up for the hi-di-hi-de-ho-man. And it a Lexington I don't hardly recognize, it change so much. Speaking jive talk. I know it's for the hi-de-hi-de-ho-man, but it still make me feel like it a foreign country.

"Are you hep?" One man tried to talk it to me, but I just stared at him. He had better luck with Mamma Sally. She just ate it up, clicked her fingers, and they did a little dance right there on Deweese Street and Third, lined up for the Lyric. The whole Lyric line was dancing, like we some giant conga line. I swayed a little. Didn't seem polite not to. Mamma Sally must'a done a good job dressing me. A whole lot of guys—"Cats," Mamma Sally called them—tried to catch my eye. But I just smiled.

Rudy didn't need to worry. Be back in my potato sack in no time. These "cats" might not think I was so pretty then. Rudy would.

Truth was, I wasn't hep. Not like Mamma Sally. She kept up with the times. I felt more at home out in the wilds of Scott County. Didn't need city excitement. Pig killings, chicken slaughter. Shootings. Too much excitement already.

Hiding Easter eggs with Rudy as exciting as I wanted to get. Letting my children call the widow of the Grand Dragon of the Ku Klux Klan Oma—"friend"—as up to date as I wanted to be.

And Rudy? You call him hep and he probably think you speaking German. Wilma tells me he a good man. She means he know how to forgive in a way most people only read about.

He know how to love in a way I can only dream about.

That hard, sometimes. To know you come up short loving. Your children, your man. Your friends. Wilma don't need to be telling me about Rudy. He as hep as the hi-de-hi-de-ho-man.

Of course, Rudy a good man. He got plenty of help, but he a good man.

And Rudy and me, we made a good family.

ABOUT THE AUTHOR

Joseph G. Anthony, a New Jersey-born Kentucky author, moved in 1980 from what he considered the center of the country—Manhattan's Upper West Side—to Hazard, Kentucky. "It was a place so isolated and obscure that I at first felt as lost as a missing person. But it was, I discovered, its own country."

In fiction he began to explore its beauty, its many problems, its strengths, and its weaknesses. "Fiction feels and understands: racism is in your face, poverty on your back. News stories can only report."

Anthony, an English professor for 35 years, is a hybrid-Kentuckian now. His accent might still be North Eastern, but he sees with an insider-outsider's eye. He regularly contributes essays and poems to local periodicals and anthologies, including a poem and story in *Kentucky's Twelve Days of Christmas*. He's a "Kentucky Colonel" (someone once sent his name in), but he's more Kentucky peasant. He lives in Lexington, Kentucky, with his wife of 36 years, Elise Mandel, also a hybrid Kentuckian. They have three grown children.

His previous books include two novels, *Peril, Kentucky,* and *Pickering's Mountain,* plus two short story collections, *Camden Blues,* and *Bluegrass Funeral.*

RECENT BOOKS BY BOTTOM DOG PRESS

Jack's Memoirs: Off the Road
By Kurt Landefeld, 590 pgs. $19.95
Daughters of the Grasslands: A Memoir
By Mary Woster Haug, 200 pgs. $18
Lake Winds: Poems
By Larry Smith, 220 pgs. $18
Echo: Poems
By Christina Lovin, 114 pgs. $16
Stolen Child: A Novel
By Suzanne Kelly, 338 pgs. $18
The Canary: A Novel
By Michael Loyd Gray, 196 pgs. $18
On the Flyleaf: Poems
By Herbert Woodward Martin, 106 pgs. $16
The Harmonist at Nightfall: Poems of Indiana
By Shari Wagner, 114 pgs. $16
Painting Bridges: A Novel
By Patricia Averbach, 234 pgs. $18
Ariadne & Other Poems
By Ingrid Swanberg, 120 pgs. $16
The Search for the Reason Why: New and Selected Poems
By Tom Kryss, 192 pgs. $16
Kenneth Patchen: Rebel Poet in America
By Larry Smith, Revised 2nd Edition, 326 pgs. Cloth $28
Selected Correspondence of Kenneth Patchen,
Edited with introduction by Allen Frost, Paper $18/ Cloth $28
Awash with Roses: Collected Love Poems of Kenneth Patchen
Eds. Laura Smith and Larry Smith
With introduction by Larry Smith, 200 pgs. $16

COLLECTIONS AND ANTHOLOGIES
d.a.levy and the mimeograph revolution
Eds. Ingrid Swanberg and Larry Smith, 276 pgs. $20
Come Together: Imagine Peace
Eds. Ann Smith, Larry Smith, Philip Metres, 204 pgs. $16
Evensong: Contemporary American Poets on Spirituality
Eds. Gerry LaFemina and Chad Prevost, 240 pgs. $16
America Zen: A Gathering of Poets
Eds. Ray McNiece and Larry Smith, 224 pgs. $16
Family Matters: Poems of Our Families
Eds. Ann Smith and Larry Smith, 232 pgs. $16

RECENT BOOKS BY BOTTOM DOG PRESS

APPALACHIAN WRITING SERIES
Wanted: Good Family: A Novel
By Joseph G. Anthony, 212 pgs. $18
Gifted and Talented: A Novel
By Julia Watts, 218 pgs. $18
Sky Under the Roof: Poems
By Hilda Downer, 126 pgs. $16
Green-Silver and Silent: Poems
By Marc Harshman, 90 pgs. $16
Sinners of Sanction County: Stories
By Charles Dodd White, 160 pgs. $17
Learning How: Stories, Yarns & Tales
By Richard Hague, 216 pgs. $18
The Homegoing: A Novel
By Michael Olin-Hitt, 180 pgs. $18
*She Who Is Like a Mare: Poems of Mary Breckinridge
and the Frontier Nursing Service*
By Karen Kotrba, 96 pgs. $16
Smoke: Poems
By Jeanne Bryner 96 pgs. $16
Broken Collar: A Novel
By Ron Mitchell, 234 pgs. $18
The Pattern Maker's Daughter: Poems
By Sandee Gertz Umbach, 90 pages $16
The Free Farm: A Novel
By Larry Smith, 306 pgs. $18
The Long River Home: A Novel
By Larry Smith, 230 pgs. cloth $22; paper $16
Eclipse: Stories
By Jeanne Bryner 150 pgs. $16

APPALACHIAN ANTHOLOGIES
*Degrees of Elevation: Short Stories of
Contemporary Appalachia*
Eds. Charles Dodd White and Page Seay 186 pgs. $18

Bottom Dog Press, Inc.
PO Box 425/ Huron, Ohio 44839
Order Online at:
http://smithdocs.net/BirdDogy/BirdDogPage.html

CPSIA information can be obtained
at www.ICGtesting.com
Printed in the USA
BVHW080900020123
655389BV00002B/339